Samuel Laing

A Modern Zoroastrian

Samuel Laing

A Modern Zoroastrian

ISBN/EAN: 9783743331600

Manufactured in Europe, USA, Canada, Australia, Japa

Cover: Foto ©Andreas Hilbeck / pixelio.de

Manufactured and distributed by brebook publishing software
(www.brebook.com)

Samuel Laing

A Modern Zoroastrian

A MODERN ZOROASTRIAN.

A MODERN ZOROASTRIAN.

1000 *copies printed, February,* 1888.
1000 „ „ *March,* 1889.
1000 „ „ *March,* 1890.
1000 „ „ *June,* 1890.
1000 „ , *March,* 1891.
1000 „ „ *June,* 1892.
1000 „ „ *February,* 1893.
1000 „ „ *November,* 1893.
1000 „ „ *October,* 1894.
1000 „ „ *September,* 1895.
1000 „ „ *January,* 1898.

A MODERN ZOROASTRIAN

BY

S. LAING,

AUTHOR OF

"MODERN SCIENCE AND MODERN THOUGHT," "PROBLEMS OF THE FUTURE,"
"HUMAN ORIGINS."

Eleventh Thousand.

LONDON: CHAPMAN AND HALL, Ld.
1898.

PREFACE TO NEW EDITION.

FROM some of the criticisms on the First Edition of this work I fear that the distinction I endeavoured to draw between the use of the term "polarity" in the inorganic and in the spiritual worlds has not been made sufficiently clear. I stated in the Introduction "That while the principle of polarity pervades both worlds, I am far from assuming that the laws under which it acts are identical; and that virtue and vice, pain and pleasure, are products of the same mathematical laws as regulate the attractions and repulsions of molecules and atoms." But this warning has been apparently overlooked by some readers who have assumed that instead of analogy I meant identity, and that it was a mistake to use the same word "polarity" for phenomena so essentially distinct as those of the material and the spiritual worlds.

Thus my "guide, philosopher, and friend," Professor Huxley, for whose authority I have the highest respect, observed in a recent article, that he had long ago acquired a habit, if he came across the word polarity applied to anything but magnetism and electricity,

of throwing down the book and reading no farther.
I must confess that I felt a little disconcerted when
I read this passage; but I was soon consoled, for,
in a month or two afterwards, I came across another
passage in the same Review which said, "However revolting may be the accumulation of misery at the negative
pole of Society, in contrast with that of monstrous
wealth at the positive pole, this state of things must
abide and grow continuously worse, as long as Istar
(the dual Goddess of the Babylonians) holds her way
unchecked."

Surely, I thought, here is a case in which the
Professor must have thrown down the Review when
he came to these words: but when I came to the
end, I found that it was not the Review, but the
pen, which must have been thrown down, for the
article is signed "T. Huxley." Can there be a more
conclusive proof that there are a vast variety of facts outside of magnetism and electricity, connected by an under-
lying idea, which inevitably suggests analogy to them,
and which can be most conveniently expressed by the
word "polarity"? Words after all are only coins to facili-
tate the interchange of ideas, and the best word is that
which serves the purpose most clearly and concisely.
Thus instead of using a waggon load of copper, or
the verbiage of a conveyancer's deed, to express the
ideas comprised in such words as "theism," " pantheism,"
or " agnosticism," we coin them for general use, as
Huxley did the word "agnosticism," in order to convey
our meaning.

Polarity is such a word. It sums up what Emerson says in his Essay on Compensation: " Polarity, or action and reaction, we meet in every part of Nature; in darkness and light; in the ebb and flow of waters; in male and female; in the inspiration and expiration of plants and animals; in the undulations of fluids and of sound; in the centripetal and centrifugal gravity; in electricity, galvanism, and chemical affinity. Superinduce Magnetism at one end of a needle, the opposite Magnetism takes place at the other end. If the South attracts, the North repels. An inevitable dualism besets nature, so that each thing is a half, and suggests another to make it whole: as spirit, matter; man, woman; odd, even; subjective, objective; in, out; upper, under; motion, rest; yea, nay."

These, by whatever name we like to call them, are facts and not fancies, and facts which enter largely into all questions, whether of science, philosophy, religion, or practical policy. Every one who wishes to keep at all abreast with modern culture, ought to have some general knowledge of the ideas and principles which underlie them and which are embraced in the comprehensive word " polarity." My object in this book has been to assist the reader, who is not a specialist, in arriving at some general understanding of the subjects treated of, and I may hope, in awakening such an interest in them as may induce him to prosecute further researches. If I succeed in this, my object will have been attained.

PREFACE.

THE reception given to my former work, on 'Modern Science and Modern Thought,' has induced me to write this further one. I refer not so much to the reviews of professional critics, though as a rule nothing could be more courteous and candid, but rather to the letters I have received from readers of various age, sex, and condition, saying that I had assisted them in understanding much interesting matter which had previously been a sealed book to them.

If I am good for anything, it is for a certain faculty of lucid condensation, and I have thought that I might apply this to some of the less-known branches of modern science, such as the new chemistry and physiology, as well as, in my first work, to the more familiar subjects of astronomy and geology; while at the same time I might extend it to some of the more obvious problems of religion, morals, metaphysics, and practical life, which force themselves, more and more every day, on the attention of intelligent thinkers.

As in the former work the scientific speculations were linked together by the leading idea of the universality of law, so, in this, unity is given to them by the all-pervading principle of polarity, which manifests

x PREFACE.

itself everywhere as the fundamental condition of the material and spiritual universe.

For the scientific portion of the work I am indebted to the most approved authorities, such as Darwin, Huxley, Haeckel, and Professor Cooke's volume on the New Chemistry in the International Scientific Series. For the religious and philosophical speculations I am myself responsible; for, although I have derived the greatest possible pleasure and profit from Herbert Spencer's writings, I had arrived at my principal conclusions independently before I had read any of his works. I can only hope that I may have succeeded in presenting a good many abstruse questions in a popular form, intelligible to the average mind of ordinary readers, and calculated, if it teaches nothing else, to teach them a practical philosophy which inculcates tolerance and charity, and assists them in finding

Sermons in stones and good in everything.

CONTENTS.

CHAPTER IX.

PRIMITIVE POLARITIES—HEREDITY AND VARIATION.

CHAPTER X.

THE KNOWABLE AND UNKNOWABLE—BRAIN AND THOUGHT.

CHAPTER XI.

RELIGIONS AND PHILOSOPHIES.

CHAPTER XII.

CHRISTIANITY AND MORALS.

CHAPTER XIII.

ZOROASTRIANISM.

CHAPTER XIV.

FORMS OF WORSHIP.

CHAPTER XV.

PRACTICAL POLARITIES.

A MODERN ZOROASTRIAN.

CHAPTER I.

INTRODUCTORY.

Experiment with magnet—Principle of polarity—Applies universally—
Analogies in spiritual world—Zoroastrian religion—Changes in modern
environment—Require corresponding changes in religions and philosophies.

SCATTER a heap of iron filings on a plate of glass ; bring
near it a magnet, and tap the glass gently, and you will
see the filings arrange themselves in regular forms.

If one pole only of the magnet is brought near the
glass the filings arrange themselves in lines radiating
from that pole.

Next lay the bar-magnet on the glass so that the
filings are influenced by both poles ; they will arrange
themselves into a series of regular curves.

In other words, the Chaos of a confused heap of inert
matter has become a Cosmos of harmonious arrangement assuming definite form in obedience to law.

As the old saying has it, that 'every road leads to
Rome,' so this simple experiment leads up to a principle
which underlies all existence knowable to human faculty
—that of Polarity. Why do the iron filings arrange

themselves in regular curves ?   Because they are magnetised by the influence of the larger magnet, and each

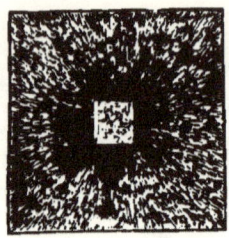 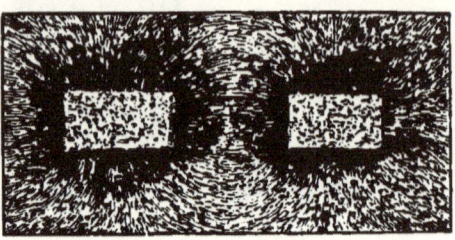

little particle of iron is converted into a little magnet
with two opposite poles attracting and repelling.

What is a magnet?   It is a special manifestation of
the more general principle of polarity, by which energy,
when it passes from the passive or neutralised into the
active state, does so under the condition of developing
opposite and conflicting energies : no action without
reaction, no positive without a negative, and, as we see
it in the simplest form in our magnets, no North Pole
without a South Pole—like ever repelling like and
attracting unlike.   The magnet, again, may be considered as a special form of electricity, for if we send an
electric current through a coil of copper wire encircling
a bar of soft iron, the bar is at once converted into a
magnet ; so that a magnet may be considered as the
summing up, at two opposite extremities or poles, of
the attractive and repulsive effects of electric currents
circulating round it.   But this electricity is itself subject to the law of polarity, whether developed by chemical
action in the form of a current or electricity in motion,
or by friction in the form of statical electricity of small
quantity but high tension.   In all cases a positive implies
a negative ; in all, like repels like and attracts unlike.

Conversely, as polarity produces definite structure. so definite structure everywhere implies polarity.

The same principle prevails not only throughout the inorganic or world of matter, but throughout the organic or world of life, and specially throughout its highest manifestations in human life and character, and in the highest products of its evolution, in societies, religions, and philosophies. To show this by some familiar and striking examples is the main object of this book.

But here let me interpose a word of caution. I must avoid the error which vitiates Professor Drummond's interesting work on 'Natural Law in the Spiritual World,' of confounding analogy and identity. Because the principle of polarity pervades alike the natural and spiritual worlds, I am far from assuming that the laws under which it acts are identical ; and that virtue and vice, pain and pleasure, ugliness and beauty, are products of the same mathematical changes of sign and inverse squares or cubes of distances, as regulate the attractions and repulsions of molecules and atoms. All I say is, that the same pervading principle may be traced wherever human thought and human knowledge extend ; that it is apparently, for some reason unknown to us, the essential condition of all existence within the sphere of that thought and that knowledge ; and that what lies beyond it is the great unknown, behind the impenetrable veil which it is not given to mortals to uplift. In like manner, if I call myself 'a modern Zoroastrian,' it is not that I wish or expect to teach a new religion or revive an old one, to see Christian churches dedicated to Ormuzd, or right reverend bishops exchanging the apron and shovel-hat for the mitre and flowing robes of the ancient Magi ;

but simply this. All religions I take to be 'working hypotheses,' by which successive ages and races of men try to satisfy the aspirations and harmonise the knowledge which in the course of evolution have come to be, for the time, their spiritual equipment. The best proof of any religion is, that it exists—i.e. that it is part of the same evolution, and that on the whole it works well, i.e. is in tolerable harmony with its environment. When that environment changes, when loftier views of morality prevail, when knowledge is increased and the domain of science everywhere extends its frontier, religions must change with it if they are to remain good working, and not become unworkable and unbelievable hypotheses.

Now of all the religious hypotheses which remain workable in the present state of human knowledge, that seems to me the best which frankly recognises the existence of this dual law, or law of polarity, as the fundamental condition of the universe, and, personifying the good principle under the name of Ormuzd, and the evil one under that of Ahriman, looks with earnest but silent and unspoken reverence on the great unknown beyond, which may, in some way incomprehensible to mortals, reconcile the two opposites, and give the final victory to the good.

> Oh ! yet we hope that somehow good
> Will be the final goal of ill.

So sings the poet of the nineteenth century : so, if we understand his doctrine rightly, taught the Bactrian sage, Zoroaster, some forty centuries earlier.

This, and this alone, seems to me to afford a working hypothesis which is based on fact, can be brought into harmony with the existing environment, and embraces, in a wider synthesis, all that is good in other philosophies and religions.

When I talk of our new environment, it requires one who, like the author, has lived more than the Scriptural threescore and ten years, and has, so to speak, one foot on the past and one on the present, to realise how enormous is the change which a single generation has made in the whole spiritual surroundings of a civilised man of the nineteenth century. When I was a student at Cambridge, little more than fifty years ago, Astronomy was the only branch of natural science which could be said to be definitely brought within the domain of natural law. And that only as regards the law of gravity, and the motions of the heavenly bodies, for little or nothing was known as to their constitution. Geology was just beginning the series of conquests by which time and the order and succession of life on the earth have been annexed by science as completely as space by astronomy; and theories of cataclysms, universal deluges, and special recent creations of animals and man, still held their ground, and were quoted as proofs of a universe maintained by constant supernatural interference.

And when I say that space had been annexed to science by astronomy, it was really only that half of space which extends from the standpoint of the human senses in the direction of the infinitely great. The other equally important half which extends downwards to the infinitely small was unknown, or the subject only of the vaguest conjectures.

Chemistry was, to a great extent, an empirical science, and molecules and atoms were at best guesses at truth, or rather convenient mathematical abstractions

with no more actual reality than the symbols of the
differential calculus. The real causes and laws of heat,
light, and electricity, were as little known as those of
molecular action and of chemical affinity. The great
laws of the indestructibility of matter, the correlation of
forces, and the conservation of energy, were unknown,
or only just beginning to be foreshadowed. As regards
life, protoplasm was a word unheard of ; scientific
biology, zoology, and botany were in their infancy ;
and the gradual building up of all living matter from a
speck of protoplasm, through a primitive cell, was not
even suspected. Above all, the works of Darwin had
not been published, and evolution had not become the
general law of modern thought ; nor had the discovery
of the antiquity of man, and of his slow development
upwards from the rudest origins, shattered into fragments established beliefs as to his recent miraculous
creation.

Science and miracle have been fighting out their
battle during the last fifty years along the whole
line, and science has been at every point victorious.
Miracle, in the sense in which our fathers believed in
it, has been not only repulsed, but annihilated so completely, that really little remains but to bury the dead.

The result of these discoveries has been to make a
greater change in the spiritual environment of a single
generation than would be made in their physical environment if the glacial period suddenly returned and
buried Northern Europe under polar ice. The change
is certainly greater in the last fifty years than it had
been in the previous five hundred, and in many respects
greater than in the previous five thousand.

It may be sufficient to glance shortly at the equally

great corresponding changes which this period has witnessed in the practical conditions of life and of society. If astronomy and geology have extended the dominion of the mind over space and time, steamers, railways, and the electric telegraph have gained the mastery over them for practical purposes. Commerce and emigration have assumed international proportions, and India, Australia, and America are nearer to us, and connected with us by closer ties, than Scotland was to England in my schoolboy days. Education and a cheap press have even in a greater degree revolutionised society, and knowledge, reaching the masses, has carried with it power so that democracy and free-thought are, whether for good or evil, everywhere in the ascendant, and old privileges and traditions are everywhere decaying.

With such a great change of environment it is evident that many of the old creeds, institutions, and other organisms, adapted to old conditions, must have become as obsolete as a schoolboy's jacket would be as the comfortable habiliment of a grown-up man. But as a lobster which has cast its shell does not feel at ease until it has grown a new one, so thinking men of the present day are driven to devise, to a great extent each for themselves, some larger theory which may serve them as a 'working hypothesis' with which to go through life, and bring the ineradicable aspirations and emotions of their nature into some tolerable harmony with existing facts.

To me, as one of those thinking units, this theory, of what for want of a better name I call 'Zoroastrianism,' has approved itself as a good working theory, which reconciles more intellectual and moral difficulties, and affords a better guide in conduct and practical life than any other; and, in a word, enables me to reduce my own individual Chaos into some sort of an intel-ligible and ordered Cosmos. I feel moved, therefore, to preach through the press my little sermon upon it, for the benefit of those whom it may concern, feeling as-sured that the process of evolution, by which

> The old order changes, giving place to new,

can best be assisted by the honest and unbiassed expres-sion of the results of individual thought and experience on the part of any one of those units whose aggregates form the complicated organisms of religions and philo-sophies, of societies and of humanity.

CHAPTER II.

Matter consists of molecules—Nature of molecules—Laws of their action in gases—Law of Avogadro—Molecules composed of atoms—Proved by composition of water—Combinations of atoms—Elementary substances—Qualities of matter depend on atoms—Dimensions and velocities of molecules and atoms—These are ascertained *facts*, not theories.

IF in building a house that is to stand when the rains fall and the winds blow, it is requisite to go down to the solid rock for a foundation, so much the more is it necessary in building up a theory to begin at the beginning and give it a solid groundwork. Nine-tenths of the fallacies current in the world arise from the haste with which people rush to conclusions on insufficient premises. Take, for instance, any of the political questions of the day, such as the Irish question : how many of those who express confident opinions, and get angry and excited on one side or the other, could answer any of the preliminary questions which are the indispensable conditions of any rational judgment ? How many marks would they get for an examination paper which asked what was the population of Ireland ; what proportion of that population was agricultural ; what proportion of that agricultural population consisted of holders of small tenements ; what was the scale of rents compared with that for small holdings in other countries;

how much of that rent was levied on them for their own improvements ; and other similar questions which lie at the root of the matter ?   In how many cases would it be found that the whole superstructure of their confident and passionate theories about the Irish difficulty was based on no more solid foundation than their like or dislike of a particular statesman or of a particular party.

I propose therefore to begin at the beginning, and, taking the simplest case, that of dead or inorganic matter, show how the material universe is built up by the operation of the all-pervading law of polarity ? What does matter consist of ? Of molecules, and molecules are made up of atoms, and these are held together or parted, and built up into the various forms of the material universe, primarily by polar forces.

Let me endeavour to make this intelligible to the intelligent but unscientific reader.   Suppose the Pyramid of Cheops shown for the first time to a giant whose eye was on such a scale that he could just discern it as a separate object.   He might make all sorts of ingenious conjectures as to its nature, but if microscopes had been invented in Giant-land and he looked through one, he would find that it was built up, layer by layer, on a regular plan and in determinate lines and angles, by molecules, or what seemed to him almost infinitely small masses, of squared stone.   For pyramid write crystal, and we may see by the human sense, aided by human instruments and human reason, a similar structure built up in the same way by minute particles. Or again, divide and subdivide our iron filings until we reach the limit of possible mechanical division discernible by the microscope ; each one remains essentially a bar of iron, as capable of being magnetised, and showing the same qualities and behaviour under chemical tests as the original bar of iron from which the filings were taken. This carries us a long way down towards the infinitely small, for mechanical division and microscopic visibility can be carried down to magnitudes which are of the order of $\frac{1}{100000}$th part of an inch.

But this is only the first step ; to understand our molecules we must ascertain whether they are infinitely divisible, and whether they are continuous, expanding by being spread out thinner and thinner like gold-beater's skin : or are they separate bodies with intervals between them, like little planets forming one solar system and revolving in space by fixed laws. Ancient science guessed at the former solution and embodied it in the maxim ' that nature abhors a vacuum ': modern science proves the latter.

In the first place bodies combine only in fixed proportions, which is a necessary consequence if they consist of definite indivisible particles, but inconceivable if the substance of each is indefinitely divisible. Thus water is formed in one way and one only : by uniting one volume or molecule of oxygen with two of hydrogen, and any excess of one or the other is left out and remains uncombined. But if the molecules could be divided into halves, quarters, and so on indefinitely, there can be no reason why their union should take place always in this one proportion and this only.

A still more conclusive proof is furnished by the behaviour of substances which exist in the form of gases. If a jar is filled with one gas, a second and third gas can be poured into it as readily as into a vacuum, the result being that the pressure on the sides of the jar is exactly equal to the sum of the separate pressures of each separate gas. This evidently means that the first gas does not occupy the whole space, but that its particles are like a battalion of soldiers in loose skirmishing order, with such intervals between each unit that a second and third battalion can be marched in and placed on the same ground, without disturbing the formation, and with the result only of increasing the intensity of the fire.

Now gas is matter as much as solids or liquids, and in the familiar instance of water we see that it is merely a question of more or less heat whether the same matter exists as ice, water, or steam. The number and nature of the molecules is not changed, only in the one case they are close to one another and solidly linked together ; in the other, further removed and free to move about one another, though still held together as a mass by their mutual attractions ; and in the third, still further apart, so that their mutual attraction is lost and they dart about, each with its own proper motion, bombarding the surface which contains them, and by the resultant of their impacts producing pressure.

In this latter and simpler form of gas the following laws are found to prevail universally for all substances. Under like conditions volumes vary directly as the temperature and inversely as the pressure. That is to say, the pressure which contains them remaining the same, equal volumes of air, steam, or any other substance in the state of gas, expand into twice the volume if the temperature is doubled, three times if it is tripled, and so on ; contracting in the same way if the temperature is lowered. If on the other hand the temperature remains constant, the volume is reduced to one

half or one third, if the pressure is doubled or tripled.
From these laws the further grand generalisation has
been arrived at, that all substances existing in the form
of gas contain the same number of molecules in the
same volume.

This, which is known as the Law of Avogadro,
from the Italian chemist by whom it was first discovered, is the fundamental law of modern chemistry,
and the key to all certain and scientific knowledge of
the constitution of matter and of the domain of the
infinitely small, just as much as the law of gravity is to
action of matter in the mass, and the resulting conditions and motions of mechanics and astronomy.

This conclusion obviously follows from it, that
difference of weight in different substances arises not
from one having more molecules in the same volume
than another, but from the molecules themselves being
heavier. If we weigh a gallon or litre of hydrogen gas,
which is the lightest known substance, and then weighing an equal volume of oxygen gas find that it is sixteen times heavier, we know for certain that the molecule or ultimate particle of oxygen is sixteen times
heavier than that of hydrogen.

It is evident that in this way the molecules of all
simple substances which can exist in the form of pure
gas can be weighed, and their weight expressed in terms
of the unit which is generally adopted, that of the molecule of the lightest known substance, hydrogen. But
science, not content with this achievement, wants to
know not the relative weight only, but the absolute
dimensions, qualities, and motions of these little bodies;
and whether, although they cannot be divided further
by mechanical means, and while retaining the qualities

of the substances they build up, they are really ultimate and indivisible particles or themselves composites.

Chemistry and electricity give a ready answer to this latter question. Molecules are composites of still smaller bodies, and to get back to the ultimate particle we must go to atoms. All chemical changes resolve themselves into the breaking up of molecules and re-arrangement of their constituent atoms. If the opposite poles of a voltaic battery are inserted in a vessel containing water, molecules of water are broken up, bubbles of gas rise at each pole, and if these are collected, the gas at the positive pole is found to be oxygen, and that at the negative pole hydrogen. Nothing has been added or taken away, for the weight of the two gases evolved exactly equals that of the water which has disappeared. But the molecules of the water have been broken up, and their constituents reappear in totally different forms, for nothing can well be more unlike water than each of the two gases of which it is composed. That it is composed of them can be verified by the reverse experiment of mixing the two gases together in the same proportion of two volumes of hydrogen to one of oxygen as was produced by the decomposition of water, passing an electric spark through the vessel containing the mixture, when with a loud explosion the gases reunite, and water is formed in precisely the same quantity as produced the volumes of gas by its decomposition. Can the ultimate particles of these gases be further subdivided; can they, like those of water, be broken up and reappear in new forms? No; there is no known process by which an atom of oxygen can be made anything but oxygen, or an atom of hydrogen anything but hydrogen.

The only thing which is compound in the composition of oxygen is that its molecules consist of two atoms linked together. This appears from the fact that while the weight of oxygen, and therefore that of its molecules, is sixteen times greater than that of an equal volume of hydrogen, and therefore of hydrogen molecules, it combines with it in the proportion not of sixteen, but of eight to one. If, therefore, the molecule were identical with the atom of oxygen, we must admit that the atom could be halved, which is contrary to its definition as the ultimate indivisible particle of the substance oxygen. But if the oxygen molecule consists of two linked atoms, O—O, and the hydrogen molecule equally of two, H—H, as can be proved by other considerations, everything is explained by assuming that the molecule of water consists of two atoms of hydrogen linked to one of oxygen, or H_2O, and that when this molecule is broken up by electricity, its constituents resolve themselves into atoms, which recombine so as to form twice as many molecules of hydrogen, H—H, as of oxygen, O,—i.e. into two volumes of hydrogen gas to one of oxygen.

Taking the single hydrogen atom as the unit of weight as being the lightest known ponderable body, and calling this weight a microcrith, or standard of the smallest of this order of excessively small weights, this is equivalent to saying that the weight of an oxygen atom is equal to 16 microcriths, and as water is composed of one such atom plus two of hydrogen, the weight of its molecule ought to be $16 + 2 = 18$, which is in fact the exact ratio in which the weight of a volume of steam, or water in the form of gas, is heavier than an equal volume of hydrogen.

This key unlocks the whole secret of the chemical changes and combinations by which matter assumes all the various forms known to us in the universe.

Thus oxygen enters into a great variety of combinations forming different substances, but always in the proportion which is either 16, or some multiple of 16, such as 32, 48, 64. That is, either 1, 2, 3, or 4 atoms of oxygen unite with other atoms to form the molecules from which these other substances are made.

One atom of oxygen weighing 16 microcriths combines, as we have seen, with two atoms of hydrogen weighing 2, to form a molecule of water weighing 18 mc. In like manner one atom of oxygen, 16 mc., combines with one of carbon, which weighs 12 mc., to form a molecule of carbonic oxide weighing 28 mc.; and two of oxygen, 32 mc., with one of carbon, 12 mc., to form a molecule of carbonic dioxide weighing 44 mc.

The same applies to all elementary substances. Thus hydrogen, two atoms of which combine with one of oxygen to form water, combines one atom to one with chlorine to form the molecule of hydrochloric acid, which weighs 36·5 mc., being the united weights of one atom of chlorine, 35·5 mc., and one of hydrogen, 1 mc. These, with hundreds of similar instances, are the results not of theories as to molecules and atoms, but of actual facts, ascertained by innumerable experiments made independently by careful observers over long periods of years, many of them dating back to the labours of the alchemists of the middle ages in pursuit of gold. The atomic theory is the child and not the parent of the facts, and is indeed nothing but the summary of the vast variety of experiments which led up to it, as Newton's law of gravity is of the facts

known to us with regard to the attractions and motions
of matter in the mass. But as Newton's law enables
us to predict new facts, to calculate eclipses and the
return of comets beforehand, and to compile nautical
almanacs ; so the new chemistry, based on the atomic
theory, affords the same conclusive proof of its truth
by enabling us in many cases to predict phenomena
which are subsequently verified by experiment, and to
infer beforehand what combinations are possible, and
what will be their nature.

The actual existence, therefore, of molecules and
atoms is as well-ascertained a fact, as that of cwts. and
lbs., or of planets and stars, of solar systems and nebulæ.

The researches of chemists have succeeded in dis-
covering about 70 substances, of which the same may
be said as of the oxygen and hydrogen into which
water is decomposed, viz. that they cannot be decomposed by any known process, and must therefore be
considered as ultimate and elementary. Their atoms
differ widely in size and weight : that of mercury, for
instance, being 200 times heavier than that of hydrogen,
and the weights varying from 1 mc. for the hydrogen
atom, up to 240 for that of uranium. When we call
them elementary substances, we merely mean that we
know no means of decomposing them. It is possible
that all of them may be compounds which we cannot
take to pieces of some substratum of uniform matter, and
it is remarkable that the weight of nearly all of these
elementary atoms is some simple multiple of that of
hydrogen, pointing to their being all combinations of
one common substratum of matter ; but this is merely
conjecture, and in the present state of our knowledge
we must assume these 66 or 71 ultimate particles

c

or atoms to be the indivisible units out of which all the complicated puzzle of the material universe is put together. They are not all equally important to us. Of the 71 elementary substances enumerated in chemical treatises, 5 are doubtful, and 30 to 35 of the remainder are either known only to chemists in minute quantities, or exist in nature in small quantities, having no very material bearing upon man's relation to matter. The most important are oxygen, hydrogen, nitrogen, and carbon. Oxygen diluted by nitrogen gives us the air we breathe, combined with hydrogen the water we drink, and with metals and other primitive bases the solid earth on which we tread. Carbon again is the great basis of organised matter and life, to which it leads up by a variety of complex combinations with oxygen, hydrogen, and nitrogen.

The qualities and relations of elementary atoms afford a subject of great interest, but of such vast extent that those who wish to understand it must be referred to professed works on modern chemistry. For the present purpose it is sufficient to say that the following conclusions are firmly established.

All the various forms of matter are composed of combinations of primitive atoms which form molecules, the molecules being neither more nor less than very small pieces of ordinary matter.

The qualities of this matter, or, what is the same thing, of its molecules, depend partly on the qualities of the atoms, which are something quite distinct from those of the molecules, and partly on their mode of aggregation into molecules, affecting the form, size, stability, and other attributes of the molecule.

All matter, down to the smallest atom, has definite weight and is indestructible. No man by taking thought can add the millionth of a milligramme to the weight of any substance, or make it either more or less than the sum of the weights of its component factors, any more than he can add a cubit to his stature. When Shelley sang of the cloud,

I change, but I cannot die,

he enunciated a scientific axiom of the first importance. Creation, in the sense of making something out of nothing, is a thing absolutely unknown and unknowable to us. If we say we *make* a ship or a steam-engine, we simply mean that we transform existing matter and existing energies into new combinations, which give results convenient for our purpose. So if we talk of making a world, our idea really is that if our powers and knowledge were indefinitely increased we might be able, given the atoms and energies with their laws of existence, to put them together so as to produce the desired results. But how the atoms and their inherent laws got there is a question as to which knowledge, or even conceivability, is impossible, for it altogether transcends human experience.

Before finally taking leave of atoms it may be well to state shortly that science, not content with having proved their existence and weighed them in terms of the lightest element, the hydrogen atom, has attempted, not without success, to solve the more difficult problem of their real dimensions, intervals, and velocities. This problem has been attacked by Clausius, Sir W. Thomson, Clerk Maxwell, and others, from various sides : from a comparison with the wave-lengths of light ; with the tenuity of the thinnest films of soap-bubbles just before they burst, and when they are presumably reduced to a single layer of molecules ; and from the kinetic theory of gases, involving the dimensions, paths, and velocities of elastic bodies, constantly colliding, and by their impacts producing the resulting pressure on the confining surface. All these methods involve such refined mathematical calculations that it is impossible to explain them popularly, but they all lead to nearly identical results, which involve figures so marvellous as to be almost incomprehensible. For instance, a cubic centimetre of air is calculated to contain 21 trillions of molecules— i.e. 21 times the cube of a million, or 21 followed by 18 ciphers; the average distance between each molecule equals 95 millionths of a millimetre, which is about 25 times smaller than the smallest magnitude visible under a microscope ; the average velocity of each molecule is 447 metres per second ; and the average number of impacts received by each molecule in a second is 4,700 millions.

CHAPTER III.

ETHER.

PERHAPS the best way to convey some idea of this order of magnitudes to the ordinary reader is to quote Sir W. Thomson's illustration, that if we could suppose a cubic inch of water magnified to the size of the earth—i.e. to a sphere 24,000 miles in circumference—the dimensions of its ultimate particles, magnified on the same scale, or, as he expresses it, its degree of coarse-grainedness, would be something between the size of rifle-bullets and cricket-balls.

Extraordinary as these dimensions are, they are not more so than those at the opposite extremity of the scale, where the distance of stars and nebulæ has to be measured by the number of thousand years their light, travelling at the rate of 192,000 miles per second, takes to reach us. Infinitely small, however, as those dimensions appear to our original conceptions derived from our natural senses, they are certain and ascertained facts, if not as to the precise figures, yet beyond all doubt as to the orders of magnitude. In dealing with them also we are to a great extent on familiar ground.

Molecules are nothing more nor less than small pieces of ordinary matter; and atoms are also matter, for they obey the law of gravity, have definite weights, and build up molecules as surely as molecules build up ordinary matter, and as squared stones build up pyramids.

But to understand the constitution of the material universe we must go a step further, part from the familiar world of sense, and deal with an all-pervading medium, which is at the same time matter and not matter, which lies outside the laws of gravity, and yet obeys other laws intelligible and calculable by us; of which it may be said we know it and we know it not. We call it Ether.

Ether is a medium assumed as a necessary consequence from the phenomena of light, heat, and electricity—primarily from those of light. Respecting light two facts are known to us with absolute certainty.

1st. It traverses space at the rate of 192,000 miles per second.

2nd. It is propagated not by particles actually travelling at this rate, but, like sound through air, by the transmission of waves.

The first fact is known from the difference of time at which eclipses of Jupiter's satellites are seen according as the earth is at the point of its orbit nearest to or farthest from Jupiter—i.e. from the time light takes to traverse the diameter of the earth's orbit, which is about 180 millions of miles; and this velocity of light is confirmed by direct experiments, as by noting the difference of time between seeing the flash and hearing the sound of a gun, which gives the velocity of light compared with the known velocity of sound.

The second fact is equally certain from the phenomena of what are called interferences, when the crest of
one wave just overtakes the hollow of a preceding one,
so that, if the two waves are of equal magnitude, the
oscillations exactly neutralise one another, and two
lights produce darkness. This is shown in a thousand
different ways, and for all the different colours depending on different waves into which white light is analysed
when passed through a prism. It is a certain result of
wave-motion, and of wave-motion only, and therefore
we know without a doubt that light is propagated by
waves.

But waves imply a medium through which wave-
forms are transmitted, for waves are nothing but the
rhythmic motion of something which rises and falls, or
oscillates symmetrically about a mean position of rest,
slowly or quickly according to the less or greater
elasticity of the medium. The waves which run along
a large and slack wire are large and slow, those along a
small and tightly stretched wire are small and quick ;
and from the data we possess as to light, its velocity
of transmission, its refraction when its waves pass from
one medium into another of different density, and from
the distance between the waves as shown by interference, it is easy to calculate the lengths and vibratory
periods of the waves, and the elasticity of the medium
through which such waves are transmitted.

The figures at which we arrive are truly extraordinary. The dimensions and rates of oscillations of
the waves which produce the different colours of visible light have been measured and calculated with the
greatest accuracy, and they are as follows :

DIMENSIONS OF LIGHT-WAVES.

Colours	No. of waves in one inch	No. of oscillations in one second
Red	39,000	477,000,000,000,000
Orange . . .	42,000	506,000,000,000,000
Yellow . . .	44,000	535,000,000,000,000
Green	47,000	577,000,000,000,000
Blue	51,000	622,000,000,000,000
Indigo . . .	54,000	658,000,000,000,000
Violet . . .	57,000	699,000,000,000,000

The elasticity of this wonderful medium is even more extraordinary.

The rapidity with which wave-motion is transmitted depends, other things being equal, on the elasticity of the medium, which is proportional to the square of the velocity with which a wave travels through it. As the velocity of the sound-wave in air is about 1,100 feet in a second, and that of the light-wave about 192,000 miles in the same time, it follows that the velocity of the latter is about a million times greater than that of the former, and if the density of ether were the same as that of air, its elasticity must be about a million million times greater. But the elasticity is the same thing as the power of resisting compression, which in the case of air we know to be about 15 pounds to the square inch ; so that the ether, if equally dense, would balance a pressure of 15 million million pounds to the square inch—that is, it would require a pressure of about 750 millions of tons to the square inch to condense ether to the density of air. On the other hand, its density, if any, must be so infinitesimally small that the earth moving through it in its orbit with a velocity of 1,100 miles a minute suffers no perceptible retardation.

Consider what this means. Air blowing at the rate

of 100 miles an hour is a hurricane uprooting trees and levelling houses. If ether were as dense as air the resistance to the earth in passing through it would be 600 times that of going dead to windward in a tropical hurricane. But in point of fact there is no sensible resistance, for the earth and heavenly bodies move in their calculated paths according to the law of gravity exactly as they would do if they were moving in a vacuum. Even the comets, which consist of such excessively rare matter that when one of them got entangled among the satellites of Jupiter it did not affect their movements, are not retarded by the ether, or so slightly, that any retardation in the case of one or two of them is suspected rather than proved. But, if the ether has no weight, how can we call it material, weight being, as we have seen, the invariable test and measure of all matter down to the minutest atom? And yet how can we deny its existence when it is demonstrably necessary to account for undoubted facts revealed to us every day by the prism, the spectroscope, electricity, and chemical action, and deductions from these facts based on the strict laws of mathematical calculation? For the existence of the ether is not based only on the phenomena of light: it is an equally necessary postulate to explain those of heat, electricity, and chemical action. We must conceive of our atoms and molecules as forming systems and performing their movements, not in vacuo, but in an all-pervading medium of this ether, to which they impart, and from which they receive, impulses.

These impulses are excessively minute, and when they occur in irregular order they produce no appreciable effect; but when the vibrations of the ether keep time with those of the atoms, the multitude of small effects becomes summed up into one considerable enough to produce great changes.   Just so a rhythmic succession of tiny ripples may set a heavy buoy oscillating, and the footfalls of a regiment of soldiers marching over a suspension-bridge may make it swing until it breaks down, while a confused mob could traverse it in safety. The latter affords a good illustration of the way in which molecular structures may be broken down, and their atoms set free to enter into other combinations, by the action of heat, light, or chemical rays beyond the visible end of the spectrum.

Conversely the phenomena of the spectroscope all depend on the fact that the vibrations of atoms and molecules can propagate waves through the ether, as well as absorb ether-waves into their own motions, and thus give spectra distinguished by bright or dark lines peculiar to each substance, by which it can be identified. Whatever ether may be, this much is certain about it : it pervades all space.   That it extends to the boundaries of the infinitely great we know from the fact that light reaches us from the remotest stars and nebulæ, and that in this light the spectroscope enables us to detect waves propagated and absorbed by the very same vibrations of the same familiar atoms at these enormous distances as at the earth's surface.   Glowing hydrogen, for instance, is a principal ingredient of the sun's atmosphere and of those distant suns we call stars, and it affects the ether and is affected by it exactly in the same manner as the hydrogen burning in an ordinary gas-lamp.

In the direction also of the infinitely small, ether permeates the apparently solid structure of crystals, whose molecules perform their limited and rigidly definite movements in an atmosphere of it, as is shown by the fact that in so many cases light and heat penetrate through them. A whole series of remarkable pheno-mena arise from the manner in which the vibrations of ether which cause light are affected by the structure of the molecules of crystals through which they pass. In certain cases they are what is called polarised, or so affected that while they pass freely if the crystal is held in one direction, they are stopped if it is turned round through an angle of 90° to its former position, so that one and the same crystal may be alternately transparent and non-transparent. It would seem as if its structure were like that of wood, grained, and more easy to pene-trate if cut with the grain than against it, so that when a ray of light attempted to penetrate, its vibrations were resolved into two, one with the grain which got through, the other against it which was suppressed ; so that the emerging ray, which entered with a circular vibration, got out with only one rectilinear vibration parallel to the diameter which coincided with the grain.

Other crystals of more complicated structure affect transmitted light in a more complex way, developing a double polarity very similar to that induced in the iron filings when brought under the influence of the two poles of the magnet. With this polarised light the most beau-tiful coloured rings can be produced from the waves of the different colours into which the white light has been analysed in passing through the crystal, which alter-nately flash out and disappear as the crystal is turned round its axis, and which present a remarkable analogy to the curves into which the iron filings form them-selves under the single or double poles of the magnet.

The importance of this will appear afterwards, but for

the present it is sufficient to show that the waves of ether which cause light really penetrate through the molecules of crystals, but in doing so may be affected by them.

RINGS OF POLARISED LIGHT,
UNIAXIAL CRYSTALS.

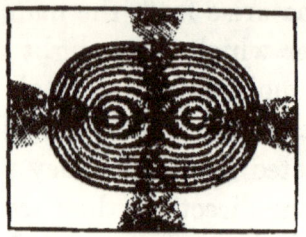

RINGS OF POLARISED LIGHT,
BIAXIAL CRYSTALS.

In dealing with these excessively small magnitudes it may assist the reader who has some acquaintance with mathematics in forming some conception of them, to refer to that refinement of calculation, the differential and integral calculus. And even the non-mathematical reader may find it worth while to give a little attention in order to gain some idea of this celebrated calculus which was the key by which Newton and his successors unlocked the mysteries of the heavens. The first rough idea of it is gained by considering what would happen if, in a calculation involving hundreds of miles, we neglected inches. Suppose we had a block of land to measure, 300 miles long and 200 wide ; as there are, say, 5,000 feet in a mile, and the error from omitting inches could not exceed a foot, the utmost error in the measurement of length could not exceed $\frac{1}{1500000}$th, and in width $\frac{1}{1000000}$th part of the correct amount. In the area of $300 \times 200 = 60,000$ square miles, the limit of error would, by adding or omitting the rectangle formed by multiplying together these two small errors, not exceed $\frac{1}{1500000} \times \frac{1}{1000000} = \frac{1}{1500000000000}$th part. It is evident that the first error is an excessively small part of the true figure, and the second error a still more excessively small part of the first error. But, as we are dealing with abstract numbers, we can just as readily conceive our initial error to be the $\frac{1}{100}$th or $\frac{1}{1000}$th of an inch, as one inch ; and, in fact, diminish it until it becomes an infinitesimally small or evanescent quantity. In doing so, however, it is evident that we shall make the second error such a still more infinitesimally small fraction of the first that it may be considered as altogether disappearing.

The first error is called a differential of the first order and denoted by d, the second a differential of the second order denoted by d_2. Thus if we call the base of our rectangle x and its height y, the area will be xy. Let us suppose x to receive the addition of a very small increment dx, and y the corresponding increment dy, what will be the corresponding increment of the area, or $d.xy$? Clearly the difference between the old area xy and the new area $(x+dx)$ multiplied by $(y+dy)$. This multiplication gives

$$
\begin{array}{l}
x + dx \\
\underline{y + dy} \\
xy + ydx \\
\quad\quad x\,dy + dx.dy \\
\overline{xy + xdy + ydx + dx.dy}
\end{array}
$$

The difference between this and xy is $xdy + ydx + dx.dy$. But $dx.dy$ is, as we have seen, a differential of the second order and may be neglected. Therefore $dxy = xdy + ydx$. In like manner $dx^2 = (x+dx)^2 - x^2 = 2xdx + dx^2$, which last term may be neglected, and $dx^2 = 2xdx$. In this way the differentials of all manner of functions and equations of symbols representing dimensions and motions may be found. Conversely the wholes may be considered as made up of an infinite number of these infinitely small parts, and found from them by summing up or integrating the differentials. Thus if we had the equation

$$x\,dy + y\,dx = 2\,z\,dz$$

we know that the left-hand side is the differential of $x\,y$, and therefore that by integrating it we shall get $x\,y$; while the right side is the differential of z^2 which we shall get by integrating it. The relation expressed therefore is that $x\,y = z^2$, or, in other words, that a rectangle whose sides are x and y exactly equals a square whose side is z.

The use of this device in assisting calculation will be apparent if we take the case of an area bounded by a curved line. We cannot directly calculate this area, but we can easily tell that of a rectangle. Now it is evident that if we inscribe rectangles in this area A B C,

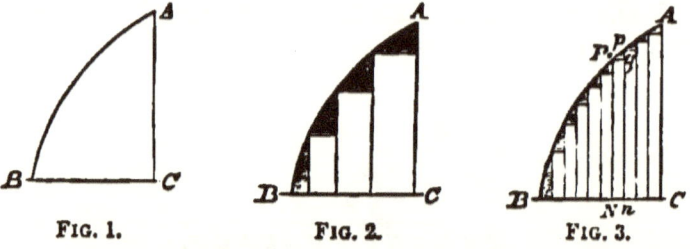

FIG. 1.　　　FIG. 2.　　　FIG. 3.

the more rectangles we inscribe the less will be the error in taking their sum as equal to the curved area. This is apparent if we compare fig. 2 with fig. 3. Suppose we take a point P on the curve, call $BN = x$ and $PN = y$, and suppose Nn to be dx, the differentially small increment of x, and $pq = dy$ the corresponding small increment of y. The area of the rectangle $PqnN = PN \times$

$N n = y\,dx$, and differs from the true curvilinear area
$P p n N$ by less than the little rectangle of $P q \times p q$ or of
$dx.dy$. But, as we have seen, if we push our division
to the first infinitesimal order, or make $N n$ and $p q$ differentials of x and y, $dx.dy$ may be neglected—i.e.
multiply the number of rectangles indefinitely, and the
sum of their areas will differ from the true area inclosed
by the curve by an error which is evanescent.

If then x and y are connected by some fixed law, as
must be the case if the extremity of y traces out some
regular curve, the relation between them may be expressed by an equation, which will remain one however
often it may be differentiated or again integrated, and
whatever modifications or transformations it may receive by mathematical processes which do not alter the
essential equality of the two sides connected by the
symbol of equality $=$. Thus by differentiating and
casting off as evanescent all differentials of a lower
order than that which we are working with, we may
arrive at forms of which we know the integrals, and by
integrating get back to the results in ordinary numbers,
which we were in search of but could not attain directly.

The same thing will apply if our symbols are
more numerous, and if they express relations of
motion as well as of space, or, in fact, any relations
which are governed by fixed laws expressible by equations. If I have succeeded in conveying to the readers
any idea of this celebrated calculus, they will perceive
what an analogy it presents to the idea of modern
physical and chemical science, that of molecules, atoms,
and ether, forming differentials of successive orders of
the infinitely small. It is certainly most remarkable
that while the former was a purely intellectual idea based

on mathematical abstractions, and which was invented and worked as an instrument for solving the most intricate astronomical problems for nearly two centuries, without a suspicion that it represented any objective reality : the latter idea, based on actual experiment, seems to show that differentials and integrals have their real counterpart in nature and represent fundamental facts in the constitution of the universe.

Those who are of a mystic or metaphysical turn of mind may discern in this, arguments for matter and laws of matter being after all only manifestations of one universal, all-pervading mind; but in following such speculations we should be deserting the solid earth for cloudland, and passing the limit of positive knowledge into the region where reflections of our own hopes, fears, religious feelings, and poetical sentiments form and dis- solve themselves against the background of the great unknown. For the present, therefore, I confine myself to pointing out how these undoubted truths of mathe- matical science, which have verified themselves in the practical form of enabling us to predict eclipses and construct nautical almanacs, correspond with and throw light upon the equally certain facts of this succession of infinitely small quantities of successive orders in the constitution of matter.

An attempt has recently been made, based on abstruse mathematical calculations, to carry our knowledge of the constitution of matter one step further back, and identify atoms with ether. This is attempted by the vortex theory of Helmholz, Sir W. Thomson, and Pro- fessor Tait. It is singular how some of the ultimate facts discovered by the refinements of science corre- spond with some of the most trivial amusements Thus the blowing of soap-bubbles gives the best clue to the movement of waves of light, and through them to the dimensions of molecules and atoms ; and the collision of billiard-balls, knocked about at random, to the movements of those minute bodies, and the kinetic theory of gases. In the case of the vortex theory the idea is given by the rings of smoke which certain adroit smokers amuse themselves by puffing into the air. These rings float for a considerable time, retaining their circular form, and showing their elasticity by oscillating about it and returning to it if their form is altered, and by rebounding and vibrating energetically, just as two solid elastic bodies would do, if two rings come into collision. If we try to cut them in two, they recede before the knife, or bend round it, returning, when the external force is removed, to their original form without the loss of a single particle, and preserving their own individuality through every change of form and of velocity. This persistence of form they owe to the fact that their particles are revolving in small circles at right angles to the axis or circumference of the larger circle which forms the ring ; motion thus giving them stability, very much as in the familiar instance of the bicycle. They burst at last because they are formed and rotate in the air, which is a resisting medium ; but mathematical calculation shows that in a perfect fluid free from all friction these vortex rings would be indivisible and indestructible : in other words, they would be atoms.

The vortex theory assumes, therefore, that the universe consists of one uniform primary substance, a fluid which fills all space, and that what we call matter consists of portions of this fluid which have become

D

animated with vortex motion. The innumerable atoms which form molecules, and through molecules all the diversified forms of matter of the material universe, are therefore simply so many vortex rings, each perfectly limited, distinct, and indestructible, both as to its form, mass, and mode of motion. They cannot change or disappear, nor can they be formed spontaneously. Those of the same kind are constituted after the same fashion, and therefore are endowed with the same properties.

The theory is a plausible one, and the reputation of its authors must command for it respectful consideration; but it is as yet a long way from being an established theory which can be accepted as a true representation of facts. In the first place it is based solely on mathematical theory, and not, as in the case of atoms and light-waves, upon actual facts of weight and measurement tested by experiment, and to which mathematical reasoning affords only an aid and supplement. No one has proved the existence of such a medium or of such vortex rings, much less weighed or measured them.

Moreover the theory is open to some very obvious objections. How can aggregations of imponderable matter acquire weight, and become subject to the law of gravity, which, as we have seen, is one of the essential and permanent qualities of atoms? If a cubic millionth of a millimetre of ether formed into a big vortex ring of, say, an atom of mercury, has a weight equal to 200 times that of an atom of hydrogen, which itself has a definite weight, why has it no weight in its original form? And if it had weight, however small, how could the enormous mass of ether filling all space produce no perceptible effect on bodies, even of attenuated cometic vapour, revolving through it with immense velocities? Again, how could these innumerable vortex rings be formed out of the ether without disturbing the uniformity and continuity of the medium, which are essential for the propagation of the light-waves through it? And how could the motions requisite to form the vortex rings be impressed on them *de novo* consistently with the principle of the conservation of energy ? Energy can no more be created out of nothing than matter, by any process known in nature or conceivable by the human intellect ; and to assume it is simply a more refined manner of falling back on the supernatural, which is itself only a more refined manner of saying that we know nothing.

For the present, therefore, we must be content with atoms and ether as the ultimate terms of our knowledge of the material or quasi-material components of the universe.

CHAPTER IV.

ENERGY.

Energy of motion and of position—Energy can be transformed, not created or destroyed—Not created by free will—Conservation of mechanical power—Convertibility of heat and work—Nature of heat—The steam-engine—Different forms of energy—Gravity—Molecular energy—Chemical energy—Dynamite—Chemical affinities—Electricity—Produced by friction—By the voltaic battery—Electric currents—Arc light—Induction—Magnetism—The magnetic needle—The electric telegraph—The telephone—Dynamo-electric engine—Accumulator.

THOSE ultimate elements, however, atoms and ether, only give us what may be called the dead half of the universe, which could not exist without the constant presence of the animating principle of force or energy. Energy is the term generally adopted in the language of science, for force is apt to be associated with human effort and with actual motion produced, while energy is a comprehensive term, embracing whatever produces or is capable of producing motion. Thus, if we bend a cross-bow, the force with which it is bent may either reappear at once in the flight of the arrow, if we let go the string; or it may remain stored up, if we fix the string in the notch, ready to reappear when we pull the trigger. In the former case it is called energy of motion, in the latter energy of position. It is important to realise this distinction clearly, for many of the ordered and harmonious arrangements of the universe depend on the polarity, or conflict with alternate victories and defeats, between those two forms of energy.

Thus if A B is a pendulum suspended at the point A, if we move it from its position of rest A C to A B and hold it there, its whole energy is that of position. If we let it go it swings backwards and forwards between the positions A B and A D, and but for the resistance of the air and the friction at the point of suspension, it would so swing for ever. But in thus swinging what happens? From A B to A C energy of motion keeps

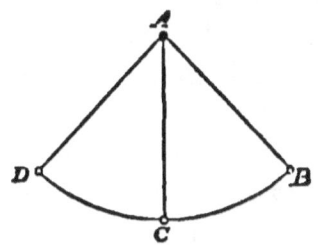

gaining on energy of position, until when the pendulum reaches C, it has annihilated it. Energy of position has entirely disappeared, and the whole original force expended in raising the pendulum to A B exactly reappears in the force or momentum of the pendulum at its lowest point. But is this victory final? By no means; energy of position having touched bottom, gathers, like Antæus, fresh vigour for the contest, and from the position A C upwards it gains ground on its adversary until when the pendulum reaches A D it is in its turn completely victorious.

The same alternation between energy of motion and of position takes place in all rhythmical movements such as waves, which, whether in water, air, or ether, are propagated, as in the case of the pendulum, by particles forced out of their position of rest and oscillating between the two energies.

Thus if waves run along an elastic wire A B, the particle P, which has been forced into the position p, oscillates backwards and forwards between p and q,

beginning with nothing but energy of position at p, losing it all for energy of motion at P, and regaining it at q. All wave-motions therefore—that is to say, all sound, light, and heat—depend on this primitive polarity.

If we have got this definition of the two forms of energy clearly into our heads, we shall be the better prepared for this further generalisation—the grandest, perhaps, in the whole range of modern science—that energy, like matter, is indestructible, and can only be transformed, but never created or annihilated.

This is at first sight a more difficult proposition to establish in the case of energy than in that of matter. In the latter case we have nothing in our experience that can lead us to suppose that we have ever created something out of nothing; but in the former, our first impression undoubtedly is that we do create force. If I throw a stone at a bird I have an instinctive impression that the force which projects the stone is the creation of my own conscious will; that I had the choice either to throw or not to throw; and that if I had decided not to throw, the impelling force would never have existed. But, if we look more closely at the matter, it is not really so. The chain of events is this: the first impulse proceeds from the visual rays, which, concentrated by the lens of the eye on the retina, give an image of the bird; this sends vibrations along the optic nerve to the brain, setting in motion certain molecules of that organ; these again send vibrations along other nerves to certain muscles of the arm and hand, which contract, and by doing so give out the energy of movement which throws the stone. All this process is strictly mechanical; the eye acts precisely like a camera obscura in forming the image; the nerve-vibrations, though not identical with those of the wires of an electric telegraph, are of the same nature, their velocity can be measured, and their presence detected by the galvanometer; the energy of the muscle is stored there by the slow combustion of the food we have eaten, in the oxygen of the air we have breathed. Take any of these conditions away, and no effort of the will can produce the result. If the nerve is paralysed, or the muscle, from prolonged starvation, has no energy left, the stone will not be thrown, however much we may desire to kill the bird.

Again, precisely the same circle of events takes place in numerous instances without any intervention of this additional factor of conscious will. We breathe mechanically, the muscles of the chest causing it to rise and fall like the waves of the ocean, without any deliberate intention of taking air into the lungs and exhaling it. Nay more, there are instances of what was at first accompanied by the sensation of conscious will, ceasing to be so when the molecular movements had made channels for themselves, as when a piano-player, who had learned his notes with difficulty, ends by playing a complicated piece automatically. The case of animals also raises another difficulty. Suppose a retriever dog sees his master shoot at and miss a hare :

shall he obey the promptings of his animal instinct and
give chase, or those of his higher moral nature which
tell him that it is wrong to do so without the word of
command ?   It is hard to see how this differs from the
case of a man resisting or yielding to temptation ; and
how, if we assign conscious will to the man, we can
deny it to the dog.

Reasoning from these premises, some philosophers
have come to the conclusion that man and all animals
are but mechanical automata, cleverly constructed to
work in a certain way fitting in with the equally pre-
ordained course of outward phenomena ; and that the
sensation of will is merely an illusion arising as a last
refinement in the adjustment of the machinery.   But
here comes in that principle of duality or polarity, by
which a proposition may be at once true and untrue,
and two contradictory opposites exist together.   No
amount of philosophical reasoning can make us believe
that we are altogether machines and not free agents ; it
runs off us like water from a duck's back, and leaves us
in presence of the intuitive conviction that to a great
extent

Man is man and master of his fate.

If this be an illusion, why not everything—evidence of
the senses, experiment, natural law, science, as well as
morality and religion ?

To pursue this farther would lead us far astray into
the misty realm of metaphysics, and I refer to it only
as showing that the principle of the conservation of
energy, standing as it does in apparent contradiction to
our natural impressions, requires a fuller demonstration
than the kindred principle of the indestructibility of
matter.

In the case of ordinary mechanical power it had been long known that the intervention of machinery did not create force, but only transformed it. If a weight of 1 lb., A, just balances a weight of 2 lb., B, by aid of a pulley, and by the addition of a minute fraction, such as a grain, raises it 1 foot, it will be invariably found that A has descended 2 feet. In other words, 1 lb. working through 2 feet does exactly the same work as 2 lbs. working through 1 foot. And whatever may be the intervening machinery the same thing holds good, and the work put in at one end comes out, neither more nor less, at the other, except for a minute loss due to friction and resistance of air. If a force equal to 1 lb. is made, by multiplying the intermediate machinery, to raise a ton a foot from the ground, exactly as much force must have been exerted as if the ton had been divided into 2,240 parts of 1 lb. each, and each part separately lifted.

But although energy cannot be created, at first sight it seems as if it might be destroyed, as when the ton falls to the ground and seems to have lost all its energy, whether of motion or of position. But here science steps in and shows us that it is not destroyed, but simply transformed into another sort of motion, which we call heat.

Some connection between mechanical work and heat had long been known, as in the familiar experiment of rubbing our hands together to warm them ; and the practice known to most primitive races of obtaining fire by twirling a stick rapidly in a hole drilled in a block of wood ; a practice described by the old Sanskrit word 'pramantha,' which means an instrument for obtaining fire by pressure or friction, and which, translated into Greek, has been immortalised by the legend of Prometheus. But it was reserved for recent years, and for an English philosopher, Dr. Joule, to give scientific precision and generality to this idea, by actually measuring the amount of heat produced by a given amount of work, and showing that they were in all cases convertible terms, so much heat for so much work, and so much work for so much heat. He did this by measuring accurately by a thermometer the heat added to a given amount of water by the work done by a set of paddles revolving in it, set in rapid motion by a known weight descending through a known space. The unit of work being taken as that sufficient to raise 1 kilogramme through 1 metre, and that of heat as that required to raise the temperature of one kilogramme of water by 1° Centigrade, the relation between them, as found by a vast number of careful experiments, is that of 424 to 1. That is, one unit of heat is equal to 424 units of work.

In this, and all cases requiring scientific precision, it is better to use the units of the metrical system than our clumsy English standards; but it may be sufficient for the ordinary reader to take the metre, which is about 39·37 inches, as practically a yard, and the kilogramme, which is 15,432 English grains, as practically equal to 2 lbs. This is sufficient to show the much greater energy of the invisible forces which act at minute distances, than that of gravity and other forces which do appreciable mechanical work, the energy of a weight falling from a height of more than 1,300 feet being only sufficient to heat its own weight by 1°.

This proof of the convertibility of work into heat

gives much greater precision to our ideas respecting the real nature of heat and its kindred molecular and atomic energies. Heat is clearly not a material substance, for a body does not gain weight by becoming hotter. In the case of all ponderable matter down to the atoms, which are only of the size of cricket-balls compared to that of the earth, any combination which adds matter adds weight, and the weight of the product exactly equals the sum of the weights of the separate factors which have united to form it. Thus, if iron is burnt in oxygen gas, the product, oxide of iron or rust, weighs more than the original iron by just as much as the weight of the oxygen which has been consumed. But heat, light, and electricity add nothing to the weight of a body when they are added to it, and take nothing away when they are subtracted. The inference is unavoidable that heat, like light, is not ponderable matter, but an energy transmitted by waves of the imponderable medium known as ether. This is confirmed by finding that when a ray from the sun is analysed by passing through a refracting prism, one part of the spectrum shows light of various colours, while another gives heat. The hottest part of the spectrum lies in the red and beyond it, showing that the heat-waves are longer, and their oscillations slower, than those of light. Heat-waves also may be made to interfere, and to become polarised, in a manner analogous to the phenomena exhibited by those of light.

There can be no doubt, therefore, that heat, like light, is an energy or mode of motion, transmitted by waves of an imponderable ether, and that it acts on the molecules and atoms of matter by the accumulated successive impulses of those waves on the molecules and atoms which are floating in it, or rather which are revolving in it, in definite groups and fixed orbits, like miniature solar systems or starry universes. We can now see how heat performs work, and why work can be transformed into it.

Heat performs work in two ways. First, it expands bodies—that is, it draws their molecules farther apart against the force of cohesion which binds them together or keeps them moving in definite orbits at definite distances. It is as if it increased the velocity, and therefore the centrifugal force of a system of planets, and so caused them to revolve in wider orbits. The expansion of mercury in a thermometer affords a familiar instance of this effect of heat and the readiest measure of its amount. Secondly, it increases the energy of the molecular motions, so that they dart about, collide, and vibrate with greater force. Thus, as heat increases, evaporation increases, for molecules on the surface are projected with so much force as to get beyond the sphere of the cohesive attraction which binds them to the system, and they dart off like comets into space. Finally, as heat increases, and more and more work is done, against the centripetal force of cohesion, most substances, and doubtless all if we could get heat enough, are converted from solids into fluids, and ultimately into gases, in which latter state the molecules have got altogether beyond the sphere of their mutual attraction, and tend to dart off indefinitely in the direction of their own proper centrifugal motions, unless confined, in which case they dart about, collide, rebound, and exercise pressure on the containing surface.

Conversely, if heat expands bodies, it is given out when they contract. Thus the enormous quantity of heat poured out for millions of years by the sun, is probably owing mainly to the mechanical force of contraction of the original cosmic matter condensing about the solar nucleus.

Again, when gases suddenly expand, their temperature falls, which is the principle by which artificial ice is procured, and frozen beef and mutton are brought from America and Australia, producing, such are the complicated relations of modern society, agricultural depression, fall of rents, and a serious aggravation of the Irish question.

As an example of the converse proposition of the transformation of heat into mechanical work, the steam-engine affords the aptest illustration. The original power came from the sun millions of years ago, and did work by enabling the leaves of plants to overcome the strong mutual affinity of carbon and oxygen in the carbonic dioxide in the air, and store up the carbon in the plant, where it remained since the coal era in the form of energy of position. By lighting the coal, or in other words separating its molecules more widely by heat, we enable them to exert once more their natural affinity for oxygen, and burn, that is re-combine into carbonic dioxide. The heat thus produced turns water into steam, which passes through a cylinder, either into a condenser if the steam is at low pressure, or into the outer air if it has been superheated and brought to a higher pressure than that of the atmosphere. The difference of the pressure or elasticity of the steam in the boiler, and of the same steam when it is condensed or liberated, is available for doing work, and, being admitted and released alternately at the two ends of the cylinder, drives a piston up and down, which, by means of cranks and shafts, turns a wheel or does whatever work is required of it. In doing this, heat disappears, being converted into work, and the amount of heat would exactly equal that into which the work would be converted according to Joule's law, if it could all be utilised without the loss necessarily incurred by friction, radiation, and the still more important absorption of latent heat required to convert water at boiling-point into vapour of the same temperature. This latter is not really an annihilation of the heat, but its conversion into work done in separating the molecules against the force of cohesion. The whole heat, therefore, is transformed into work, mainly molecular work in tearing molecules asunder, and the residue into mechanical work turning spindles and driving locomotives and steamboats.

The intermediate machinery here, including the water in the boiler, is merely the means of applying the original energy in the particular way we desire. The essential thing is the transformation of a certain amount of heat into work by passing, in accordance with the laws of heat, from a hotter to a colder body. The last condition is indispensable, for the nature of heat is to seek an equilibrium by passing from hot to cold, and no work can be got out of it in the reverse way. On the contrary, work must be expended and turned into heat to restore the temperature which has run down. The case is analogous to that of water, which, if raised by evaporation or stored up in reservoirs at a level above the sea, can be made to turn a wheel while it is running down; but when it has all run down to the sea level, can do no more work, and can only be pumped up again to a higher level by the expenditure of fresh work. Owing to this tendency of heat we can see that, although matter and energy are to all appearance indestructible, the present constitution of the universe is not eternal. The animating energy of heat is always tending to obliterate differences of temperature, and bring all energy down to one uniform dead level of a common average, in which no further life, work, or motion are possible. Fortunately this consummation is far off, and for many tens or hundreds of millions of years the inhabitants of this tiny planet may feel fairly secure, and need not, like the late Dr. Cumming, of millenarian celebrity, introduce breaks in the leases of their houses to provide against the contingency of the world coming to an end at an early date.

Dismissing, then, to the remote future any speculations as to the failure of this essential element of active energy, let us rather consider the various protean forms in which it shows itself.

1. The energy of visible motion, which, as we have seen, may be transformed into an equivalent amount of energy of position.

2. Molecular energy, which causes the cohesive attraction, repulsion, and other proper motions of these minute and invisible particles of matter.

3. Energy of heat and light, which are transmitted by waves of the assumed imponderable medium called ether.

4. Energy of chemical action, by which the small ultimate particles of ponderable matter, called atoms, separate and combine into the various combinations of molecules constituting visible matter, in obedience to certain affinities, or inherent attractions and repulsions.

5. Electrical energy, which includes magnetism as a special instance.

All these forms of energy may exist, as in the case of visible energy, either as energies of motion or of position, and the actual constitution of the universe is due in a great measure to the alternation of these two energies.   Thus all wave-motion, whether it be of the waves of the sea grinding down a rocky coast, of the air transmitting sound, or of ether transmitting light and heat, are instances of energies of motion and of position, conflicting with one another and alternately gaining the victory.   So also a pound of gunpowder or dynamite has an immense energy of position, which, when its atoms are let loose from their mutual unstable connection by heat or percussion, manifests itself in an enormous energy of motion, which is more or less destructive according to the rapidity with which the atoms rush into new combinations.

Let us consider these different energies a little more in detail.   The energy of visible motion is manifested principally by the law of gravity, under which all matter attracts other matter directly as the mass and inversely as the square of the distance. It is a universal and uniform law of matter, and can be traced without change or variation from the minutest atom up to the remotest double star. The energy of living force might, at first sight, be considered as another of the commonest causes of visible motion ; but, when closely analysed, it will be found that what appears as such is only the result of molecular energy of position stored up in the living body by chemical changes during the slow com-bustion of food, and that nothing has been added by any hypothetical vital force.   The conscious will seems to act in those cases simply as the signalman who shows a white flag may act on a train which has been standing on the line waiting for it. The energy which moves the train is due entirely to the difference of heat, which has been developed by the combustion of coal, between the steam in the boiler and the steam when allowed to escape into the air; and this energy came originally from the sun, whose rays enabled the leaves of growing plants to decompose carbonic dioxide and store up the carbon in the coal. Of this force of gravity causing visible motion we may say that it is comparatively a very weak force, which acts uniformly over all distances great or small.

Molecular energies, on the other hand, act with vastly greater force, but at very small distances, and appear sometimes as attractive and sometimes as repulsive forces. Thus solid bodies are held together by a force of cohesion which is very powerful, but acts only at very small distances, as we may see if we break a piece of glass and try to mend it by pressing the broken edges together. We cannot bring them near enough to bring the molecular attraction again into play and make the broken glass solid. But the same glass acts with repellent energy if another solid tries to penetrate it, so that we can walk on a glass floor without sinking into it. Heat also, by increasing the distance between the molecules, first weakens the cohesive force so that the solid becomes fluid, and finally overcomes it altogether, so that it passes into the state of gas in which the centripetal attraction of the molecules is extinguished, and they tend to recede further and further from each other under the centrifugal force of their own proper velocities. The great energy of molecular forces will be apparent from the fact that a bar of iron, in cooling 10° Centigrade, contracts with a force equal to a ton

E

for each square inch of section, as exemplified in the tubular bridge across the Menai Straits, where space has to be allowed for the free contraction and expansion of the iron under changes of temperature.

Chemical energy, or the mutual attractions and repulsions of atoms, is even more powerful than that of molecules. It displays itself in their elective affinities, or what may be called the likes and dislikes, or loves and hatreds, of these ultimate particles. Perhaps the best illustration will be afforded by that 'latest resource of civilisation,' dynamite. This substance, or to give it its scientific name, nitro-glycerine, is composed of molecules each of which is a complex combination of nine atoms of oxygen, five of hydrogen, three of nitrogen, and three of carbon. Of these, oxygen and hydrogen have a strong affinity for one another, as is seen by their rushing together whenever they get the chance, and by their union forming the very stable compound, water. Oxygen and carbon have also a very strong affinity, and readily form the stable product carbonic dioxide gas. Nitrogen, on the other hand, is a very inert substance; its molecule consists of two atoms of itself which are bound together by a strong affinity, and can only be coaxed with difficulty into combinations with other elements, forming compounds which are, as it were, artificial structures, and very unstable. We see this in the air, which consists mainly of oxygen and nitrogen, but not in chemical combination, the oxygen being simply diluted by the nitrogen, as whisky is with water, with the same object of diluting the too powerful oxygen or too potent alcohol, and enabling the air-breather or whisky-drinker to take them into the system without burning up the tissues too rapidly.

If nitrogen had more affinity for oxygen it would combine chemically with it, and we should live in an atmosphere of nitrous oxide, or laughing gas.

The molecule, therefore, of nitro-glycerine resembles a house of cards, so nicely balanced that it will just stand, but will fall to pieces at the slightest touch. When this is supplied by a slight percussion the molecule falls to pieces and is resolved into its constituent atoms, which rush together in accordance with their natural affinities, forming an immense volume of gas, partly of water in the form of steam where oxygen has combined with hydrogen, and partly of carbonic dioxide where it has combined with carbon, leaving the nitrogen atoms to pair off, and revert to their original form of two-atom molecules of nitrogen gas. It is as if ill-assorted couples, who had been united by matrimonial bonds tied by the manœuvres of Belgravian mothers, found themselves suddenly freed by a decree of divorce *a vinculo matrimonii*, and rushed impetuously into each other's arms, according to the laws of their respective affinities. So striking is the similitude that one of Goethe's best-known novels, the 'Wahlverwandschaften,' takes its title from the human play of these chemical reactions. The enormous energy developed when these atomic forces are let loose and a vast volume of gas almost instantaneously created, is attested by the destructive force by which the hardest rocks are shattered to pieces and the strongest buildings overthrown.

These loves and hatreds, or, as they are termed, chemical affinities and repulsions of the atoms, are the principal means by which the material structure of the universe is built up from the original elements. The earth, or solid crust of the planet we inhabit, consists mainly of oxidised bases, and is due to the affinity of oxygen for silicon, calcium, aluminium, iron, and other primary elements of what are called metals. This affinity enables them to make stable compounds, which, under the existing conditions of temperature and otherwise, hold together and are not readily decomposed. Water in like manner, in all its forms of waves, seas, lakes, rivers, clouds, and invisible vapour, is due to the affinity between oxygen and hydrogen forming a stable compound. Salt again is owing to the affinity of chlorine for sodium, and so for nearly all the various products with which we are familiar, oxygen and nitrogen in the air we breathe being almost the only elements which exist in their primary and uncombined state in any considerable quantities, and form an essential part of the conditions which render our planet a habitable abode for man and other forms of life.

We shall see presently something more of the nature of these affinities, and the laws by which they act; but before entering on this branch of the subject we must consider the remaining form in which the one indestructible energy of the universe manifests itself, viz. that of electricity.

Electricity is the most subtle and the least understood of these forms. In its simplest form it appears as the result of friction between dissimilar substances. Thus if we rub a glass rod with a piece of silk, taking care that both are warm and dry, we find that the glass has acquired the property of attracting light bodies, such as little bits of paper, or balls of elder-pith. Other substances, such as sealing-wax and amber, have the same property. Pursuing our research further we find that this influence is not, like that of gravity, uniform and always acting in the same direction, but of two kinds, equal and opposite. If we touch the pith-ball by the excited glass rod, it will after contact be repelled ; but if we bring the ball which has been excited by contact with the glass within the influence of a stick of sealing-wax which has been excited by rubbing it with warm dry flannel, the ball instead of being repelled is attracted.

Conversely, if the pith-ball has been first touched by excited sealing-wax, it will afterwards be repelled by excited sealing-wax and attracted by excited glass. It is clear, therefore, that there are two opposite electricities, and that bodies charged with similar electricities repel, and with unlike electricities attract, one another. For convenience, one of these electricities, that developed in glass, is called positive, and the other negative ; and it has been clearly proved that one cannot exist without the other, and that whenever one electricity is produced, just as much is produced of an opposite description. If positive electricity is produced in glass by rubbing it with silk, just as much negative electricity is produced upon the silk.

Another primary fact is that some substances are able to carry away and diffuse or neutralise this peculiar influence called electricity, while others are unable to do so and retain it. The former are called conductors, the latter non-conductors. Thus, glass is an insulator or non-conductor, while metal is a conductor of electricity ; and the reason why the substances rubbed together, as glass and silk, must be dry is that water, in all its forms, is a conductor which carries away the electricity as fast as it is produced.

These facts have given rise to a theory—which is

after all not so much an explanation as a convenient mode of expressing the facts—of the existence of two opposite electric fluids, which, in the ordinary or unexcited body, are combined and neutralise one another, but are separated by friction, and flow in opposite directions, accumulating at opposite poles, or, it may be, one being accumulated at one pole, while the other is diffused through some conducting medium and lost sight of. The active electricity, be it positive or negative, thus accumulated at one pole, and retained there by the substance in contact with it being a non-conductor, disturbs by its influence the electrical equilibrium of any body brought near to it, separates its two fluids, and attracts the one opposite to itself. This attraction draws the light body towards it until contact ensues, when the electric fluid of the excited body flows into the smaller one, so that its opposite electricity is expelled, and it is in the same condition as its exciter, and therefore liable to be repelled by a similar exciter, or attracted by an opposite one which formerly repelled it.

It is evident, without going further, that there is a great analogy between electrical energy and those of heat and of chemical affinity. The same mechanical work—viz. friction—which generates heat, generates electricity. The chief difference seems to be that friction may be transformed into heat when the same substances are rubbed together, as in the case of obtaining fire by the friction of wood; but electricity can only be obtained by friction between dissimilar substances. Thus no electricity is obtained by rubbing glass upon glass, or silk upon silk, or upon glass covered with silk, though a slight difference of texture is sometimes sufficient to separate the electric fluids. Thus if two pieces of the same silk ribbon are rubbed together, lengthways, no electricity is produced, but if crossways, one is positively, and the other negatively, electrified. In this respect the analogy is evident to chemical affinity, which, in like manner, only acts between dissimilar bodies.

In order, however, to carry the proof of the identity of these forms of energy beyond the sphere of vague analogy, we must follow up electricity far beyond the simple manifestations of the glass rod and sealing-wax, and pursue it to its origin, in the transformations of chemical action and mechanical work, in the voltaic battery, the electric telegraph, the telephone, and the dynamo.

The voltaic battery, in its simplest form, is a trough containing an acid liquid in which pairs of plates of different metals are immersed. It is evident that if the action of the acid on each metal were precisely the same, equal quantities of each would be dissolved in the acid, and the equilibrium of chemical energies would not be affected. But, the action being different, this equilibrium is disturbed, and if the sum of these disturbances for a number of separate pairs of plates can be accumulated, it will become considerable. This is done by connecting the plates of the same metal in each cell by a metallic wire covered by some non-conducting substance. There are, therefore, two wires, one to the right hand, the other to the left, the loose extremities of which are called the poles of the battery. If we test these poles as we did the glass rod and stick of sealing-wax, we find that one pole is charged with positive and the other with negative electricity. In other words, the chemical energy, whose equilibrium was disturbed by the unequal action of the acid on the plates of different metals, has been transformed into electrical energy manifesting itself, as it always does, under the condition of two equal and opposite polarities. If we connect these two poles with one another the two electricities rush together and unite, and there is established what is called an electrical current circulating round the battery. As the chemical action of the acid on the metals is not momentary but continuous, the acid taking up molecule after molecule of the metal, so also the current is continuous. When we call it a current, the term is used for the sake of convenience, for as the current, as we shall presently see, will flow along the wire or other conducting substance for immense distances, as across the Atlantic, with a velocity of many thousands of miles per second, we can, no more than in the case of light, figure it to ourselves as an actual transfer of material particles swept along as by a river running with this enormous velocity, but necessarily as a transmission of some form of motion travelling by waves or tremors through the all-pervading ether in which the atoms of the conducting wire are floating. Be this as it may, the effect of these electric currents is very varied and very energetic. It can produce intense heat, for if, instead of uniting the two poles, we connect them by a thin platinum wire, it will, in a few seconds, become heated to redness. If the connecting wire is thicker, heat will equally be generated but less intense, thus maintaining the analogy to the current which rushes with more impetuosity through a narrow than through a wide channel. If the poles are tipped with a solid substance like carbon, whose particles remain solid under great heat, when they are brought nearly together intense light is produced and the carbon slowly burns away. This produces what is called the arc light, which gives such a strong illuminating power and is coming into general use for lighting up large spaces.

Another transformation is back again into chemical energy, which is shown by the power of the electric current to decompose compound substances. If, for instance, the poles of a battery are plunged into a vessel containing water, the molecules of the water will be decomposed and bubbles of oxygen gas will rise from the positive, and of hydrogen from the negative, pole.

Another effect of electrical currents is that of attraction and repulsion on one another. If two parallel wires, free to move, carry currents flowing in the same direction as from positive to negative, or *vice versâ*, they will attract one another ; if in opposite directions, they will repel. Electrical currents also work by way of induction, that is, they disturb the electrical equilibrium of bodies brought within their influence and induce currents in them. Thus, if we have two circular coils of insulated wire placed near each other, one on the right hand, the other on the left, and connect the extremities of the right-hand coil with the poles of a battery, when the connection is first made and the current begins to flow, a momentary current in the opposite direction will pass through the left-hand coil. This will cease, and as long as the current continues to flow through the right-hand coil there will be no current through the other ; but if we break the contact between the right-hand coil and the battery, there will be again a momentary current through the left-hand coil, but this time in the same direction as the other.

The same effect will be produced if, instead of making and breaking contact in the right-hand coil, we keep the current constantly flowing through it, and make the right-hand coil alternately approach and recede from the other coil. In this case, when the right-hand coil approaches, it induces an opposite current in the left-hand one ; and when it recedes, one in the same direction as that of the primary.

These phenomena of induction prepare us to understand the nature of magnets, and the magnetic effects produced by electrical currents. If an insulated wire is wrapped round a cylinder of soft or unmagnetic iron, and a current passed through the wire, the cylinder is converted into a magnet and becomes able to sustain weights. If the current ceases, the cylinder is no longer a magnet, and drops the weight. A magnet is therefore evidently a substance in which electric currents are circulating at right angles to its axis, and a permanent magnet is one in which such currents permanently circulate from the constitution of the body without being supplied from without. The earth is such a magnet, and also iron and other substances, under certain conditions.

This being established, it is easy to see why an electrical current deflects the magnetic needle. If such a needle is suspended freely near a wire parallel with it, on a current being passed through the wire it must attract if similar, or repel if dissimilar, the currents which are circulating at right angles to the axis of the needle, and thus tend to make the needle swing into a position at right angles with the wire so that its currents may be parallel to that of the needle. This is the reason why the needle in its ordinary condition points

to the north and south, or rather to the magnetic poles
of the earth, because its currents are influenced by the
earth currents which circulate parallel to the magnetic
equator.   The deviation of the needle from this direction, caused by any other current, like that passed along
the wire, will depend on the strength of the current,
which may be measured by the amount of deflection of
the needle.   The direction in which the needle deflects,
viz. whether the north pole swings to the right or to the
left, will depend on the direction of the current through
the wire.   The direction of the circular currents which
form a magnet is such that if you look towards the
north pole of a freely suspended cylindrical magnet—i.e.
if you stand on the north of it and look southwards—the
positive current will ascend on your right hand, or on
the west side, and descend on the east.   It follows that
unlike poles must necessarily attract, and like poles repel
one another, for in the former case the circular currents
which face each other are going in the same, and in the
latter in opposite directions.

The reader is now in a position to understand the
principle of the electric telegraph, that wonderful invention which has revolutionised human intercourse and,
to a great extent, annihilated space and time.   It originated in the discovery made by Oersted, a Danish
savant, that the effect of an electric current was to make
a magnet swing round, in the endeavour to place itself
at right angles to it.   The conducting power of insulated copper wire is such that it practically makes no
difference whether one of the wires connected with the
pole of a battery is two feet or 2,000 miles in length,
and the earth, being a conducting medium, supplies
an equal extension from the other pole, so that a closed

electric circuit may be established across the Atlantic as easily as within the walls of a laboratory.

• If, therefore, a magnetic needle is suspended at the American end, it will respond to every electrical current, and to any interruption, renewal, or reversal of that current established in England. The needle may thus be made to swing to the right or left, by forming or reversing a current through the wire ; and it will return to its position whenever the current is interrupted, and repeat its movement whenever the current is renewed. In fact it may be made to move like the arm of the old-fashioned telegraph, or of a railway signal. It only remains to have a machine by which the operator can form and interrupt currents rapidly, and a code by which certain movements of the needle stand for certain letters of the alphabet, and you have the electric telegraph.

There are many ingenious applications of the machinery, but in principle they all resolve themselves into transformations of energy. Chemical energy is transformed into electric energy, and that again into mechanical work in moving the needle.

The telephone is another instance of similar transformations. Here spoken words create vibrations of the air, which cause corresponding vibrations in a thin plate or disc of metal at one end, which are conveyed by intermediate machinery to a similar disc at the other end, whose vibrations cause similar vibrations in the air, reproducing the spoken words at a distance which may be a great many miles from the speaker.

The great inventions of modern science which have so revolutionised society are all instances of the laws of the conservation of energy. Man makes the powers of nature available for his purposes by transforming them backwards and forwards, now into one, now into another form of energy, as required for the result he wishes to attain. He wants mechanical power to pump water or drive a locomotive or steamboat : he gets it from the steam-engine, by transforming the energy of heat in coal, which came ages ago from the energy of chemical action produced by the sun's rays in the green leaves of growing plants. He wants to send messages in a few seconds across the Atlantic : he does it by transforming chemical energy into electricity in a voltaic battery, sending its vibrations along a conducting wire, and converting it at the far end into mechanical power, making a magnetic needle turn on its axis and give signals. If, instead of sending a message, he wants to hold a conversation at a distance, he invents the telephone, by which sound-vibrations of air are transformed into vibrations of a disc, then into electric currents, then into vibrations of a distant disc, and finally back again to spoken words. Or, if he wants light, he turns electricity into it by tipping the poles of his battery with carbon and bringing them close together.

The latest inventions of electrical science—the dynamo and the accumulator—afford remarkable instances of this convertibility of one primitive energy into different forms. In the instance just quoted of obtaining light from electricity by the voltaic battery, the cost has hitherto proved an obstacle to its adoption. The electrical energy is all obtained from the transformation of the heat produced in the cells by the chemical action on the metal used, which is commonly zinc. Now, the heat of combination of zinc with oxygen is only about one-sixth of that of coal, while the cost of zinc is about

twenty times as great. Theoretically, therefore, energy
got by burning zinc costs 120 times as much as that
got by burning coal. Practically the difference is not
nearly so great, for there is very little loss of energy in
the battery by the process of conversion, while the best
steam-engine cannot convert into work as much as
twenty per cent. of the heat energy in the coal consumed.
Still, after making every allowance, the cost of energy
from zinc remains some twenty times as great as from
coal, so that unless some process is found for obtaining
back the zinc as a residual product, there is no prospect
of this form of electricity being generally available for
light or for mechanical power.

The dynamo is an instrument invented for the mechanical generation of electricity by taking advantage
of the principle that electrical energy is produced by
moving magnets near coils of wire, or coils of wire near
magnets. A current is thus started by induction, and,
once started, the mechanical power exerted in making
the magnet or coils revolve is continually converted
into electricity until the accumulated electrical energy
becomes very powerful. The original energy comes of
course from the coal burned in the steam-engine which
makes the magnet or coils revolve.

The principle of the conservation of energy is well
illustrated by the fact that as the dynamo generates an
electric current if made to revolve, conversely it may
be made to revolve itself if an electric current is sent
through it from an exterior source. It is, therefore,
available not only as a source of light in the former case,
but as a direct source of mechanical power in the latter.
It is on this principle that electric engines are constructed
and electric railways are worked. Here also it is a ques-

tion of cost and convenience, for you can only get electricity enough either to light a street or to drive an engine, by an original steam-engine or other motive power to work the dynamo, and a system of conducting wires to convey the electricity to the place where the light or power is wanted. Where the motive power is supplied by nature, as in the case of tidal or river currents or waterfalls, it is quite possible that power may be obtained in this way to compete with that obtained directly from the steam-engine ; but there are as yet considerable practical difficulties to be overcome in the transmission of any large amount of energy for long distances.

To overcome some of these difficulties the accumulator has been invented, which affords yet another remarkable instance of the transformation of energy. It consists of two lead plates immersed in acidulated water. When a strong electrical current is sent through the water, it decomposes it, the oxygen going to one lead plate and the hydrogen to the other. The oxygen attacks the lead plate to which it goes, forming peroxide of lead; while the hydrogen reduces any oxide in the other plate, producing pure lead, and leaving a film of surplus hydrogen on the surface. The charging current is then reversed, so that the latter plate is now attacked and the former one reduced, when the current is again reversed. By continuing this process the surfaces of both lead plates become porous, so that they present a large surface, and can therefore hold a great deal of peroxide of lead. The charging current being now broken, the oxygen which has been forcibly separated from the liquid seeks to recombine with hydrogen ; and if the two lead plates are joined by a wire, this effort of the oxygen generates an electrical current in the opposite direction to the original one, which is the current utilised. Electricity is thus stored up in a portable box, where it can be kept till wanted, when it is drawn out by connecting the plates, and as a large amount of energy has been accumulated the current which is produced lasts for a considerable time.

Unfortunately accumulators are bulky, heavy, and expensive, and nearly half the energy of the original charging current is lost in obtaining the reversed or working current. They are therefore not as yet adapted for general use, though perfectly capable of supplying either light or motive power, for both which purposes they have been successfully applied in special cases. The future both of electric power and electric lighting is now reduced entirely to a question of cost; and though it is hard to beat gas and the steam-engine, with cheap coal, and air and water for nothing, it is possible that by using natural sources of power to move dynamos, and by obtaining zinc back as a residual product in batteries, electricity may in certain cases carry the day.

CHAPTER V.

POLARITY IN MATTER.

Ultimate elements of universe—Built up by polarity—Experiment with magnet—Chemical affinity—Atomic poles—Alkalies and acids—Quantivalence — Atomicity — Isomerism — Chemical stability — Thermochemistry—Definition of atoms—All matter built up by polar forces.

I ALMOST fear that by this time some of my readers may think that I have seduced them under false pretences to read long chapters of dry science, when they had been led from the introduction to anticipate discussions on the more immediately interesting topics of morals, religions, and philosophies. My excuse must be that these scientific subjects are really of extreme interest in themselves and indispensable as a solid basis for the superstructure to be raised on them. How can I attempt to show that the law of polarity extends to the more complex problems of human thought and life, if I fail in establishing its application to the simpler case of inorganic force and matter? It must be recollected also that among the primitive polarities is that of author and reader. It is my part to endeavour to present the leading facts and laws of the material universe in such plain and popular language that the ordinary reader who has neither time nor faculty for special studies may apprehend them clearly without excessive effort, or extraordinary intelligence. But it is the reader's part to supply a fair average amount of attention, and above all to feel an interest in interesting matters. Cleverness and curiosity are very much convertible terms, and the clearest exposition is thrown away on the torpid mind which views the marvellous universe in which he has the privilege to live, with the stupid apathy of the savage, taking things as they come without caring to know anything about them.

For the reader's part of the work I am not responsible ; but for my own I am, and I proceed therefore to give in my own way, and with the best faculty that is in me, a clear summary of such of the fundamental facts and laws of nature as seem necessary for the work I have undertaken.

From the preceding chapters we are now able to realise what are the ultimate elements of the material universe, and it remains to show how they are put together. The elements are ether, energy, and matter.

First, ether : a universal, all-pervading medium, imponderable or infinitely light, and almost infinitely elastic, in which all matter, from suns and planets down to molecules and atoms, float as in a boundless ocean, and whose tremors or vibrations, propagated as waves, transport the different forms of energy, light, heat, and electricity, across space.

Secondly, energy : a primitive, indestructible something, which causes motion and manifests itself under its many diversified forms, such as gravity, mechanical work, molecular and atomic forces, light, heat, electricity, and magnetism, all of which are merely Protean transformations of the one fundamental energy, and convertible into each other.

Thirdly, matter : the ultimate elements of this are atoms, which combined form molecules, or little pieces of ordinary matter with all its qualities, which are the bricks used in building all the varied structures of the organic and inorganic worlds. Of these atoms some seventy have never yet been divided, and therefore, although we may suspect that they are merely combinations or transformations of one original matter, we must be content for the present to consider them as elementary. In like manner we may suspect that matter is in reality only another form of energy, and that the impression of solidity is given by the action of a repellent force which is very energetic at short distances. If this were established we might look forward to the generalisation that energy was the one reality of nature ; but for the present it is a mere speculation, and we must be content with over seventy elementary atoms as ultimate facts. In any case this much is certain, that matter, like energy, is indestructible. We have absolutely no experience of either of them being created or annihilated. Nay, more, we have no faculties to enable us even to conceive how something can be made out of nothing, and all we know, or can ever know, about these primitive constituents of the universe is of their laws of existence, their evolutions and their transformations.

Minute as the atoms and molecules are, we must conceive of them not as stationary and indissolubly connected, but rather as little solar systems in which revolving atoms form the molecule, and revolving molecules form the matter, held together as separate systems by their proper energies and motions, until some superior force intruding breaks up the system and sets its components free to form new combinations.

What is the principle which thus forms, un-forms, and re-forms the various combinations of atomic and molecular systems by which the world is built up from its constituent elements ?   It is polarity.

As I began with the illustration of the magnet introducing order and harmony into the confused mass of iron filings, let me take this other illustration from the same source. If we place an iron bar in contact with the pole of a magnet, the bar becomes itself a magnet with opposite poles to the original one, so that as opposite poles attract, the iron bar adheres to it. Bring a lump of nickel in contact with the further end or free pole of the iron bar, and the nickel also will be magnetised and adhere.   Let the lump of nickel be as large as the pole of the iron bar is able to support, and now bring a lump of soft iron near this pole.   It will drop the nickel and take the iron.   This is exactly similar to those cases of chemical affinity in which a molecule drops one of its factors and takes on another to which its attraction is stronger.   If iron rusts in water it is because the oxygen atom drops hydrogen to take iron just as the magnet dropped nickel.

The polarity of chemical elements is attested by the fact that when compounds are decomposed by the electric current, the different elementary substances appear at different poles of the battery.   Thus, oxygen, chlorine, and non-metallic substances appear at the positive pole; while hydrogen, potassium, and metals generally, appear at the negative one.   The inference is irresistible that the atoms had in each case an opposite polarity to that of the poles to which they were attracted.   This is confirmed by the fact that the radicals, i.e. the elementary atoms or groups of atoms which have opposite polarities, combine readily ; while those which have the same polarity, as two metals, have but slight affinity for each other. Like therefore attracts unlike, as in all cases of polarity, and the greater the degree of unlikeness the stronger is the attraction. Thus, the radicals of all alkalies are electro-positive, and appear at the negative pole of a battery : while those of acids are all electro-negative, and the higher each stands in its respective scale of polarity the more strongly does it show the peculiar qualities of acid or alkali and the more eagerly does it combine with its opposite.

Acids and alkalies are, in fact, all members of the same class of compounds called *hydrates*, because a single atom of hydrogen is a common feature in their composition. This atom is coupled with a single atom of oxygen, which may be conceived of as the central magnet holding the hydrogen atom at one pole, while at the other it holds either a single atom of some metallic element, such as potassium or sodium, or a group consisting of such an element together with atoms of oxygen, so constituted as to present a single pole to the attraction of the central oxygen atom. Thus, if K stands for kali or potassium, N for nitrogen, O for oxygen, and H for hydrogen, we may have the compounds

$$\text{H} - \text{O} - \text{K}$$

and

$$\text{H} - \text{O} - \left(\text{N} \underset{\text{O}}{\overset{\text{O}}{\underset{\displaystyle -}{\displaystyle -}}} \right).$$

The former is the molecule of potassic hydrate, which is the most caustic or strongest of alkalies; the latter, that of nitric acid, the most corrosive or powerful of acids. These are the extremes of the series, of which there are many intermediate members, all being more or less alkaline, that is caustic and turning litmus-paper blue, when the third element is a simple metallic atom; and acid, corrosive, and turning litmus-paper red, when it is a compound radical of a group of metallic and oxygen atoms. This shows to what an extent whole classes of substances may have a general resemblance in their constitution, and yet differ most widely in their qualities by the substitution of one element for another.

These special qualities may be made to diminish and finally disappear by mixing the two opposite substances, or, as it is called, neutralising an acid by an alkali or an alkali by an acid. Thus, if hydrochloric acid, $H Cl$, be poured into a solution of sodic-hydrate, $Na - O - H$, the alkaline qualities of the latter diminish and finally disappear, the result of the neutral solution being water, $H - O - H$, and sodic-chloride, or common salt, $Na - Cl$. It is evident that this result has been produced by the hydrogen atom in $H - Cl$ and the sodium atom in $Na - O - H$ changing places, the former preferring to unite with oxygen to form water, while the displaced sodium atom finds a refuge with chlorine. The oxygen atom has dropped sodium and taken hydrogen, just as the magnet dropped nickel and took iron.

This polarity of chemical elements manifests itself in different ways. In some cases it appears like that of a magnet, in which there are two opposite poles, and two only, one at each end. Thus oxygen (O) is bipolar, and its atom holds together two atoms of hydrogen (H) in forming the molecule of water, which may be represented as $H + - O + - H$, which is equivalent to $\boxed{\text{N}}$ s $\overline{\underset{\text{iron}}{\text{magnet}}}$ N $\boxed{\text{s}}$. Others again, like hydrogen and chlorine, seem to have only a single pole, as in the case of electricity in an excited glass rod, and have to create for themselves the opposite pole, which is the indispensable condition of all polarity, by induction in another body. Thus, muriatic or hydrochloric acid is formed by the union of a single atom of chlorine, which is strongly negative, with a single atom of hydrogen, in which it appears to have induced a positive pole : though the combination is not a very stable one, for if an element with a stronger positive pole of its own is presented to the chlorine, it drops the hydrogen, just as the magnet drops the nickel. Other atoms are multipolar, and seem as if made up of more than one magnet, or rather as if the atom had regular shape like a triangle, square, or pentagon, and each angle was a pole, thus enabling it to unite with three, four, five, or more atoms of other substances. Thus, one atom of nitrogen unites with three of hydrogen, one of carbon with four of hydrogen, and so on. Every substance has, therefore, what is called its 'quantivalence,' or power of uniting with it a greater or less quantity of other atoms, and conversely that of replacing in combinations other atoms, or groups of atoms, the sum of whose quantivalence equals its own. Thus, one atom of carbon, which has four poles, combines with four atoms of hydrogen or chlorine, which is unipolar, but with only two of oxygen, which are bipolar ; while the oxygen atom combines with two of hydrogen, and that of chlorine with one atom only of hydrogen. The analogy between the single atomic and electrical poles on the one hand, and the dual and magnetic poles on the other, will be evident if we consider what occurs if a pith-ball, electrified positively, is brought near a similar ball electrified negatively. They attract each other, and the one becomes the pole of the other ; but if separated, each carries with it its own electrical charge. But the separate balls or poles, though no longer influencing each other, are not isolated, for each draws by induction an electrical charge opposite to its own to the extremity of the nearest conductor, and thus creates for itself a new or second pole. Polarity, in fact, involves · opposition of relations, or two poles, and electrical only differs from magnetic polarity in the fact that in the latter the two poles are in the same body, while in the former they are in separate bodies.

For pith-balls read atoms, and we have an explana- tion of the univalent atoms like those of chlorine and sodium which act as single poles ; and this is confirmed by the fact that such atoms are never found isolated, but are always associated in a molecule with at least one other atom which forms the opposite pole of the mole- cular system. Bivalent or magnetic atoms, on the other hand, which have two poles, like those of mercury and zinc, may constitute a complete polar system and be found isolated, and form the class of molecules which consist of single atoms.

This conception of the polarity of atoms enables us to understand the way in which the almost infinite variety of substances existing in the world is built up from a comparatively few simple elements. Atoms and radicals, which are multipolar, can attract and form molecules with as many other atoms or radicals as they have poles. This is called their degree of atomicity, which is the same as their quantivalence ; and each of these atoms or radicals may be replaced by some other atom or radical, which presents to any pole a more powerful polarity. Thus, compounds may be built up of great and varied complexity, for the quality of any compound may be greatly altered by any one of the substitutions at any one of the poles. And the molecules, or small specimens of matter, may be thus built up into very complex aggregations of atoms, some single molecules containing more than a hundred atoms. Thus, carbon has four poles, or is quadrivalent, and its atoms possess the power of combining among themselves to an almost indefinite extent and forming groups of great stability. Thus, carbon radicals may be formed in very great number, each affording a nucleus upon which compound radicals may be built up, so that carbon has been aptly called the skeleton of almost all the varied compounds of the more complex forms of inorganic matter as well as the principal foundation of organic life.

Nor is this all, for the qualities of substances depend not only on the qualities of their constituent elements, but also on the manner in which these elements are grouped. Two substances may have exactly the same chemical composition and yet be very different. We may suppose that the same elements affect us differently according as they are grouped. Thus, the same bricks may be built up either into a cube or pyramid, which forms are extremely stable and can only be taken in pieces brick by brick; or into a Gothic arch, which all tumbles to pieces if a single brick forming the keystone is displaced. As an instance of this, butyric acid, which gives the offensive odour to rancid butter, has exactly the same composition as acetic ether, which gives the flavour to a ripe apple. They consist of the same number of atoms of the same elements

—carbon, hydrogen, and oxygen—united in the same proportions. This applies to a number of substances, and is called Isomerism, or formation of different wholes from the same parts.

The principle of polarity, therefore, aided by the subsidiary conditions of quantivalence, atomicity, and isomerism, gives the clue to the construction of the inorganic world out of some seventy elementary substances. Of the substances thus formed, whether of molecules or of combinations of molecules, some are stable and some unstable. As a rule the simpler combinations are the most stable, and instability increases with complexity. Thus the diamond, which is merely a crystal of pure carbon, is very hard and indestructible; while dynamite, or nitro-glycerine, which is a very complex compound, explodes at a touch.

The stability of a substance depends partly on the stable structure of its component elements, and partly on their mutual affinity being strong enough to keep them together in presence of the attractions of other outside elements, which, in the case of most natural substances at the surface of the earth, consist principally of air and water. Thus, the rocks, earths, metallic oxides, water, carbonic dioxide, and nitrogen are extremely stable, and resist decomposition, or chemical union with other substances, with great energy. With regard to all substances this law holds good, that the tendency is to fall back from a less stable to a more stable condition, and that such a falling back is always attended with an evolution of heat ; while, on the other hand, heat is always absorbed and disappears whenever the elements of a more stable substance are made to enter into a less stable condition. Thus, when wood burns, there is a falling back from a substance unstable, on account of its affinity for the oxygen in the air, into the stable products, carbonic dioxide and water, and the heat evolved is the effect of this fall.

As the tendency of all changes is towards stability we arrive at the following law, which is one of the most recent generalisations of modern chemistry : In all cases of chemical change the tendency is to those products whose formation will determine the greatest evolution of heat.

This, however, does not imply that the tendency may not be overcome and unstable products formed, for just as a weight may be lifted against the force of gravity, so may the chemical tendency be overcome by a sufficient energy acting against it. Heat is the principal means of supplying this energy, and by increasing it sufficiently not only are molecules drawn apart and most solids converted into fluids and finally into gases, but there is reason to believe that at extremely high temperatures, such as may prevail in the sun, all matter would be resolved into isolated or dissociated atoms. Thus, water at a temperature of 1,200° is resolved into a mixture of oxygen and hydrogen atoms no longer chemically united into water-molecules ; and iodine-vapour, which below 700° degrees consists of molecules of two atoms, above that temperature consists of single atoms only.

The subject might be pursued further, but enough has been said for the present purpose to show that the universe consists of atoms which are endowed with polarity, and that as diminished temperature allows these atoms to come closer together and form compounds, matter in all its forms is built up by the action of polar forces.

CHAPTER VI.

POLARITY IN LIFE.

Contrast of living and dead—Eating and being eaten—Trace matter upwards and life downwards—Colloids—Cells—Protoplasm—Monera—Composition of protoplasm—Essential qualities of life—Nutrition and sensation—Motion—Reproduction—Spontaneous generation—Organic compounds—Polar conditions of life.

POLARITY having been established as the universal law of the inorganic world, we have now to pass to the organic, or world of life. At first sight there seems to be a great gulf fixed between the living and the dead which no bridge can span. But first impressions are very apt to deceive us, and when things are traced up to their origins we often find them getting nearer and nearer until it is difficult to say where one begins and the other ends. Take for instance such an antithesis as 'eating or being eaten.' If a hunter meets a grizzly bear in the Rocky Mountains, one would say that no distinction can be sharper than whether the bear eats the man, or the man the bear. In the one case there is a man, and in the other a bear, less in the world. But look through a microscope at a glass of water, and you may see two specks of jelly-like substance swimming in it. They are living creatures, for they eat and grow, and thrust out and retract processes of their formless mass, which serve as temporary legs and arms for seizing food and for voluntary motion. In short, they are each what may be called strictly individual amœbæ, forming separate units of the animated creation as much as the man and the bear. But if the two happen to come in contact, what happens? The two slimy masses involve one another and coalesce, and the resulting amœba swims away merrily as two gentlemen rolled into one.

Now in his case what became of their individualities: did amœba A eat amœba B, or *vice versa*, and is the resulting amœba a survival of A or of B, or of both or neither of them? And what becomes of the antithesis of 'eating or being eaten' which was so clear and distinct in the highly specialised forms of life, and is so evanescent in the simpler forms? This illustration may serve to teach us how necessary it is to trace things up to their origins, before expressing too trenchant and confident opinions as to their nature and relations.

In the case of the organic and inorganic worlds the proper course obviously is, not to draw conclusions from extreme and highly specialised instances, but to follow life downwards to its simplest and most primitive form, and matter upwards to the form which approaches most nearly to this form of life. Following matter upwards, we find a regular progression from the simple to the complex. Take the diamond, which is one of the simplest of substances, being merely the crystallised form of a single ultimate element, carbon. It is extremely hard and extremely stable. Ascending to compounds of two, three, or more elements, we get substances which are more complex and less stable; and at last we arrive at combinations which involve many elements and are extremely complex. Among these latter substances are some, called colloids, which are neither solid, like crystals, nor fluid, like liquids, but in an intermediate state, like jelly or the white of an egg, in which the molecules have great mobility and are at a considerable distance apart, so that water can penetrate their mass. These colloids are for the most part very complicated compounds of various elements based on a nucleus of carbon, which, from its atom having four poles with strong mutual attractions, is eminently qualified for forming what may be called the inner skeleton of these complex combinations. Colloids of this description form the last stage of the ascending line from inorganic matter to organic life.

Next let us trace life downwards towards matter. There is a constant succession from the more to the less complex and differentiated: from man, through mammals, reptiles, fishes, and a long chain of more simple forms, until at its end we come to the two last links, which are the same for all animals, all plants, and all forms of animated existence. The last link but one is the cell, the last of all is protoplasm.

Protoplasm, or, as Huxley calls it, 'the physical basis of life,' is a colourless jelly-like substance, absolutely homogeneous, without parts or structure, in fact a mere microscopic speck of jelly.

The cell is the first step in the specialisation of protoplasm, the outer layer of which, in contact with the surrounding environment, becoming hardened so as to form an enclosing cell-wall, while a portion of the enclosed protoplasm condenses into a nucleus, in which a further condensation makes what is called the nucleolus or second smaller nucleus. This constitutes the nucleated cell, whose repeated subdivision into other similar cells in geometrical progression furnishes the raw material out of which all the varied structures of the world of life are built up. Plants and animals, bones, muscles, and organs of sense, are all composed of modified cells, hardened, flattened, or otherwise altered, as the case may require. If we trace life up to its origin in the individual instead of in the species, we arrive at the same result. All plants and animals, whether of the lowest or highest forms, fish, reptile, bird, mammal, man, begin their individual existence as a speck of protoplasm, passing into a nucleated cell, which contains in it the whole principle of its subsequent evolution into the mature and completed form.

Protoplasm is, therefore, evidently the nearest approach of life to matter; and if life ever originated from atomic and molecular combinations, it was in this form. To suppose that any more complex form of life, however humble, could originate from chemical combinations, would be a violation of the law of evolution, which shows a uniform development from the simple to the complex, and never a sudden jump passing at a bound over intermediate grades. To understand life, therefore, we must understand protoplasm; for protoplasm, closely as it approximates to colloid matter, is thoroughly alive. A whole family, the Monera, consist simply of a living globule of jelly, which has not even begun to be differentiated. Every molecule, as in a crystal, is of homogeneous chemical composition and an epitome of the whole mass. There are no special parts, no organs told off for particular functions, and yet all life-functions—nutrition, reproduction, sensation, and movement—are performed, but each by the whole body. The jelly-speck becomes a mouth to swallow, and turning inside out, a stomach to digest. It shoots out tongues of jelly to move and feel with, and presently withdraws them.

With these attributes it is impossible to deny to protoplasm the full attributes of life, or to doubt that, like the atom in the material world, it is the primary element of organic or living existence. Given the atom, we can trace up, step by step, the whole evolution of matter ; so given the protoplasm, we can trace up the evolution of life by progressive stages to its highest development—man. To understand life, therefore, we must begin by trying to understand protoplasm.

What is protoplasm? In its substance it is a nitrogenous carbon compound, differing only from other similar compounds of the albuminous family of colloid by the extremely complex composition of its atoms. It consists of five elements, and its average composition is said by chemists to be 52·55 per cent. carbon, 21·23 oxygen, 15·17 nitrogen, 6·7 hydrogen, 1·2 sulphur. Its peculiar qualities, therefore, including life, are not the result of any new and peculiar atom added to the known chemical compounds of the same family, but of the manner of grouping and motions of these well-known material elements. It has in a remarkable degree the faculty of absorbing water, so that its molecules seem to float in it in a condition of semi-fluid aggregation, which seems to be necessary for the complex molecular movements which are the cause or accompaniment of life. Thus, many seeds and animalculæ, if perfectly dry, may remain apparently as dead and as unchanging as crystals, for years, or even, as in the case of the mummy wheat, for centuries, to revive into life when moistened.

But in addition to those material qualities in which

protoplasm seems to differ only from a whole group of similar compounds of the type of glycerine, by the greater complexity and mobility of its molecules, it has developed the new and peculiar element which is called life. Life in its essence is manifested by the faculties of nutrition, sensation, movement, and reproduction.

As regards nutrition there is this essential difference between living and non-living matter. The latter, if it feeds and grows at all, does so only by taking on fresh molecules of its own substance on its outer surface, as in the case of a small nucleus-crystal of ice in freezing water. If it feeds on foreign matter and throughout its mass, it does so only in the way of chemical combination, forming a new product. Living matter, on the other hand, feeds internally, and works up foreign substances, by the process we call digestion, into molecules like its own, which it assimilates, rejecting as waste any surplus or foreign matter which it cannot incorporate. It thus grows and decays as assimilation or waste preponderates, remaining always itself. The distinction will be clear if we consider what happens when water rusts iron. In a certain sense the iron may be said to eat the oxygen, reject the hydrogen, and grow, or increase in weight by what it feeds on; but the result is not a bigger piece of iron, but a new substance, rust, or oxide of iron. That living matter should feed internally is not so wonderful, for its semi-fluid condition may well enable foreign molecules to penetrate its mass and come in contact with its own interior molecules; but it is an experience different from anything known in the inorganic world that it should be able to manufacture molecules of protoplasm like its own out of these foreign molecules, and thus grow by assimilation.

G

For instance, when amœbæ, bacteria, and other low organisms live and multiply in chemical solutions which contain no protoplasm, but only inorganic compounds containing the requisite atoms for making protoplasm, or when a plant not only chemically decomposes carbonic dioxide, exhaling the oxygen and depositing the carbon in its stem and leaves, but also from this and other elements drawn from the soil or air manufactures the living protoplasm which courses through its channels, the result is that life has manufactured life out of non-living materials.

If we take sensation, this, in its last analysis, is change, or molecular motion, induced in a body by the action of its environment. Here there is a certain analogy between living and non-living matter, for the latter does respond to changes in the surrounding environment, as in the case of heat, electricity, and otherwise; but living matter is far more sensitive, the changes are far more frequent and complex, and in certain cases they are accompanied by a sensation of what is called consciousness, which in the higher organisms rises into a perception of voluntary effort or free-will as a factor in the transformation of energies. Thus it happens that in the case of dead matter the changes produced by a change of conditions follow fixed laws and can be predicted and calculated, while those of living matter are apparently uncertain and capricious. We can tell how much an iron bar will expand with heat; but we cannot say whether, if a particle of food is brought within reach of an amœba, it will or will not shoot out a finger to seize it. If the amœba is hungry it probably will; if it is enjoying a siesta after a full meal, it probably will not.

The case of sensation includes that of motion, which is after all only sensation applied in the liberation of energy of position which has by some chemical process become stored up, either in the living mass, or in some special organ of it, such as muscle. Iron, for instance, moves when it expands by heat or is attracted by a magnet ; but it moves, like the planets, by fixed and calculable laws : while living matter moves, as might be expected from the variable character of its sensation, in a manner which often cannot be calculated. There are cases, however, of reflex or involuntary motion, where, even in the highest living organisms, sensation and motion seem to follow change of environment, in a fixed and invariable sequence, as in shrinking from pain, touching or galvanising a nerve ; and it may be that the apparent spontaneousness and variability of living motion is only the result of the almost infinitely greater complexity and mobility of the elements of living matter.

Reproduction remains, which is the faculty most characteristic of life, and which distinguishes most sharply the organic from the inorganic world. In the inorganic there is no known process by which dead matter reproduces itself, as the cell does when it con-tracts in the middle and splits up into two cells, which in their turn propagate an endless number of similar cells, increasing in geometrical progression until they supply the raw material from which all the count-less varieties of living organisms are built up, which, in their turn, repeat the process and reproduce themselves in offspring. This is the real mystery of life ; we can partly see or suspect how its other faculties might arise from an extension of the known qualities and laws of matter and of energy ; but we can discern no analogy between the non-reproductive nitrogenous carbon compound, which makes so near an approach to protoplasm in its chemical composition, and the reproductive protoplasm, which is fertile, increases and multiplies, and replenishes the earth. Can the gap be bridged over : can protoplasm be manufactured out of chemical elements ? It is done every day by plants which make protoplasm out of inorganic elements, and by the lowest forms of life which live and multiply in chemical solutions. It is done also in the life-history of all individuals whose primitive cell or ovum makes thousands or millions of other cells, each containing within its enclosing membrane as much protoplasm as there was in the unit from which they started. But in all these instances there was the living principle to start with, existing in the primitive speck of protoplasm, from which the rest were developed. Can this primitive speck be created ; or, in other words, can protoplasm be artificially manufactured by chemical processes ?

The answer must be, No ; not by any process now known. The similarity of chemical composition, and the increasing conviction of the universality of natural law and of evolution, have led to a very general belief that such a spontaneous generation of life must be possible, and numerous experiments have been made to produce it. For a time the balance seemed to be very evenly held between the supporters and opponents of spontaneous generation. In fact, starting from the assumption, which at first was common to both sides, that heat equal to the boiling point of water destroyed all life organisms, spontaneous generation had the best of it : for it was clearly proved that living organisms did appear in infusions contained in vessels which had been hermetically sealed, after being subjected to this, or even a higher degree of heat. But subsequent and more careful experiments have shown that the germs or spores of bacteria and other animalculæ, which are generally floating in the air, can, when dry, withstand a greater degree of heat, and that when the experiments are made in optically pure air no life ever appears and the infusions never putrefy. On questions of this sort all who are not themselves expert experimentalists must be guided by authority, and we may be content to accept the dictum of Huxley that biogenesis, or all life from previous life, was 'victorious along the whole line.' But in doing so we must accept Huxley's caution, 'that with organic chemistry, molecular physics, and physiology yet in their infancy, and every day making prodigious strides, it would be the height of presumption for any man to say that the conditions under which matter assumes the qualities called vital, may not some day be artificially brought together.'

And further, 'that as a matter not of proof but of probability, if it were given me to look beyond the abyss of geologically recorded time, to the still more remote period when the earth was passing through chemical and physical conditions which it can never see again, I should expect to be a witness of the evolution of living protoplasms from non-living matter.' Such is the cautious candour with which scientific men approach problems upon which theologians dogmatise with the unerring intrepidity of ignorance.

In the meantime what may be said as to Huxley's reservations is this: A considerable step has been made in the direction indicated, by the success of recent

chemistry in forming artificially what are called organic compounds, that is, substances which were previously known only as products of animal or vegetable
secretions. Urea, for instance, the base of uric acid, with
which so many are unfortunately familiar in the form
of gout ; indigotine, the principle of the blue colouring
matter of the indigo plant ; and alizarine, that of madder ;
are all now produced artificially, and have even become
important articles of commerce. If chemists can make
the indigotine, which the growing plant elaborates at
the same time as it elaborates protoplasm, may we not
hope some day to make the latter as well as the former
product? Now organic compounds of this class are
being formed artificially every day, and it is said that
chemists have already succeeded in producing several
hundreds. But even if this expectation is never ful-
filled, we may fall back on Huxley's second reservation
of the enormous difference of chemical and physical
conditions in the early stages of the earth's life from
anything now known. It has been calculated that the
earth's temperature when it first started on its career as
an independent planet was something like 3,000,000°
Fahrenheit. At this heat probably all atoms would be
dissociated ; but as the temperature diminished they
would come closer together, but still with a great deal of
motion, and making wide excursions, which might bring
many different atoms together in complex though unstable combinations. Moreover, carbon, which is the
basis of all such combinations of the class of protoplasm, was far more abundant in those early days in
the form of carbonic dioxide gas, before the enormous
amount of vegetable matter in the form of coal and
otherwise, had been subtracted from it. In any case

the first protoplasm must be extremely ancient; for the remains of sea-weeds are found in the oldest strata, and vegetation of any sort implies the manufacture of proto-plasm from inorganic matter.

The passage from the organic into the inorganic world is best traced by following the line of Pasteur's researches on ferments. How does the world escape being choked up by the accumulation of dead organic matter throughout innumerable ages ? By what are called ferments, inducing processes of fermentation and putrefaction, by which the course of life is reversed, and the organic elements are taken to pieces and restored to the inorganic world. Pasteur proved, in opposition to the theories of Liebig and other older chemists, that this was not done directly by the oxygen of the air, but through the intermediate agency of living microbes, whose spores, floating in the air, took up their abode and multiplied wherever they found an appropriate habitation. Given an air purified from germs, or a temperature low enough to prevent them from germinating, and putrescible substances would keep sweet for ever. The practical realisation of this is seen in the enormous commerce in canned meats and fruits, and in the imports of frozen beef and mutton, causing a fall of rents and much lamentation among British landlords and farmers.

But then the question was asked, How are your microscopic organisms disposed of ? What are the ferments of your ferments ? For even microscopic bacteria and vibrios would, in time, choke up the world by their residue if not got rid of. Pasteur answered that the ferments are destroyed by a new series of organisms —aerobes—living in the air, and these by other aerobes in succession until the ultimate products are oxidised.

' Thus, in the destruction of what has lived, all is reduced
to the simultaneous action of the three great natural
phenomena—fermentation, putrefaction, and slow combustion.   A living being, animal or vegetable, or the
débris of either, having just died, is exposed to the air.
The life that has abandoned it is succeeded by life under
other forms.   In the superficial parts, accessible to the
air, the germs of the infinitely little aerobes flourish and
multiply.   The carbon, hydrogen, and nitrogen of the
organic matter are transformed by the oxygen of the air,
and under the vital activity of the aerobes, into carbonic
acid, the vapour of water, and ammonia.   The combustion continues as long as organic matter and air are
present together.   At the same time the superficial combustion is going on, fermentation and putrefaction are
performing their work in the midst of the mass by
means of the developed germs of the original microbes,
which, note, do not need oxygen to live, but which
oxygen causes to perish.   Gradually the phenomena of
destruction are at last accomplished through the work
of latent fermentation and slow combustion.'

This seems a complete demonstration of the passage
of the organic into the inorganic world in the way of
analysis, or taking the puzzle to pieces.   In the opposite
way of synthesis, or putting it together, the nearest
approach yet made has been in the manufacture of those
organic compounds already referred to, such as urea, alizarine, indigotine and other products which had hitherto
only been known as products of animal or vegetable
life.   Of these a vast number have been already formed
from inorganic elements by chemical processes, and
almost every day announces some fresh discovery.

Under these circumstances it is unsafe to affirm

either, on the one hand, that the problem has been solved
and that life has ever been made in a laboratory ; or,
on the other hand, that there is any such great gulf fixed
between the organic and the inorganic, that we can
assume a break requiring secondary supernatural inter
ference to surmount it, and ignore the good old maxim
that 'Natura nihil facit per saltum.' Positive proof is
wanting, but the probabilities point here, as they do
everywhere else throughout the universe, to the truth
of the theory of 'original impress' as opposed to that
of 'secondary interference.'

It remains to show how the fundamental law of
polarity affects the more complex relations of life and
of its various combinations. And here it is important
to bear in mind that as the factors of the problem become more intricate and complex, so also do the laws
which regulate their existence and action. Polarity is
no longer a simple question of attraction and repulsion
at the two ends of a magnet or at the opposite poles of
an atom. It appears rather as a general law under
which as the simple and absolute becomes differentiated
by evolution into the complex and manifold, it does so
under the condition of developing contrasts. For every
plus there is a *minus*, for every like an unlike ; one cannot exist without the other ; and, although apparently
antagonistic, harmonious order is only possible by their
co-existence and mutual balance.

This is so important that it may be well to make the
idea clearer by an illustration. The earth revolves round
the sun in its annual orbit under the influence of two
forces : the centripetal, or force of gravity tending to
draw it towards the sun ; and the centrifugal, tending to
make it dart away into infinite space. During half the

orbit the centripetal seems to be gaining ground on the
centrifugal, and the earth is approaching nearer to the
sun.   If this continued it would revolve ever nearer and
soon fall into it ; but the centrifugal force is gradually
recruiting its strength from the increased velocity of
the earth, until it first equals the centripetal, and finally
outstrips it, and for the remaining half of the orbit it is
constantly gaining ground.   If this went on, the earth
would fly off into the chilly regions of outer space ;
but the centripetal force in its turn regains the ascendency ; and thus by the balance of the two forces our
planet describes the beautiful ellipse, its harmonious
orbit as a habitable globe ; while comets in which one
or the other force unduly preponderates for long periods
are alternately drawn into fiery proximity to the sun,
and sent careering through regions void of heat.

Compare this passage from Herbert Spencer : ' As
from antagonist physical forces, as from antagonist
emotions in each man, so from the antagonist social
tendencies man's emotions create, there always results
not a medium state, but a rhythm between opposite
states.   The one force or tendency is not continuously
counterbalanced by the other force or tendency ; but
now the one greatly preponderates, and presently by
reaction there comes a preponderance of the other.'

And again : ' There is nowhere a balanced judgment and a balanced action, but always a cancelling
of one another by opposite errors.   Men pair off in
insane parties, as Emerson puts it.'

The reader will now begin to understand the sense
in which polarity applies to these complex conditions
of an advanced evolution.

To return, however, from this digression to the

point at which it began, viz. the origin of life, we have to show how the law of polarity prevails in the organic as well as in the inorganic world. In the first place the material to which all life is attached, from the speck of protoplasm to the brain of man, is strictly a chemical product of atoms and molecules bound together by the same polar laws as those of inorganic matter.

In like manner all the essential processes by which life lives, moves, and has its being, are equally mechanical and chemical. If the brain, receiving a telegram from without through the optic nerve, sends a reply along another nerve which liberates energy stored up in a muscle and produces motion, the messages are received and transmitted like those sent by a voltaic battery along the wires of a telegraph, and the energy is stored up by the slow combustion of food in oxygen, just as that of the steam-engine is produced by the combustion of coal. All this is mechanical, inorganic, and therefore polar.

But when we come to the conditions of life proper, we find the influence of polarity mainly in this : that as it develops from simpler into more complex forms, it does so under the law of developing contrasts or opposite polarities, which are necessary complements of each other's existence. Thus, as we ascend in the scale of life, we find two primitive polarities developed : that of plant and animal, and that of male and female.

CHAPTER VII.

PRIMITIVE POLARITIES—PLANT AND ANIMAL.

Contrast in developed life—Plants producers, animals consumers—Differences disappear in simple forms—Zoophytes—Protista—Nummulites—
Corals—Fungi—Lichens—Insectivorous plants—Geological succession
—Primary period, Algæ and Ferns—Secondary period, Gymnosperms
—Tertiary and recent, Angiosperms—Monocotyledons and Dicotyledons—Parallel evolution of animal life—Primary, protista, mollusca,
and fish—Secondary, reptiles—Tertiary and recent, mammals.

ANIMALS or plants ? Judging by first impressions,
nothing can be more distinct. No one, whether scientific or unscientific, could mistake an oak tree for an
ox. To the unscientific observer the tree differs in
having no power of free movement, and apparently no
sensation or consciousness ; in fact, hardly any of the
attributes of life. The scientific observer sees still
more fundamental differences, in the fact that the plant
feeds on inorganic ingredients, out of which it manufactures living matter, or protoplasm ; while the animal
can only provide itself with protoplasm from that
already manufactured by the plant. The ox, who
lives on grass, could not live on what the grass thrives
on, viz. carbon, oxygen, hydrogen, and nitrogen. The
contrast is so striking that the vegetable world has
been called the producer, and the animal world the
consumer, of nature.

Again, the plant derives the material framework of

its structure from the air, by breathing in through its leaves the carbonic dioxide present in the atmosphere, decomposing it, fixing the carbon in its roots, stem, and branches, and exhaling the oxygen. The animal exactly reverses the process, inhaling the oxygen of the air, combining it with the carbon of its food, and exhaling carbonic dioxide. Thus, a complete polarity is established, as we see in the aquarium, where plant and animal life balance each other, and the opposites live and thrive, where the existence of either would be impossible without the other.

Sharp, however, as the contrast appears to be in the more specialised and developed specimens of the two worlds, we have here another instance of the difficulty of trusting to first impressions, and have to modify our conceptions greatly, if we trace animal and vegetable life up to their simplest forms and earliest origins. In the first place, each individual vegetable or animal begins its existence from a simple piece of pure protoplasm. This develops in the same way into a nucleated cell, by whose repeated subdivision the raw material is provided for both structures alike. The chief difference at this early stage is that the animal cells remain soft and naked, while those of vegetables secrete a comparatively solid cell-wall, which makes them less mobile and plastic. This gives greater rigidity to the frame and tissues of the plant, and prevents the development of the finer organs of sensation and other vital processes, which characterise the animal. But this is a difference of development only, and the origination of the future life from the speck of protoplasm is the same in both worlds.

If, instead of looking at the origin of individuals, we

trace back the various forms of animal and vegetable life from the more complex to the simpler forms, we find the distinctions between the two disappearing, until at last we arrive at a vanishing point where it is impossible to say whether the organism is an animal or a plant.

A whole family, comprising sponges, corals, and jelly-fish, are called Zoophytes, or plant-animals, from the difficulty of assigning them to one kingdom or the other. On the whole they rather more resemble animals, and are generally classed with them, though they lack many of their most essential qualities, and in form often bear a close resemblance to plants. But when we descend a step lower in the scale of existence we come to a large family—the Protista—of which it is impossible to say that they are either plants or animals. In fact, scientific observers have classed them sometimes as belonging to one and sometimes to the other kingdom ; and it was an organism of this class, looking at which through a microscope Huxley pronounced it to be probably a plant, while Tyndall exclaimed that he would as soon call a sheep a vegetable. They are mostly microscopic, and are the first step in organised development from the Monera, which are mere specks of homogeneous protoplasm. Small as they are they have played an important part in the formation of the earth's crust, for the little slimy mass of aggregated cells has in many instances the power of secreting a solid skeleton, or a minute and delicate envelope or shell, the petrified remains of which form entire mountains. Thus the nummulitic limestone, which forms high ranges on the Alps and Himalayas, and of which the Pyramids are built, consists of the petrified skeletons of a species of

Radiolaria, or many-chambered shells, forming the complicated and elegant mansion with many rooms and passages, of the formless, slimy mass which constitutes the living organism. Chalk also, and the chalk-like formation which is accumulating at the bottom of deep oceans, are the results of the long-continued fall of the microscopic snowdrift of shells of the Globigenera and other protistic forms swimming in the sea ; and in a higher stage of development the skeletons of corals, one of the family of Zoophytes or plant-animals, form the coral reefs and islands so numerous in the Pacific and Indian Oceans, and are the basis of the vast masses of coralline limestone deposited in the coal era and other past geological periods.

As development proceeds the distinction between plants and animals becomes more apparent, though even here the simplest and earliest forms often show signs of a common origin by interchanging some of the fundamental attributes of the two kingdoms. Thus, the essential condition of plant existence is to live on inorganic food, which they manufacture into protoplasm, by working up simple combinations into others more complicated. Their diet consists of water, carbonic dioxide, and ammonia ; they take in carbonic dioxide and give out oxygen, while animals do exactly the reverse. But the fungi live, like animals, upon organic food consisting of complicated combinations of carbon, which they assimilate ; and, like animals, they inhale oxygen and give out carbonic dioxide.

Lichens afford a very curious instance of the association of vegetable and animal functions in the same plant. They are really formed of two distinct organisms : a body which is a low form of Alga or sea-weed, and a parasitic form of fungus, which lives upon it. The former has a plant life, living on inorganic matter and forming the green cells, or chlorophyll, which are the essential property of plants, enabling them under the action of the sun's rays to decompose carbonic dioxide · while the parasite lives like an animal on the formed protoplasm of the parent stem, forming threads of colourless cells which env lop and interlace with the original lichen of which they constitute the principal mass, as in a tree overgrown with ivy.

Even in existing and highly developed plants we find some curious instances of reversion towards animal life. Certain plants, for instance, like the Dionæa or Venus' fly-trap, finding it difficult to obtain the requisite supply of nitrogenous food in a fluid state from the arid or marshy soil in which they grow, have acquired a habit of supplying the deficiency by taking to an animal diet and eating flies. Conjoined with this is a more highly developed sensitiveness, and power of what appears to be voluntary motion, and a faculty of secreting a sort of gastric juice in which the flies are digested. The fundamental property also of decomposing carbonic dioxide and exhaling oxygen depends on light stimulating a peculiar chemical action of the chlorophyll, and at night leaves breathe like lungs, exhaling not oxygen, but the carbonic dioxide.

The records of geology, imperfect as they are, show a continued progression from these simple and neutral organisms to higher and more differentiated forms, both in the animal and vegetable worlds. These records are imperfect because the soft bodies of the simpler and for the most part microscopic forms of protoplasm and cell life are not capable of being preserved in petrifactions, and it is only when they happen to have secreted shells or skeletons that we have a chance of identifying them. Still we have a sufficient number of remains in the different geological strata to enable us to trace development. Thus, in the vegetable world, in the earliest strata, the Laurentian, Cambrian, and Silurian, forming the primordial period, which forms a thickness of some 70,000 feet of the earth's crust—or more than that of the whole of the subsequent strata, Primary, Secondary, Tertiary, and Quaternary, taken together—we find only vegetable remains of the lowest group of plants, that of the Tangles or Algæ, which live in water. Forests of these sea-weeds, like those of the Aleutian Islands, in some of which single tangles stream to the length of sixty feet, and floating masses, like those of the Sargasso Sea, appear to have constituted the sole vegetation of these primæval periods.

The Primary epoch, which comes next, comprises the Devonian or Old Red Sandstone, the Carboniferous or Coal system, and the Permian, the average thickness of the three together amounting to about 42,000 feet. In these the family of Ferns predominates, the remains of which constitute the bulk of the large strata of coal, forming in modern times our great resource for obtaining the energy which, in a transformed shape, does so much of our work. Pines begin to appear, though sparingly, in this epoch.

The Secondary epoch comprises the Triassic, the Jurassic, and the Cretaceous or Chalk formation, the average thickness of the three amounting to about 15,000 feet. In this era a higher species of vegetation predominates, that of the Gymnosperms, or plants having naked seeds, of which the pines, or Coniferæ, and the palm-ferns, or Cycadeæ, are the two principal classes. As in the case of the former epoch, traces of the approaching higher organisation in the form of leaf-bearing trees began to appear towards its close.

The Tertiary period extends from the end of the Chalk to the commencement of the Quaternary or modern period. It is divided into the Eocene or older, the Miocene or middle, and the Pliocene or newest Tertiary system; though the division is somewhat arbitrary, depending on the number of existing species, mostly of shell-fish, which have been found in each. The average thickness of the three together is about 3,000 feet. In this formation a still higher class of vegetation of the same order as that now existing, which made its first appearance in the Chalk period, has become predominant. It is that of Angiosperms, or plants with covered seeds, forming leafy forests of true trees. This group is divided into the two classes of monocotyledons or single-seed-lobed plants, and dicotyledons or plants with double seed-lobes. The monocotyledons spring from a single germ leaf, and are of simpler organisation than the other class. They comprise the grasses, rushes, lilies, irids, orchids, sea-grasses, and a number of aquatic plants, and in their highest form develop into the tree-like families of the palms and bananas.

The dicotyledons include all forms of leaf-bearing forest trees, almost all fruits and flowers, in fact by far the greater part of the vegetable world familiar to man, as coming into immediate relation with it, except in the case of the cultivated plants, which are developments of the monocotyledon grasses.

We see, therefore, in the geological record a confirmation of the evolution over immense periods of time of the more complex and perfect from the simple and primitive.

If we turn to the same geological record to trace the development of animal life, we find it running a parallel course with that of plants. The earliest known fossil, the Eozoon Canadiense, from the Lower Laurentian, is that of the chambered shell of a protista of the class of Rhizopods, whose soft body consists of mere protoplasm which has not yet differentiated into cells. As we ascend the scale of the primordial era, traces of marine life of the lower organisms begin to appear, until in the Silurian they become very abundant, consisting however mainly of mollusca and crustacea, and in the Upper Silurian we find the first traces of fishes.

In the Primary era the Devonian and Permian formations are characterised by a great abundance of fishes, of the antique type, which has no true bony skeleton, but is clothed in an armour of enamelled scales, and whose tail, instead of being bi-lobed or forked, has one lobe only—a type of which the sturgeon and garpike are the nearest surviving representatives. In the Coal formation are found the first remains of land animals in the form of insects and a scorpion, and a few traces of vertebrate amphibious animals and reptiles; while higher up in the Permian are found a few more highly developed reptiles, some of which approximate to the existing crocodile. Still fishes greatly predominate, so that the whole Primary period may be called the age of fishes, as truly as, looking at its flora, it may be called the age of ferns.

In the Secondary period reptiles predominate, and are developed into a great variety of strange and co·lossal forms. The first birds appear, being obviously developed from some of the forms of flying lizards, and having many reptilian characters. Mammals also put in a first feeble appearance, in the form of small, marsupial, insectivorous creatures.

In the Tertiary period the class of mammals greatly predominates over all other vertebrate animals, and we can see the principal types slowly developing and differentiating into those at present existing. The human type appears plainly in the middle Miocene, in the form of a large anthropoid ape, the Dryopithecus, and undoubted human remains are found in the beginning of the Quaternary, if not, as many distinguished geologists believe, in the Pliocene and even in the Miocene ages.

So far, therefore, there seems to be a complete parallelism between the evolution of animal and vegetable life from the earliest to the latest, and from the simplest to the most complex forms. These facts point strongly to a process of evolution by which the animal and vegetable worlds, starting from a common origin in protoplasm, the lowest and simplest form of living matter, have gradually advanced step by step, along diverging lines, until we have at last arrived at the sharp antithesis of the ox and the oak tree. It is clear, however, that this evolution has gone on under what I have called the generalised law of polarity, by which contrasts are produced of apparently opposite and antagonistic qualities, which however are indispensable for each other's existence. Thus animals could not exist without plants to work up the crude inorganic materials into the complex and mobile molecules of protoplasm, which are alone suited for assimilation by the more delicate and complex organisation of animal life. Plants, on the other hand, could not exist without a supply of the carbonic dioxide, which is their principal food, and which animals are continually pouring into the air from the combustion of their carbonised food in oxygen, which supplies them with heat and energy. Thus nature is one huge aquarium, in which animal and vegetable life balance each other by their contrasted and supplemental action, and, as in the inorganic world, harmonious existence becomes possible by this due balance of opposing factors.

CHAPTER VIII.

PRIMITIVE POLARITIES—POLARITY OF SEX.

Sexual generation—Base of ancient cosmogonies—Propagation non-sexual in simpler forms—Amœba and cells—Germs and buds—Anemones—Worms—Spores—Origin of sex—Ovary and male organ—Hermaphrodites—Parthenogenesis—Bees and insects—Man and woman—Characters of each sex—Woman's position—Improved by civilisation—Christianity the feminine pole—Monogamy the law of nature—Tone respecting women test of character—Women in literature—In society—Attraction and repulsion of sexes—Like attracts unlike—Ideal marriage—Woman's rights and modern legislation.

'MALE and female created He them.' At first sight this distinction of sex appears as fundamental as that of plant and animal. Mankind, and all the higher forms of life with which mankind has relations, can only propagate their species in one way: by the co-operation of two individuals of the species, who are essentially like and yet unlike, possessing attributes which are complementary of one another, and whose union is requisite to originate a new living unit—in other words, by sexual propagation. So certain does this appear that all ancient religions and philosophies begin by assuming a male and female principle for their gods, or first guesses at the unknown first causes of the phenomena of nature. Thus Ouranos and Gaia, Heaven and Earth; Phœbus and Artemis, the Sun and Moon: are all figured by the primitive imagination as male and female; and the Spirit of God brooding over Chaos and producing the

world, is only a later edition, revised according to monotheistic ideas, of the far older Chaldean legend which
describes the creation of Cosmos out of Chaos by the
ro-operation of great gods, male and female. Even
in later and more advanced religions, traces of this ineradicable tendency to assume difference of sex as the
indispensable condition of the creation of new existence
are found to linger and crop up in cases where they
are altogether inapplicable. Thus, in the orthodox
Christian creed we are taught to repeat ' begotten, not
made,' a phrase which is absolute nonsense, or *nonsense*—that is, an instance of using words like counter-
feit notes, which have no solid value of an idea behind
them. For ' begotten ' is a very definite term, which
implies the conjunction of two opposite sexes to produce a new individual. Unless two deities are assumed
of different sexes the statement has no possible meaning. It is a curious instance of atavism, or the way in
which the qualities and ideas of remote ancestors sometimes crop up in their posterity.

Science, however, makes sad havoc with this impression of sexual generation being the original and
only mode of reproduction, and the microscope and
dissecting knife of the naturalist introduce us to new
and altogether unsuspected worlds of life. By far the
larger proportion of living forms, in number at any rate,
if not in size, have come into existence without the aid
of sexual propagation. When we begin at the beginning, or with those Monera which are simple specks of
homogeneous protoplasm, we find them multiplying by
self-division. Amœba A, when it outgrows its natural
size, contracts in the middle and splits into two Amœbæ,
B and C, which are exactly like one another and like

the original A. In fact B contains one half of its parent A, and C the other half. They each grow to the size of the original A, and then repeat the process of splitting and duplicating themselves.

The next earliest stage in the evolution of living matter, the nucleated cell, does exactly the same thing. The nucleus splits into two, each of which becomes a new nucleus for the protoplasmic matter of the original cell, and either multiply within it, or burst the old cell-wall and become two new cells resembling the first.

The next stage in advance is that of propagation by germs or buds, in which the organism does not divide into two equal parts, but a small portion of it swells out at its surface, and finally parts company and starts on a separate existence which grows to the size of the parent by its inherent faculty of manufacturing fresh protoplasm from surrounding inorganic materials. This process may be witnessed any day in an aquarium containing specimens of the sea-anemone, where the minute new anemones may be seen in every form, both before and after they have parted from the parent body. It remains one of the principal modes of propagation of the vegetable 'world, where plants are multiplied from buds even after they have developed the higher mode of sexual propagation by seeds. In some of the lowest animals, such as worms, the buds are reduced to a small aggregation of cells, which form themselves into distinct individuals inside the body of the parent, and separate from it when they have attained a certain stage of development.

Advancing still further on the road towards sexual reproduction, we find these germ-buds reduced to spores, or single cells, which are emitted from the parent, and afterwards multiply by division until they form a many-celled organism, which has the hereditary qualities of the original one. This is the general form of propagation of the lower plants, such as algæ, mosses, and ferns, and also of a number of the lower forms of animal-like microscopic organisms, such as bacteria, whose spores, floating in the air in enormous quantities, and multiplying when they find a fit soil with astonishing rapidity, in a few days devastate the potato crop of a whole district or bring about an epidemic of scarlet-fever or cholera. They have their use however in creation, and their action is beneficent as well as the reverse, for they are the principal cause of putrefaction, the process by which the dead organic matter, which, if not removed, would choke up the world, is resolved into the inorganic elements from which it sprang, and rendered available for fresh combinations.

We are now at the threshold of that system of sexual propagation which has become the rule in all the higher families of animals and in many plants. It may be conceived as originating in the amalgamation of some germ-cell or spore with the original cell which was about to develop into a germ-bud within the body of some individual, and by the union of the two producing a new and more vigorous originating cell which modified the course of development of the germ-bud and of its resulting organism. This organism, having advantages in the struggle for life, established itself permanently with ever new developments in the same direction, which would be fixed and extended in its descendants by heredity, and special organs developed to meet the altered conditions. Thus at length the distinction would be firmly established of a female organ or ovary containing the egg or primitive cell from which the new being was to be developed, and a male organ supplying the fertilising spore or cell, which was necessary to start the egg in the evolutionary process by which it developed into the germ of an offspring combining qualities of the two parents. This is confirmed by a study of embryology, which shows that in the human and higher animal species the distinction of sex is not developed until a considerable progress has been made in the growth of the embryo. It is only however in the higher and more specialised families that we find this mode of propagation by two distinct individuals of different sexes firmly established. In the great majority of plants, and in some of the lower families of animals —for instance, snails and earth-worms—the male and female organs are developed within the same being, and they are what is called hermaphrodites. Thus, in most of the flowering plants the same blossom contains both the stamens and anther, which are the male organ, and the style and germ, which are the female.

Another transition form is Parthenogenesis, or virginal reproduction, in which germ-cells, apparently similar in all respects to egg-cells, develop themselves into new individuals without any fructifying element. This is found to be the case with many species of insects, and with this curious result, that those same germ-cells are often capable of being fructified, and in that case produce very different individuals. Thus, among the common bees, male bees or drones arise from the non-fructified eggs of the queen bee, while females are produced if the egg has been fructified.

In the higher families however of animal life the distinction of sex in different individuals has become the universal rule, and it produces a polarity or contrast which becomes ever more conspicuous as we rise in the scale of creation, until it attains its highest development in the highest stage hitherto reached, that of civilised man and woman. Both physical and mental character-istics depend mainly on the fact that the ovary or egg-producing organ is developed in the female, and thus the whole work of reproduction is thrown on her. To perform this a large portion of the vital energy is required, which in the male is available for larger and more prolonged growth of organs, such as the brain, stature, and limbs, by which a more powerful grasp is attained of the outward environment. In other words, the female comes sooner to maturity and is weaker than the male. She is also animated by a much stronger love for the offspring, which is part of her own body, during the period of infancy; and thus, in addition to the physical attributes, such as lacteal glands and larger breasts, she inherits qualities of softness, amiability, and devotion, which fit her for the office of nurse. Her physical weakness, again, has made her, for untold ages, and even now in all the less advanced communities, and too often even in the most advanced, the slave of the stronger male. She has thus inherited many of the mental qualities which are essential to such a state : the desire to propitiate by pleasing and making herself attractive; the gentleness and submissiveness which shrink from a contest of brute force in which she is sure to be defeated; the clinging to a stronger nature for support, which in extreme cases leads to blind admira-tion of power and the spaniel-like attachment to a master whether deserving of it or not. As civilisa-tion however advances, and as intellectual and moral qualities gain ascendency over brute strength and animal instincts, the condition of woman improves, and it comes more and more to be recognised that she is not made to be man's slave or plaything, but has her own personality and character, which, if in some respects inferior, are in others better than those of the male half of creation. Tennyson, the great poet of modern thought, who sums up so many of the ideas and tendencies of the age in concise and vigorous verse, writes :—

> For woman is not undeveloped man,
> Nor yet man's opposite.

Not opposite, yet different, so that the one supplements what is wanting to the other, and the harmonious union of the two makes ideal perfection. It is the glory of European civilisation to have done so much to develop this idea of the equality of the sexes, and to have gone so far towards emancipating the weaker half of the human species from the tyranny of the stronger half.

It would be unfair to omit mention of the great part which Christianity has had in this good work; not only by direct precept and recognition of religious equality, but even more by the embodiment, as its ideal, of the feminine virtues of gentleness, humility, resignation, self-devotion, and charity. Ideal Christianity is, in fact, what may be called the feminine pole of conduct and morality, as opposed to the masculine one of courage, hardihood, energy, and self-reliance. Many of the precepts of Christianity are unworkable, and have to be silently dropped in practice. It would not answer either for individuals or nations 'when smitten on one cheek to turn the other.' When an appeal is made to *fact* to decide whether it is a right rule to live as the sparrows do, taking no thought for the morrow, the verdict of *fact* is in favour of foresight and frugality.   Herbert Spencer has stated this polarity very strongly as that of the religion of amity and the religion of enmity ; but I think he states the case too adversely for the latter, for the qualities which make men and nations good fighters and victorious in the struggle for existence, are in their way just as essential as the gentler virtues, and both alike become defects when pushed to the 'falsehood of extremes.'   Christianity, therefore, whatever may become of its dogmas, ought always to be regarded with affection and respect for the humanising effect it·has produced, especially in improving the condition of the female half of creation.

This improvement in the condition of women has brought about a corresponding improvement in the male sex, for the polarity between the two has come to be the most intimate and far-reaching influence of modern life.   Take the literature of the novel and play, which aim at holding up the mirror to human nature and contemporary manners, and you will find that they nearly all turn upon love.   The word 'immorality' has come to signify the one particular breach of the laws of morality which arises from the relations of the sexes.

In providing for the birth of nearly equal numbers of each sex, nature clearly establishes monogamy, or union of single pairs, as the condition of things most in accordance with natural laws.   The family also, the first germ of civilisation, is impossible, or can only exist in a very imperfect and half-developed state, without this permanent union of a single husband and wife.   Violations of this law lead to such disastrous consequences to individuals, and are so deteriorating to nations, that they are properly considered as the 'immorality' *par excellence*, and condemned by all right-minded opinion. And yet to observe this law is a constant lesson in self-control for a great part of the life : a lesson of the utmost value, for it is a virtue which is at the root of all other virtues. And it is formed and becomes habitual and easy by practice, for just as the muscles of the ballet-dancer's leg or black-smith's arm acquire strength and elasticity by use, so do the finer fibres of the brain improve by exercise and become soft and flabby by disuse, so that effort in the former case is a pleasure and in the latter a pain. For this reason chaste nations are generally strong and conquering nations ; dissolute Imperial Rome went down before the Goths and Germans, and polygamous Turkey perishes of dry rot in the midst of the progress of the nineteenth century. Indeed, there is no better test of the position which either an individual, a class, or a nation hold in the scale of civilisation, than the tone which prevails among the men with regard to women. Wherever Turkish ideas prevail, we may be sure that whatever may be the outward varnish of manner there is essential snobbishness.

> Up and down
> Along the scale of life, through all,
> To him who wears the golden ball,
> By birth a king, at heart a clown.

On the other hand, wherever women are regarded with a chivalrous respect and reverence, the heart of a true gentleman beats, though it be under the rough exterior of one of Bret Harte's cow-boys or Californian miners.

Nothing in fact gives one more hope in the progress of human society than to find that in the freest countries, and those farthest advanced towards modern ideas and democratic institutions, the tone with regard to women shows the greatest improvement.   There is a regular *crescendo* scale of progress from Turkey to America.   I do not refer so much to the fact that in the newer colonies and countries women can travel unprotected without fear of insult or injury, as to the almost instinctive recognition of their equal rights as intelligent and moral beings who have a personality and character of their own, which places them on the same platform as men though on opposite sides of it.

To understand rightly the real spirit of an age or country, it is not enough to study dry statistics or history in the form of records of wars and political changes. We must study the works of the best poets, novelists, and dramatists, who seek to embody types and to hold up the mirror to contemporary ideas and manners.   A careful perusal of such works as those of Dickens, Thackeray, Trollope, and George Eliot at home, and of Bret Harte, Howells, James, and Mrs. Burnett in the United States, will give a truer insight into the inner life of the country and period than any number of blue-books or consular returns.   They show what the writers of the greatest genius, that is, of the greatest insight, see as types of the actual ideas and characters surrounding them ; and the fact of their works being popular shows that the types are recognised as true.   Now it is certain that the English literature of fiction and its latest development, that of the American novelists, show an ever-increasing recognition of the female individual as an equal unit with the male in the constitution of modern society. Those dear ' school marms ' of Bret Harte's and Wendell Holmes', who career so joyously through mining camps, receiving courtesy and radiating civilising influences among the rough inhabitants ; or touch the hearts and throw a mellow light over the autumn days of middle-aged professors and philosophers, are far removed from the slaves of prehistoric savages or the inmates of a Turkish harem. So also in the more complex relations of a more crowded civilisation, in the circles of Washington, New York, and Boston, the ideal American woman is always depicted as bright, intelligent, and independent, with a character and personality of her own, and the suspicion never seems to enter the author's head that she is in any respect inferior to the male characters with whom she is associated.

The same may be said to a great extent of English literature from the time of Shakespeare downwards. No better portrait than Portia was ever drawn of the

Perfect woman, nobly planned
To soothe, to comfort, and command ;
And yet a spirit still, and bright
With something of an angel light.

And in the long gallery of good and loveable women, from Rosalind and Imogene down to Lucy Roberts and Laura Pendennis, we have not one who is a mere nonentity or child of passionate impulse. Nor is the recognition of woman's equality less marked in the bad characters. Lady Macbeth is of a stronger nature than Macbeth ; Becky Sharp more clever and full of resources than the men with whom she plays like puppets ; Maggie Tulliver, with all her wild struggles with herself and her surroundings, has far more in her than her brother Tom.   Compare these characters with those of the school of modern French novels, which turn mainly on adultery and seduction, committed for the most part not in any whirlwind of irresistible passion, but to gratify some passing caprice or vanity, and it is easy to see how wide is the gulf which separates the ideals and moral atmosphere of the two countries.

It is not therefore from any wish to indulge in what Herbert Spencer calls the ' unpatriotic bias,' and depreciate my own country, that I am disposed to think that the younger English-speaking communities are somewhat in advance of ourselves in this matter of the relations of the sexes, but simply because I think that the feeling is there more widespread and universal. We have in English society two strata in which women are still considered as inferior beings to men : a lower one, where better ideas have not yet permeated the dense mass of ignorance and brutality ; and a higher one, where among a certain portion, let us hope a small one, of the gilded youth and upper ten, luxury and idleness have blunted the finer susceptibilities, and created what may be most aptly called a Turkish tone about women.   There are many of this class, and unfortunately often in high places, where their example does widespread mischief, whose ideal might be summed up in the words of the Irish ballad :—

> I am one of the ould sort of Bradies,
>   My turn does not lie to hard work;
> But I'm fond of my pipe and the ladies,
>   And I'd make a most illigant Turk.

And most ' illigant Turks ' they make, though far worse than real Turks who are born and brought up in the ideas and surroundings of a lower civilisation; while

I

the tone of our English Turks is far more nauseous and disgusting, as denoting innate selfishness, sensuality, and vulgarity. Of these two classes there seem to be fewer in the newer English communities ; and if they exist, they are in such a small minority that they conceal their existence, and pay the homage of vice to virtue which is called hypocrisy.

To return, however, to the more scientific aspects of the question, the polarity of sex displays itself as conspicuously as that of the magnet in the fundamental law of repulsion of like for like, and attraction of like for unlike. In each case there must be an identity of essence developing itself in opposite directions. Thus, atoms attract or repel atoms, but not molecules ; for if they seem to do so, it is only in cases in which the molecule contains some atom whose atomicity or polar power has not been fully satisfied. So currents of air or water do not affect electric currents. But given the identity of substance, its differentiation takes place under an ever-increasing progression of polarity of affinities and repulsions.

A German naturalist, Brahm, discussing the question why birds sing, says, ' the male finds in the female those desirable and attractive qualities which are wanting in himself. He seeks the opposite to himself with the force of a chemical element.' This is equally true of the male and female of the human species. A masculine woman and effeminate man are equally unattractive, and if the qualities are pushed to an extreme extent, the individuals become monstrosities, and, instead of attracting, excite vehement disgust and repulsion. This, which is true physically, is equally true of moral and intellectual characteristics. Each seeks, in the happy marriage or perfect ideal union, the qualities which are most deficient in themselves : the woman, strength, active courage, and the harder qualities; the man, gentleness, amiability, and the softer virtues. In each individual, as in each union of individuals, harmony and perfection depend on the due balance of the opposite qualities, and the ' falsehood of extremes ' leads up to chaos and insanity.   The man in whom strength and hardihood are not tempered by gentleness and affection becomes brutal and tyrannical ; while the woman who has no strength of character becomes silly and frivolous.   Marriage, however, involves the highest ideal, for the well-assorted union of the two in one gives a more complete harmony and reconciliation of opposites than can be attained by the single individual, who must always remain more or less within the sphere of the polarity of his or her respective sex.   But here also the same law of polarity operates, for as happy marriage affords the highest ideal, so do unhappy and ill-assorted unions involve the greatest misery and most complete shipwreck of life.   Especially to the woman, for the man has other pursuits and occupations, and can to a great extent withdraw himself from domestic troubles ; while the woman has no defence against the coarseness, selfishness, and vulgarity of the partner to whom she is tied, and who may make her life a perpetual purgatory, and drag all her finer intellectual and moral nature down to a lower level.   Fortunately extreme cases are rare, and, though the ideal of a perfect union may seldom be attained to, the great majority of married couples manage to jog on together, and bring up families in comparative comfort and respectability. Evidently, however, in many cases the weaker party does not get fair play, and the laws which are the result of centuries of male legislation are often too oblivious of the maxim that what is ' sauce for goose is sauce for gander.' Improvement, however, is coming from the growth of the more healthy public opinion which stigmatises any invasion of woman's real rights, and any attempt on the part of her natural protector to bully and tyrannise, as utterly disgraceful ; and the waves of this public opinion are slowly but surely sapping the cliffs of legal conservatism, and forcing the intrenchments of stolid injustice behind ermine robes, horsehair wigs, and obsolete Acts of Parliament.

CHAPTER IX.

PRIMITIVE POLARITIES—HEREDITY AND VARIATION.

Heredity in simple forms of life—In more complex organisms—Pangenesis—Varieties how produced—Fixed by law of survival of the fittest—Dr. Temple's view—Examples : triton, axolotl—Variations in individuals and species — Lizards into birds — Ringed snakes — Echidna.

As the earth is kept in an orbit, which makes life possible by the balance of the antagonist centripetal and centrifugal forces, so is that life evolved and maintained by the balance of the two conflicting forces of heredity and variation. Heredity, or the principle which makes offsprings resemble their parental organisms, may be considered as the centripetal force which gives stability to species ; while variation is like the centrifugal force which tends to make them develop into new forms, and prevents organic matter from remaining ever consolidated into one uniform mass.

As regards heredity, the considerations which have been advanced in the last chapter, on the origin of sex, will enable the reader to understand the principles on which it is based. When a moneron, or living piece of pure protoplasm, or its successor the nucleated cell, propagates itself by simple division into two equal parts, it is obvious that each half must, in its atomic constitution and motions, exactly resemble the original. If amœba A divides into amœbæ B and C, both B and C

are exact facsimiles of A and of one another, and so are
the progeny of B and C through any number of generations.   They must remain identical repetitions of the
parent form, unless some of them should happen to
be modified by different actions of their surrounding
environment, powerful enough to affect the original
organisation.

In propagation by germs or buds, the same thing
must hold true, only, as the offspring carries with it
not the half, but only a small portion of the parental
organism, its impress will be less powerful, and the
new organism will more readily be affected by external
influences. When we come to propagation by spores or
single cells, and still more to sexual propagation by the
union of single cells of two progenitors, it becomes
more difficult to see how the type of the two parents, and
of a long line of preceding ancestors, can be maintained
so perfectly.

Of the fact that it is maintained there can be no
doubt. Not only do species breed true and remain
substantially the same for immense periods, but the
characters of individual parents and their ancestors
repeat themselves, to a great extent, in their offspring.
Thus the cross between the white and black varieties
of the human species perpetuates itself to such an
extent, that a single cross of black blood leaves traces
for a number of generations. In the Spanish American
States and the West Indies, where the distinction is
closely observed, the term 'octoroon' is well known,
as applied to creoles who have seven-eighths of white
to one-eighth of black blood in their composition. In
the case of what is called 'atavism,' this recurrence to
the characters of ancestors is carried to a much further

extent. In breeding animals, it is not uncommon to find the peculiar features of generations of ancestors long since extinct cropping up occasionally in individuals. Thus, stripes like those of the ass along the back and down the shoulders, occasionally appear on horses whose immediate ancestors for many generations back showed nothing of the sort; and even stripes across the legs like those of the zebra occur quite unexpectedly, and testify to the common descent of the various species of the horse tribe from a striped ancestor. How these ancestral peculiarities can be transmitted through many generations, each individual of which originated from a single microscopic cell which had been fructified by another cell, is one of the greatest mysteries of nature. It may assist us in forming some idea of the possibility of a solution to remember what has been proved as to the dimensions of atoms. Their order of magnitude is that of a cricket-ball to the earth. In a single microscopic cell, therefore, there may be myriads of such atoms circling round one another and forming infinitesimal solar systems, of infinite complexity and variety. Darwin's theory of 'Pangenesis' supposes that some of the actual identical atoms which formed part of ancestral bodies are thus transmitted through their descendants for generation after generation, so that we are literally 'flesh of the flesh' of the primæval creature who was developed into man in the later tertiary or early glacial period. Haeckel, more plausibly, suggests that not the identical atoms, but their peculiar motions and mode of aggregation have been thus transmitted: a mode of transmission which, with his prevailing tendency to invent long and learned names for everything, he calls the

'Perigenesis of plastids.' In any case, however, these must be taken not as solutions of the problem, but as guesses at the truth which show that its solution is not impossible.

The opposite principle to heredity, that of variation, is equally important and universal. It is apparent in the fact, that although every individual of every species reproduces qualities of parents and ancestors, no two individuals do so in precisely the same manner ; no two are exactly alike. This difference, or individuality, becomes more marked as the organism is higher. Thus, sheep and hounds differ from one another by slight differences which require the practised eye of the shepherd or huntsman to detect ; while human beings are so unlike, that of the many millions existing in each generation no two exactly resemble one another. The reason of this is apparent if we consider that the higher the organism the more complex does it become, and the less the chance of the whole complicated relations of parent and ancestral organisms being transmitted by single cells so solidly and completely as to overpower and remain uninfluenced by external influences. Variation evidently depends mainly on the varying influences of environment. If the exterior layer of molecules of a lump of protoplasm become differentiated from the interior ones and form a cell-wall, it is because they are in more immediate contact with the air or other surrounding medium. Internal changes depend on conditions such as temperature and nutrition. In the case of cultivated plants and domestic animals we can see most clearly how varieties are produced by adaptation to changes of environment. These variations, however, would not proceed very far, were it not for the interaction of the opposing forces of variation and heredity, by which latter the variations appearing in individuals are fixed and accumulated in descendants, until they become wide and permanent divergencies. This is done in the case of cultivated plants and domestic animals by man's artificial selection in pairing individuals who show the same variations; and in nature by the struggle for existence, giving victory and survival to those forms, and in the long run to those forms only, whose variations, slight as they may be in each generation, tend to bring individuals into better adaptation to their environment.

It is the great glory of Darwin to have established this firmly by an immense number of interesting and exhaustive instances, and thus placed evolution, or a scientific explanation of the development and laws of life, on a solid basis. Every day fresh discoveries and experiments confirm this great principle, and it has almost passed into the same phase as Newton's law of gravity, as a fundamental law accepted as axiomatic by all men of science, and as the basis of modern thought, to which all religions and philosophies have to conform, accepted by nearly all modern thinkers. I may here quote a passage from an eminent Anglican divine, Dr. Temple, for the double purpose of showing how universal has become the acceptance of this Darwinian view of evolution among intelligent men ; and how little terrible are its consequences, even to those who look at the facts of the universe through a theological medium and retain their belief in accepted creeds.

' It seems in itself something more majestic, more befitting of Him to whom a thousand years are as one day, and one day as a thousand years, thus to impress His will once for all on this creation, and provide for all its countless varieties by this one original impress, than by special acts of creation to be perpetually modifying what He had previously made.' [1]

Scientific men would be content to accept this statement of Dr. Temple's almost in his own words, except that they might consider his definition of the Great First Cause as somewhat too absolute and confident. Having had to deal so much with actual facts and accurate knowledge, they are apt to be more modest in assertion than even the most enlightened theologian, whose studies have lain rather in the direction of phrases and ideas, which, from their very nature, are more vague and indefinite, and perhaps rather guesses and aspirations after truth, than proofs of it. In any case there is the authority of a learned and liberal-minded bishop for the position that the scientific way of looking at the universe is not necessarily profane or irreligious.

To return to variation : the instances of the operation of this principle, alone or in conjunction with that of heredity, in working out the evolution of species, are exceedingly numerous and interesting. Those who wish to understand the subject thoroughly must study the works of Darwin, Haeckel, Huxley, and other modern writers ; but for my present purpose it will be sufficient to refer to a few of the most marked instances which may assist the reader in comprehending how the gradual evolution of life and creation of new species may have been brought about.

There is an amphibious animal, called the triton or water-salamander, akin to the frog, whose normal course is to begin life living in the water and breathing by gills, and end it on land with gills metamorphosed into

[1] Dr. Temple, *Religion and Science.*

lungs. If they are shut up in water and kept in a tank they never lose their gills, but continue through life in the lower stage of development, and reproduce themselves in other tritons with gills. Conversely the axolotl, a peculiar gilled salamander from the Lake of Mexico, has its normal course to live, die, and propagate its species in water, breathing by gills ; but if an axolotl happens to stray from the water and take to living on dry land, the gills are modified into lungs and the animal gains a place in the class in the school of development. This fits in remarkably with the fact that the embryo of all vertebrate mammals, including man, passes through the gilled stage before arriving at the development of lungs, which assists us in understanding two facts of primary importance in the history of evolution.

First, how terrestrial life may have arisen from aquatic life by adaptation to altered conditions.

Secondly, how the evolution of the embryo sums up in the individual, in the period of a few days or months, the various stages of evolutions which it has taken millions of years to accomplish in the species.

As a parallel to the transformation of gills into lungs, and of an aquatic into a land animal, if we turn to the geological records of the Secondary period we may trace the transformation of a water into an air population, of sea-lizards into flying-lizards, and of flying-lizards into birds. The ' Hesperornis ' is an actual specimen of the transition, being a feathered lizard, or rather winged and feathered creature which is half lizard and half bird.

A remarkable instance of the great change of functions which may be produced by a change of outward conditions is afforded by the common ringed snake, which in its natural state lays eggs which take three weeks to hatch; but if confined in a cage in which no sand is strewed it hatches the eggs within its own body, and from oviparous becomes viviparous. This may help us to understand how the lowest order of mammals, which, like the Australian echidna or duck-billed mole, lay eggs, may have developed, first into marsupial, and finally into placental mammals.

These examples may assist the reader in understanding how the infinite diversities of living species may have been developed in the course of evolution from simple origins, just as the inorganic world was from atoms, by the action and reaction of primitive polar forces between the organism and its environment, and between heredity and variation.

CHAPTER X.

Basis of knowledge—Perception—Constitution of brain—White and grey
matter—Average size and weight of brains—European, negro, and ape
—Mechanism of perception—Sensory and motor nerves—Separate
areas of brain—Sensory and motor centres—Abnormal states of brain
—Hypnotism—Somnambulism—Trance—Thought-reading—Spiritualism—Reflex action—Ideas how formed—Number and space—
Creation unknowable—Conceptions based on perceptions—Metaphysics—Descartes, Kant, Berkeley—Anthropomorphism—Laws of
nature.

BEFORE entering on the higher subjects of religions and
philosophies, it is well to arrive at some precise idea of
the limits of human knowledge, and of the boundary
line which separates the knowable from the unknowable. The ultimate basis of all knowledge is perception.
Without an environment to create impressions, and
an organ to receive them, we should know absolutely
nothing. What is the environment and what the
organ of human knowledge? The environment is the
whole surrounding universe, or, in the last analysis, the
motions, or changes of motion, by which the objects in
that universe make impressions on the recipient organ.
The organ is the grey matter of that large nervous
agglomeration, the brain. But here I must at the out-
set make two reservations. In the first place I do not
define how these impressions are made. In all ordinary

cases they are made through the channels of the senses; but it is possible that in certain exceptional cases vibrations in the brain, causing perceptions, may be conveyed to it through the nerves in other ways. In somnambulism, for instance, it seems to be an ascertained fact that a somnambulist with closed eyes securely bandaged can walk in the dark and avoid obstacles as well as if guided by the sight in full daylight. There is a great deal of evidence also that in artificial somnambulism, otherwise called mesmerism or hypnotism, and also in what is called thought-reading, perceptions may be conveyed from one brain to another otherwise than by the usual methods of speech or writing. But these phenomena, however far they may be extended, do not affect the position that impressions on the brain are the essential condition of thought. If the grey matter of the brain is deficient or diseased the mind is affected, and beyond a certain point becomes extinct.

The second and more important reservation is, that although mind and all its qualities are thus indissolubly connected with matter, it by no means follows that they are matter or mere qualities of it. In the case of the atoms and energies, we know absolutely nothing of their real essence, and cannot form even a conception of what they are, how they came there, or what will become of them. It is the same with mind, soul, or self: we feel an instinctive certainty of their existence, as we do of that of matter; and we can trace their laws and manifestations under the conditions in which they are known to us, viz. those of association with matter and motion in the brain. But of their real essence or existence we know nothing, and it is as unscientific to affirm as to deny. Directly we pass beyond the boundary of such knowledge as really can be known by human faculty, and stand face to face with the mystery of the Great Unknown, we can only bow our heads with reverence and say with the poet,

> Behold, I know not anything.

I hope thus to steer safely between Scylla and Charybdis—between the arid rocks of materialism and the whirling eddies of spiritualism.   Materialist and spiritualist seem to me very like two men disputing as to the existence of life in the sun.   'No,' argues the former ; 'for the known conditions there are totally inconsistent with any life we can conceive.'   'Yes,' says the other ; 'for the belief fits in with many things which I earnestly wish to believe respecting a Supreme Being and a future existence.'   To the first I say, ignorance is not evidence ; to the second, wishes are not proofs.   For myself, while not quarrelling with those more favoured mortals who have, or fancy they have, superior knowledge, I can only say that I really know nothing ; and this being the case, I see no use in saying that I know, and think it both more truthful and more modest to confess the limitation of my faculties.

With this caution I return to the field of positive knowledge.   The brain, spinal marrow, and nerves consist of two substances : one white, which constitutes the great mass consisting of tubes or fibres ; the other grey, which is an aggregation of minute cells, so minute that it has been computed that there are several millions of them in a space no larger than a sixpence.   The bulk of this grey nerve-tissue is found in the higher animals, and especially in man, in the outside rind which covers the brain, and its amount is greatly increased by the convolutions of that organ giving a greater extent of covering surface.   In fact the convolutions of the average human brain give as much grey matter in a head of average size, as would be given by a head of four times the size if the brain were a plane surface.   The extent of the convolutions is, therefore, a sure sign of the extent of intellect.   They are more numerous and deeper in the European than in the negro; in the negro than in the chimpanzee; in the anthropoid ape than in the monkey or lemur.   This grey nerve-tissue is the organ by which impressions from without are turned into perceptions, volitions, and evolutions of nerve force.   The white matter is simply the medium of transmission, or we may say the telegraph wires by which the impressions are conveyed to the head office and the answers sent. The cell-tissue of the grey matter is thus emphatically the organ of the mind.   In fact, if it did not sound too materialistic, we might call thought a secretion of the grey matter, only in saying so we must bear in mind that it is only a mode of expressing the fact that the two invariably go together; and that if we say with the German philosopher 'Ohne Phosphor kein Gedank,' it does not mean that thought and phosphorus are identical, but simply that the condition on which thought depends is that of the existence of a material organ of which phosphorus is an ingredient.

That this grey nerve-tissue is really the organ of thought has been firmly established by numerous ex-periments both in man and the lower animals.   Injuries to it, or diseases in it, invariably affect what is called the mind; while considerable portions of the white matter may be removed without affecting the think-ing and perceptive powers.   A certain amount of it is indispensable for the existence of intellect ; the more there is of it as the brain increases in size and the convolutions become deeper, the greater is the intellect; when these fall below certain dimensions intellect is extinguished and we have idiocy.   The average brain of the male white European weighs $49\frac{1}{2}$ ounces, of the negro a little under 47.   The maximum brains which have been accurately weighed and measured, are those of Cuvier and Daniel Webster, the weight of the former being $64\frac{1}{3}$ ounces, and the capacity of the latter being 122 cubic inches ; while the average capacity of the Teutonic race, including English, Germans, and Americans, is 92 inches, of the negro 83, and of the Australian and Hottentot 75.   The brain of the idiot seldom weighs over 23 ounces, and the minimum weight consistent with a fair degree of intelligence is about 34 ounces.

The mechanism by which correspondence is kept up between the living individual and the surrounding universe is very simple—in reality, as simple as that of any ordinary electric circuit.   In the most complex case, that of man, there are a number of nerve-endings, or small lumps of protoplasm, embedded in the tissues all over the body, or highly specialised and grouped together in separate organs such as the eye and ear, from which a nerve-fibre leads direct to the brain, or to the spinal cord and so up to the brain.   These nerve-endings receive the different vibrations by which outward energy presents itself, which propagate a current or succession of vibrations of nerve-energy along the nerve-fibre.   This nerve-fibre is a round thread of protoplasm covered by a white sheath of fatty matter which insulates it like the wire of a submarine telegraph

K

coated with gutta-percha. This nerve-wire leads up to a nerve-centre, consisting of two corpuscles of proto-plasm : the first or sensory, a smaller one, which is connected by branches with the second, a much larger one, called the motor, from which a much larger nerve-fibre or wire proceeds, which terminates in a mass of protoplasm firmly attached to a muscle. Thus, a sen-sation is propagated along the sensory nerve to the sensory nerve-centre, whence it is transmitted to the motor-centre, which acts as an accumulator of stored-up energy, a large flow of which is sent through the large conductor of the motor-nerve to the muscle, which it causes to contract and thus produces motion. It is thus that the simpler involuntary actions are produced by a process which is purely mechanical. In the more complex cases, in which consciousness and will are involved, the process is essentially the same, though more complicated. The message is transmitted to the brain, where it is received by a cluster of small sensory cells or nerve-centres, which are connected with another cluster of fewer and larger motor-centres, often at some distance from them, by a network of interlacing fibres. But it is always a case of a single circuit of wires, batteries, and accumulators, adapted for receiving, re-cording, and transmitting one sort of vibrations caused by and producing one sort of energy, and one only. The brain does not act as a whole, receiving indiscrimi-nately impressions of light, sound, and heat ; but by separate organs for each, located in separate parts of it. It is like a great central office, in one room of which you have a printing instrument reading off and record-ing messages sent through an electric telegraph ; in another a telephone ; in a third a self-registering thermometer, and so on. And the same for the motor-centres and nerves. One set is told off to move the muscles of the face, another those of the arms, others for the legs and body, and so forth. This is further complicated by the fact that the brain like the rest of the body has two sides, a right and left, and that in some cases the motor-apparatus is doubled, each working only on one side, while in others the same battery and wires serve for both. As a rule the right hemisphere of the brain works the muscles of the left side of the body, and *vice versâ*, so that an injury to one side of the brain may paralyse the voluntary motion of the limbs on the opposite side, leaving in a perfect condition those on its own side.

In the case of the higher functions involving thought, the upper part of the brain, which performs these functions, seems to be a sort of duplex machine, so that we have two brains capable of thinking, just as we have two eyes capable of seeing. It is a remarkable fact that the areas of the brain which are appropriated to the lowest and most instinctive functions, which appear first, lie lowest, and as the functions rise the position of their nerve-centres rises with them. Thus, at the very base of the frontal convolutions at the lowest end of the fissure of Rolando, we find the motor areas for the lower part of the face, by which the lowest animals and the new-born infant perform their solitary function of sucking and swallowing. Higher up are the centres in the right and left brains for moving the upper limbs, that is, for seizing food and conveying it to the mouth, which is the next function in the ascending scale. Next above these are the centres for moving the lower limbs and for co-ordinating the motions of the

arms and legs, marking the progression of an organism
which can pursue and catch as well as eat its food.
And still higher are the centres which regulate the
motions of the trunk and body in correspondence with
those of the limbs ; while highest of all, at the front
and hind ends of the enveloping cortex of the brain,
come the organs of the intellectual faculties.

It is easy to see that this corresponds with the progression of the individual, for the infant sucks and cries
for food from the first day, soon learns to extend its
hand and grasp objects, but takes some time to learn to
walk, and still longer to perform exercises like dancing
or riding, in which the motions of the whole body
have to be co-ordinated with those of the limbs. And
as the development of the individual is an epitome of
the evolution of life from protoplasm, we may well
suppose that the brain was developed in this order from
its first origin in a swelling at the end of the spinal
cord as we find it in the lowest vertebrates.

It is a singular fact that the particular motor area
which gives the faculty of articulate speech lies in a
small patch of about one and a half square inches on
the left side of the lower portion of the first brain. If
this is injured, the disease called aphasia is produced, in
which the patient loses the power of expressing ideas
by connected words. The corresponding area on the
right side cannot talk ; but in left-handed persons this
state of things is reversed, and the right side, which is
generally aphasial, can be taught to speak in young
people, though not in the aged.

Higher up in the cortex, or convoluted envelope of
the brain, come the areas for hearing and seeing, the
latter being the more extensive. These areas are filed

mainly by a great number of sensory nerve-centres or cells, connected with one another in a very complicated network.   These seem to be connected with the multitude of ideas which are excited in the brain by perceptions derived from the higher senses, especially that of sight.   The simple movements are produced by a few large motor-centres, which have only one idea and do only one thing, whether it be to move the leg or the arm.   But a sensation from sight often calls up a multitude of ideas.   Suppose you see the face of one with whom some fifty years ago you may have had some youthful love passages, but your lives drifted apart, and you now meet for the first time after these long years, how many ideas will crowd on the mind, how many nerve-cells will be set vibrating, and how many nerve-currents set coursing along intricate paths!   No wonder that the nerve-corpuscles are numerous and minute, and the nerve-channels many and complicated.

When we come to the seats of the intellectual faculties the question becomes still more obscure. They are probably situated in the hinder and front parts of the surface of the brain, and depend on the grey matter consisting of an immense number of minute sensory cells.   It has been computed that there are millions in the area of a square inch, and they are all in a state of the most delicate equilibrium, vibrating with the slightest breath of nervous impression.   They depend for their activity entirely on the sensory perceptive centres, for there is no consciousness in the absence of sensory stimulation, as in dreamless sleep.   Perception, however caused, whether by outward stimulation of real objects, or by former perceptions revived by memory, sends a stream of energy through the sense-area, which expands, like a river divided into numerous channels, fertilising the intellectual area, where it is stored up by memory, giving us the idea of continual individual existence, and by some mysterious and unknown process becoming transformed into consciousness and deliberate thought. And conversely the process is reversed when what we call will is excited, and the small currents of the intellectual area are concentrated by an effort of attention and sent along the proper nerve-channels to the motor-centres, whose function it is to produce the desired movement. This mechanical explanation, it will be observed, leaves entirely untouched the question of the real essence and origin of these intellectual faculties, as to which we know nothing more than we do of the real essence and origin of life, of matter, and of energy.

A very curious light however is thrown on them by phenomena which occur in abnormal states of the brain, as in trance, somnambulism, and hypnotism. In the latter, by straining the attention on a given object or idea, such as a coin held in the hand or a black wafer on a white wall, the normal action of the brain is, in the case of many persons—perhaps one out of every three or four—thrown out of gear, and a state induced in which the will seems to be annihilated, and the thoughts and actions brought into subjection to the will of another person. In this state also a cataleptic condition of the muscles is often induced, in which they acquire enormous strength and rigidity. In somnambulism outward consciousness is in a great measure suspended, and the somnambulist lives for the time in a walking dream which he acts and mistakes for reality. In this state old perceptions, scarcely felt at the time, seem to revive, as in dreams, with such wonderful vividness and accuracy that the somnambulist in acting the dream does things altogether impossible in the waking state. Thus an ignorant Scotch servant-maid is said to have recited half a chapter of the Hebrew version of the Old Testament : the explanation being that she had been in the service of a Scotch minister, who was studying Hebrew, and who used to walk about his room reciting this identical passage.   It would seem as if the brain were like a very delicate photograph plate, which takes accurate impressions of all perceptions, whether we notice them or not, and stores them up ready to be reproduced whenever stronger impressions are dormant and memory by some strange caprice breathes on the plate.

Most wonderful, however, are some of the pheno- mena of trance.   In this case it really seems as if two distinct individuals might inhabit the same body. Jones falls into a trance and dreams that he is Smith. While the trance lasts he acts and talks as Smith, he really is Smith, and even addresses his former self Jones as a stranger.   When he wakes from the trance he has no recollection of it, and takes up the thread of his own life, just as if he had dozed for a minute instead of being in a trance for hours.   But if he falls into a second trance, days or weeks afterwards, he takes up his trance life exactly where he dropped it, absolutely forgetting his intermediate real life.   And so he may go on alternating between two lives, with two separate personalities and consciousnesses, being to all intents and purposes now Jones and now Smith.   If he died during a trance, which would he be, Jones or Smith? The question is more easily asked than answered ; but it certainly appears as if with one mode of motion in the same brain you might have one mind and personal identity associated with it, and with another mode of motion different ones.

It would take me too far, and the facts are too doubtful, to investigate the large class of cases included under the terms thought-reading, telepathy, psychism, and spiritualism. It may suffice to say that there is a good deal of evidence for the reality of very curious phenomena, but none of any real weight for their being caused by any spiritualistic or supernatural agency. They all seem to resolve themselves into the assertion that under special conditions the perceptions of one brain can be reproduced in another otherwise than by the ordinary medium of the senses, and that in such conditions a special sort of cataleptic energy or psychic force may be developed. The amount of negative evidence is of course enormous, for it is certain that in millions upon millions of cases thought cannot be read, things are not seen beyond the range of vision, and coincidences do not occur between deaths and dreams or visions. Neither can tables be turned, nor heavy bodies lifted, without some known form of energy and a fulcrum at which to apply it.

This borderland of knowledge is, therefore, best left to time, which is the best test of truth. That which is real will survive, and be gradually brought within the domain of science and made to fit in with other facts and laws of nature. That which is unreal will pass away, as ghosts and goblins have done, and be forgotten as the fickle fashion changes of superstitious fancy. In the meantime we shall do better to confine ourselves to ascertained facts and normal conditions.

It is pretty certain that although the brain greatly preponderates as an organ of mind in man and the higher animals, the grey tissue in the spinal marrow and nervous ganglia exercises a limited amount of the same functions proportionate to its smaller quantity. The reflex or automatic actions, such as breathing, are carried on without reference to the brain, and the messages are received and transmitted through the local offices without going to the head office.   This is the case with many complicated motions which originated in the brain, but have become habitual and automatic, as in walking, where thought and conscious effort only intervene when something unusual occurs which requires a reference to the head office ; and in the still more complex case of the piano-player, who fingers difficult passages correctly while thinking of something else or even talking to a bystander.

Indeed, in extreme cases, where experiments on the brain have been tried on lower animals, it is found that it can be entirely removed without destroying life, or affecting many of the actions which require perception and volition.   Thus, when the brain has been entirely removed from a pigeon, it smoothes its feathers with its bill when they have been ruffled, and places its head under its wing when it sleeps ; and a frog under the same conditions, if held by one foot endeavours to draw it away, and if unsuccessful, places the other foot against an obstacle in order to get more purchase in the effort to liberate itself.

So much for the organ of mind; the other factor, that of outward stimulus, is still more obvious.   If thought cannot exist without grey nerve-tissue, neither can it without impressions to stimulate that tissue.   A perfect brain, if cut off from all communication with the external universe, could no more think and have perceptions, than impressions from without could generate them without the appropriate nerve-tissue. Once generated, the mind can store them up by memory, control them by reason, and gradually evolve from them ever higher and higher ideas and trains of reasoning, both in the individual and the species :—in the individual passing from infancy to manhood, partly by heredity from ancestors, and partly by education—using the word in the large sense of influences of all sorts from the surrounding environment ; in the species, by a similar but much slower development from savagery to civilisation.

Thus the whole fabric of arithmetic, algebra, and the higher calculi are built up from the primitive perception of number. The earliest palæolithic savage must have been conscious of a difference between encountering one or two cave-bears or mammoths ; and some existing races of savages have hardly got beyond this primitive perception. Some Australian tribes, it is said, have not got beyond three numerals, one, two, and a great number. But by degrees the perceptions of number have become more extensive and accurate, and the number of fingers on each hand has been used as a standard of comparison. Thus ten, or two-hand, the number of fingers on the two hands has gradually become the basis of arithmetical numeration, and from this up to Sir W. Hamilton's ' Quaternions ' the progression is regular and intelligible. But Newton could never have invented the differential calculus and solved the problem of the heavens, if thousands of centuries before some primitive human mind had not received the perception that two apples or two bears were different from one.

In like manner geometry, as its name indicates, arises from primitive perceptions of space, applied to the practical necessity of land-measuring in alluvial valleys like those of the Nile and Euphrates, where annual inundations obliterated to a great extent the dividing lines between adjoining properties. The first perceptions of space would take the form of the rectangle, or so many feet or paces, or cubits or arm-lengths, forwards, and so many sideways, to give the proper area ; but as areas were irregular, it would be discovered that the triangle was necessary for more accurate measurement. Hence the science of the triangle, circle, and other regular forms, as we see it developed in Euclid and later treatises on geometry, until we see it in its latest development in speculations as to space of four dimensions.

But in all these cases we see the same fundamental principle as prevails throughout the universe under the name of the 'conservation of energy'; always something out of something, never something out of nothing.

This, therefore, defines the limit of human knowledge, or boundary line between the knowable and the unknowable. Whatever is *transformation* according to existing laws is, whether known or unknown, at any rate, knowable—whatever is *creation* is unknowable. We have absolutely no faculties to enable us to form the remotest conception of what the essence of these primary atoms and energies really is, how they came there, and how the laws, or invariable sequences, under which they act, came to be impressed on them. We have no faculties, because we have never had any perceptions upon which the mind can work. Reason and imagination can no more work without antecedent perceptions than a bird can fly in a vacuum.

Thus, for instance, the imagination can invent dragons, centaurs, and any number of fabulous monsters, by piecing together fragments of perceptions in new combinations; but ask it to invent a monster whose head shall be that of an inhabitant of Saturn and its body that of a denizen of Jupiter, and where is it? Of necessity all attempts to define or describe things of which we have never had perceptions, must be made in terms of things of which we have had perceptions, or, in other words, must be anthropomorphic.

So far as science gives any positive knowledge as to the relations of mind to matter, it amounts to this: That all we call mind is indissolubly connected with matter through the grey cells of the brain and other nervous ganglia. This is positive. If the skull could be removed without injury to the living organism, a skilful physiologist could play with his finger on the human brain, as on that of a dog, pigeon, or other animal, and by pressure on different notes, as on the keys of a piano, annihilate successively voluntary motion, speech, hearing, sight, and finally will, consciousness, reasoning power, and memory. But beyond this physical science cannot go. It cannot explain how molecular motions of cells of nerve-centres can be transformed into, or can create, the phenomena of mind, any more than it can explain how the atoms and energies to which it has traced up the material universe were themselves created or what they really are.

All attempts to further fathom the depths of the unknown follow a different line, that of metaphysics, or, in other words, introspection of mind by mind, and endeavour to explain thought by thinking. On entering into this region we at once find that the solid earth is giving way under our feet, and that we are attempting to fly in an extremely rare atmosphere, if, indeed, we are not idly flapping our wings in an absolute vacuum. Instead of ascertained facts which all recognise, and experiments which conducted under the same conditions always give the same results, we have a dissolving view of theories and intuitions, accepted by some, denied by others, and changing with the changing conditions of the age, and with individual varieties of characters, emotions, and wishes. Thus, mind and soul are with some philosophers identical, with others mind is a product of soul ; with some soul is a subtle essence, with others absolutely immaterial ; with some it has an individual, with others a universal, existence ; by some it is limited to man, by others conceded to the lower animals ; by some located in the brain, by others in the heart, blood, pineal gland, or dura mater ; with some it is pre-existent and immortal, with others created specially for its own individual organism ; and so on *ad infinitum*. The greatest philosophers come mostly to the conclusion that we really know nothing about it. Thus Descartes, after having built up an elaborate metaphysical theory as to a spiritual, indivisible substance independent of the brain and cognisable by self-consciousness alone, ends by honestly confessing ' that by natural reason we can make many conjectures about the soul, and have flattering hopes, but no assurance.' Kant also, greatest of metaphysicians in demolishing the fallacies of former theories, when he comes to define his 'noumenon,' has to use the vaguest of phrases, such as ' an indescribable something, safely located out of space and time, as such not subject to the mutabilities of those phenomenal spheres, . . . and of whose ontological existence we are made aware by its phenomenal projections, or effects in consciousness.' The sentence takes our breath away, and makes us sympathise with Bishop Berkeley when he says, ' We metaphysicians have first raised a dust, and then complain we cannot see.' It prepares us also for Kant's final admission that nothing can really be proved by metaphysics concerning the attributes, or even the existence, of the soul ; though, on the other hand, as it cannot be disproved, its reality may for moral purposes be assumed.

It appears, therefore, that the efforts of the sublimest transcendentalists do not carry us one step farther than the conclusions of the commonest common-sense, viz. that there are certain fundamental conditions of thought, such as space, time, consciousness, personal identity, and freedom of will, which we cannot explain, but cannot get rid of. The sublimest speculations of a Plato and a Kant bring us back to the homely conclusions of the old woman in the nursery ballad, in whose mind grave questions as to her personal identity were raised by the felonious abstraction of the lower portion of her petticoat.

> If I be I, as I think I be,
> I've a little dog at home, and he'll know me.

It is a safe 'working hypothesis' that when I go home in the afternoon, my wife, children, and little dog will recognise me as being ' I myself I ;' but why or how I am I, whether I was I before I was born, or shall be so after I am dead, I really know no more than the little dog who wags his tail and yelps for joy when he recognises my personal identity as something distinct from his own, when he sees me coming up the walk.

Our conceptions, therefore, are necessarily based on our perceptions, and are what is called anthropomorphic. The term has almost come to be one of reproach, because it has so often been applied to religious conceptions of a Deity with human, though often not very humane, attributes; but, if considered rightly, it is an inevitable necessity of any attempt to define such a being or beings. We can only conceive of such as of a magnified man, indefinitely magnified no doubt, but still with a will, intelligence, and faculties corresponding to our own. The whole supernatural or miraculous theory of the universe rests on the supposition that its phenomena are, in a great many cases, brought about, not by uniform law, but by the intervention of some Power, which, by the exercise of will guided by intelligent design, alters the course of events and brings about special effects. As long as the theory is confined to knowable transformations of existing things, like those which are seen to be affected by human will, it is not necessarily inconceivable or irrational. Inferring like effects from like causes, the hypothesis was by no means unreasonable that thunder and lightning, for instance, were caused by some angry invisible power in the clouds. On the contrary, the first savage who drew the deduction was a natural philosopher who reasoned quite justly from his assumed premises. Whether the premises were true or not was a question which could only be determined centuries later by the advance of accurate knowledge.

When do we say we know a thing? Not when we know its essence and primary origin, for of these the wisest philosopher is as ignorant as the rudest savage; but when we know its place in the universe, its relation to other things, and can fit it in to that harmonious sequence of events which is summed up in what are called Laws of Nature. The highest knowledge is when we can trace it up to its earliest origin from existing matter and energy, and follow it downwards so as to be able to predict its results. The force of gravity affords a good illustration of this knowledge, both where it comes up to, and where it falls short of, perfection.

Newton's law leaves nothing to be desired as regards its universal application and power of prediction; but we do not yet fully understand its mode of action or its relation to other forms of energy. It is probable that some day we may be able to understand how the force of gravity appears to act instantaneously at a distance, and how all the transformable forces, gravity, light, heat, electricity, and molecular or atomic forces, are but different manifestations of one common energy. But in the meantime we know this for certain, that the law of gravity is not a local or special phenomenon, but prevails universally from the fixed stars to the atoms, from the infinitely great to the infinitely small. This is a *fact* to which all other phenomena, which are true facts and not illusions, must conform.

In like manner, if we find in caves or river-gravels, under circumstances implying enormous antiquity, and associated with remains of extinct animals, rude implements so exactly resembling those in use among existing savages, that if the collection in the Colonial Exhibition of stone celts and arrow-heads used by the Bushmen of South Africa were placed side by side with one from the British Museum of similar objects from Kent's Cavern or the caves of the Dordogne, no one but an expert could distinguish between them, the conclusion is inevitable that Devonshire and Southern France were inhabited at some remote period by a race of men not more advanced than the Bushmen. Any theory of man's origin and evolution which is to hold water must take account of this fact and square with it. And so of a vast variety of facts which have been reduced to law and become certainly known during the last half-century. A great deal of ground remains unexplored or only partially explored; but sufficient has been discovered to enable us to say that what we know we know thoroughly, and that certain leading facts and principles undoubtedly prevail throughout the knowable universe, including not only that which is known, but that which is as yet partially or wholly unknown. For instance, the law of gravity, the conservation of energy, the indestructibility of matter, and the law of evolution, or development from the simple to the complex

HAVING thus, I may hope. given the reader some precise ideas of what are the boundaries and conditions of human knowledge, we may proceed to consider their application to the highest subjects, religions and philosophies.

In the introductory chapter of this work I have said that all religions are in effect 'working hypotheses,' by which men seek to reconcile the highest aspirations of their nature with the facts of the universe, and bring the whole into some harmonious concordance. I said so for the following reasons. In a discussion at the Metaphysical Society on the uniformity of laws of nature, recorded in the 'Nineteenth Century,' Huxley is represented as saying that he considered this uniformity, not as an axiomatic truth like the first postulates of geometry, but as a 'working hypothesis'; adding, however, that it was an hypothesis which had never been known to fail. To this some distinguished advocates of Catholic theology replied, that their conviction was of a higher nature, for their belief in God was a final truth which was the basis of their whole intellectual and moral nature, and which it was irrational to question. This is in effect Cardinal Newman's celebrated argument of an 'illative sense,' based on a complete assent of all the faculties, and which was therefore a higher authority than any conclusions of science. The answer is obvious, that complete assent, so far from being a test of truth, is, on the contrary, almost always a proof that truth has not been attained, owing either to erroneous assumptions as to the premises, or to the omission of important factors in the solution of the problem. To give an instance, I suppose there could not be a stronger case of complete assent than that of the Inquisitors who condemned the theories of Galileo. They had in support of the proposition that the sun revolved round the earth the testimony of the senses, the universal belief of mankind in all ages, the direct statement of inspired Scripture, the authority of the infallible Church. Was all this to be set aside because some 'sophist vainly mad with dubious lore' told them, on grounds of some new-fangled so-called science, that the earth revolved round its axis and round the sun? 'No ; let us stamp out a heresy so contrary to our " illative sense," and so fatal to all the most certain and cherished beliefs of the Christian world, to the inspiration of the Word of God, and to the authority of His Church.' 'E pur si muove,' and yet the earth really did move ; and the verdict of *fact* was that Galileo and science were right, and the Church and the illative sense wrong.

In truth the distinction between the conclusions of science and those of religious creeds might be more properly expressed by saying that the former are 'working hypotheses' which never fail, while the latter are 'working hypotheses' which frequently fail. Thus, the fundamental hypothesis of Cardinal Newman and his school of a one infinite and eternal personal Deity, who regulates the course of events by frequent miraculous interpositions, so far from being a necessary and axiomatic truth, has never appeared so to the immense majority of the human race : and even at the present day, in civilised and so-called Christian countries, its principal advocates complain that ninety-nine out of every hundred practically ignore it.   It is not so with the uniformity of the laws of nature.   No palæolithic savage ever hesitated about putting one foot after another in chase of a mammoth from a fear that his working hypothesis of uniform law might fail, the support of the solid earth give way, and with his next step he might find himself toppling over into the abyss of an infinite vacuum.   In like manner Greeks and Romans, Indians and Chinese, monotheists, polytheists, pantheists, Jews and Buddhists, Christians and Mahometans, all use standard weights in their daily transactions without any misgivings that the law of gravity may turn out not to be uniform.   But religious theories vary from time to time and from place to place, and we can in a great many cases trace their origins and developments like those of other political and social organisms.

To trace their origins we must, as in the case of social institutions, look first at the ideas prevailing among those savage and barbarous races who are the best representatives of our early progenitors ; and secondly at historical records.   In the first case we find the earliest rudiments of religious ideas in the universal belief in ghosts and spirits.   Every man is conceived of as being a double of himself, and as having a sort of shadowy self, which comes and goes in sleep or trance, and finally takes leave of the body, at death, to continue its existence as a ghost.   The air is thus peopled with an immense number of ghosts who continue very much their ordinary existence, haunt their accustomed abodes, and retain their living powers and attributes, which are exerted generally with a malevolent desire to injure and annoy.   Hence among savage races, and by survival even among primitive nations of the present day, we find the most curious devices to cheat or frighten away the ghost, so that he may not return to the house in which he died.   Thus, the corpse is carried out, not by the door, but by a hole made for the purpose in the wall, which is afterwards built up, a custom which prevails with a number of widely separated races—Greenlanders, Hottentots, Algonquins, and Fijians ; and the practice even survives among more civilised nations, such as the Chinese, Siamese, and Thibetans ; nor is it wholly extinct in some of the primitive parts of Europe.

This idea obviously led to the practice of constructing tents or houses for the ghosts to live in, and of depositing with them articles of food and weapons to be used in their ghostly existence.   In the case of great chiefs, not only their arms and ornaments are deposited, but their horses, slaves, and wives were sacrificed and buried with them, so that they might enter spirit-land with an appropriate retinue.   The early Egyptian tombs were as nearly as possible facsimiles of the house in which the deceased had lived, with pictures of his geese, oxen, and other possessions painted on the walls, evidently under the idea that the ghosts of these objects would minister to the wants and please the fancy of the human ghost whose eternal dwelling was in the tomb where his mummy was deposited.

Another development of the belief in spirits is that of fetish-worship, in which superstitious reverence is paid to some stock or stone, tree or animal, in which a mysterious influence is supposed to reside, probably owing to its being the chosen abode of some powerful spirit. This is common among the negro races, and it takes a curious development among many races of American Indians, where the tribe is distinguished by the totem, or badge of some particular animal, such as the bear, the tortoise, or the hare, which is in some way supposed to be the patron spirit of the clan, and often the progenitor from whom they are descended. This idea is so rooted that intermarriage between men and women who have the same totem is prohibited as a sort of incest, and the daughter of a bear-mother must seek for a husband among the sons of the deer or fox. Possibly a vestige of the survival of this idea may be traced in the coat-of-arms of the Sutherland family, and the wild cat may have been the totem of the Clan Chattan, while the oak tree was that of the Clan Quoich, with whom they fought on the Inch of Perth. Be this as it may, it is clearly a most ancient and widespread idea, and prevails from Greenland to Australia ; while it evidently formed the oldest element of the prehistoric religion of Egypt, where each separate province had its peculiar sacred animal, worshipped by the populace in one nome, and detested in the neighbouring one.

By far the earliest traces of anything resembling religious ideas are those found in burying-places of the neolithic period. It is evident that at this remote period ideas prevailed respecting ghost or spirit life and a future existence very similar to those of modern savages. They placed weapons and implements in the graves of the dead, and not infrequently sacrificed human victims, and held cannibal feasts. Whether this was done in the far more remote palæolithic era is uncertain, for very few undoubted burials of this period have been discovered, and those few have frequently been used again for later interments. We can only draw a negative inference from the absence of idols which are so abundant in the prehistoric abodes explored by Professor Schliemann, among the very numerous carvings and drawings found in the caves of the reindeer period in France and Germany, that the religion of the palæolithic men, if they had any, had not reached the stage when spirits or deities were represented by images.

For the first traces therefore of anything like what is now understood by the term religion, we must look beyond the vague superstitions of savages, at the historical records of civilised nations. As civilisation advanced population multiplied, and rude tribes of hunters were amalgamated into agricultural communities and powerful empires, in which a leisured and cultured class arose, to whom the old superstitions were no longer sufficient. They had to enlarge their 'working hypothesis' from the worship of stocks and stones and fear of ghosts, to take in a multitude of new facts and ideas, and specially those relating to natural phenomena which had roused their curiosity, or become important to them as matters of practical utility. The establishment of an hereditary caste of priests accelerated this evolution of religious ideas, and from time to time recorded its progress. The oldest of such records are those of Egypt and Chaldæa, where the fertility of alluvial valleys watered by great rivers had led to the earliest development of a high civilisation. The records also of the Chinese, Hindoos, Persians, and other nations take us a long way back towards the origins of religions.

In all cases we find them identical with the first origins of science, and taking the form of attempted explanations of natural phenomena, by the theory of deified objects and powers of nature. In the Vedas we see this in the simplest form, where the gods are simply personifications of the heavens, earth, sun, moon, dawn, and so forth; and where we should say the red glow of morning announces the rising of the sun, they express it that Aurora blushes at the approach of her lover the mighty Sun-god. It is very interesting to observe how the old Chaldæan legend of the creation of the world has been modified in the far later Jewish edition of it in Genesis, to adapt it to monotheistic ideas. The Chaldæan legend begins, like that of Genesis, with an 'earth without form and void,' and darkness on the chaotic deep. In each legend the Spirit of God, called Absu in the Chaldæan, moves on the face of the waters, and they are gathered together and separated from the land. But here a difference begins: in the original Chaldæan legend ' the great gods were then made ; the gods Lakman and Lakmana caused themselves to come forth ; the gods Assur and Kesar were made ; the gods Anu, Bel, and Hea were born.'

The appearance of the gods Lakman and Lakmana

was the primitive mode of expressing the same idea as that which is expressed in Genesis by saying that God created the firmament separating the heaven above from the earth beneath ; Assur and Kesar mean the same thing as the hosts of heaven and the earth ; the god Bel is the sun, and so forth.   It is evident that the first attempts to explain the phenomena of nature originated in the idea that motion and power implied life, personality, and conscious will ; and therefore that the earth, sky, sun, moon, and other grand and striking phenomena, must be regarded as separate gods.

As culture advanced astronomy became more and more prominent in these early religions, and solar myths became a principal part of their mythologies, while astrology, or the influence of planets and stars on human affairs, became an important part of practical life.   The Chaldæan legend referred to contains a mass of astronomical knowledge, which in the Genesis edition is reduced to ' He made the stars also.'   It describes how the constellations were assigned their forms and names, the twelve signs of the zodiac established, the year divided into twelve months, the equinoxes determined, and the seasons set their bounds.   Also how the moon was made to regulate the months by its disc, ' horns shining forth to lighten the heavens, which on the seventh day approaches a circle.'

In the still older Egyptian pyramids we find proof of the long previous existence of great astronomical knowledge and refined methods of observation, for these buildings, which are at once the largest and the oldest in the world, are laid down so exactly in a meridian line, and with such a close approximation to the true latitude, as would have otherwise been impossible.   In fact there is every reason to believe that while they were constructed as tombs for kings, they were at the same time intended for national observatories, for the arrangement of the internal passages as such is to make the Great Pyramid serve the purpose of a telescope, equatorially mounted, and showing the transits of stars and planets over the meridian, by reference to a reflected image of what was then the polar star, a knowledge of which was essential for accurate calculation of the calendar and seasons, for fixing the proper date of religious ceremonies, and very probably for astrological purposes.

The prevalence of these solar and astronomical myths among a number of different nations separated by wide intervals of space and time is very remarkable. Egyptians, Indians, Babylonians, Chinese, Mexicans, and Peruvians had myths which were strangely similar, indeed almost identical, based on the sun's annual passage through the constellations of the zodiac. His apparent decline and death as he approached the winter solstice, and his return to life when he had passed it, gave rise to myths of the murder of the Sun-god by some fierce wild boar, or treacherous enemy, and of his triumphant resurrection in renewed glory. Hence, also, the passage of the winter solstice was a season of general rejoicing and festivity, traces of which survive when the sirloin and turkey smoke upon the hospitable tables of modern Christmas. One remarkable myth had a very universal acceptance, that of the birth of the infant Sun-god from a virgin mother. It appears to have originated from the period, some 6,450 years ago, when the sun, which now rises at the winter solstice in the constellation of Sagittarius, rose in that of Pisces, with the constellation of the Virgin, with upraised arms marked by five stars, setting in the north-west. Anyhow, this myth of an infant god born of a virgin mother holds a prominent place in the religions of Egypt, India, China, Chaldæa, Greece, Rome, Siam, Mexico, Peru, and other nations. The resemblances are often so close that the first Jesuit missionaries to China found that their account of the miraculous conception of Christ had been anticipated by that of Fuh-ke, born 3468 B.C.; and if an ancient priest of Thebes or Heliopolis could be restored to life and taken to the Gallery of Dresden, he would see in Raffaelle's Madonna di San Sisto what he would consider to be an admirable representation of Horus in the arms of Isis.

The planets also, still more mysterious in their movements than the sun, and therefore still more endowed with human-like faculties of life, power, and purpose, were from an early period believed to exercise an influence on human affairs. Of the universality of this belief we find traces in the names of the days of the week, which are so generally taken from the sun, moon, and five visible planets—Mercury, Mars, Jupiter, Venus, and Saturn—to whom special days were dedicated. If every seventh day is a day of rest, it was originally so because it was thought unlucky to undertake any work on the Sabbath, Saturday, or day of the gloomy and malignant Saturn.

As time rolled on and civilisation advanced, this simple nature-worship and deification of astronomical phenomena developed into larger and more complex conceptions. Following different lines of evolution, polytheism, pantheism and monotheism began to emerge as religious systems with definite creeds, rituals, and sacred books These lines seem to have been determined a good deal by the genius of the race in which the religious development took place. The impressions made on the human mind by the surrounding universe are very various. Suppose ourselves looking up at the heavens on a clear starry night, what will be the impression? To one, that of awe and reverence, and he will feel crushed, as it were, into nothingness, in the presence of such a sublime manifestation of majesty and glory. Another, of more æsthetic nature, will be charmed by the beauty of the spectacle, and tempted to assign life to it, and to personify and dramatise its incidents. A third, of a scientific turn, will above all things wish to understand it.

Thus we find the impression of awe preponderating among the Semitic races generally; and as in their political relations, so in their religious conceptions, we find them prone to prostrate themselves before despotic power. With the Greeks again the æsthetic idea almost swallowed up the others, and the old astronomical myths blossomed into a perfect flower-bed of poetical and fanciful legends. The Chinese never got beyond a simple pantheism, which looked upon the universe as being alive, and saw nothing behind it; while the more metaphysical and physically feebler races of Hindoos and Buddhists refined their pantheism into a system of illusion, in which their own existence and the surrounding universe were literally

> such stuff
> As dreams are made on,

and to be 'rounded with a sleep' was the final consummation devoutly to be desired.

Monotheism developed itself later, partly from the

feeling of the unity of nature forcing itself on the more philosophical minds ; partly from that feeling of reverence and awe in presence of the Unknown which swallowed up other conceptions ; and partly, in the earlier stages, from the feeling which exalted the local god of the tribe or nation, first into a supremacy over other gods, and finally into sole supremacy, degrading all other gods into the category of dumb idols made by human hands.   In the Old Testament we can trace the development of this latter idea in its successive stages. Until the later days of the Jewish monarchy it is evident that the Jews never doubted the existence of other gods ; and their allegiance oscillated between Jehovah and the heathen deities symbolised by the golden calf, worshipped in high places, and contending for the mastership in the rival sacrifices of Elijah and the priests of Baal.   But the prophetic element gradually introduced higher ideas, and in the reigns of Hezekiah and Josiah the worship of Jehovah as the sole God became the religion of the State ; and old legends and documents were re-edited in this sense in the sacred book, which was discovered and published for the first time in the reign of the latter king.   The subsequent misfortunes of the nation, their captivity and contact with other religions in Babylonia, strengthened this monotheism into an ardent, passionate national faith, as it has continued to be with this remarkable people up to the present day.   Christianity and Mahometanism, children of Judaism, have spread this form of faith over a great part of the civilised world ; and of the three theories of polytheism, pantheism, and monotheism, it may be said that only the two latter survive.

Polytheism was bound to perish first, for slow as

the advance of science was, the uniformity of most of the phenomena, which had been attributed to so many separate gods, could not fail to make an impression; and as ideas of morality came slowly and tardily to be evolved as an element of religion, the cruel rites and scandalous fables which so generally accompanied polytheistic religions became shocking to an awakening conscience.

It is worthy of remark that this element of morality, which has now gone so far towards swallowing up the others, was the latest to appear. Even in the Jewish conception Jehovah was for a long time just as often cruel, jealous, and capricious, as just and merciful; and St. Paul's doctrine that because God had the power to do as He liked, He was warranted in creating a large portion of the human race as 'vessels of wrath,' pre-destined to eternal punishment, is as revolting to the modern conscience as any sacrifice to Beelzebub or Moloch. If we wish to see how little necessary connec-tion there is between morality and monotheism, we have only to look at Mahometanism, which, in its extremer forms, may be called monotheism run mad.

The Wahabite reformer, we are told by Palgrave, preached that there were only two deadly sins : paying divine honours to any creature of Allah's, and smoking tobacco ; and that murder, adultery, and such like trivial matters, were minor offences which a merciful Allah would condone. He held also that of the whole in-habitants of the world all would surely be damned, except one out of the seventy-two sects of Mahometans, who held the true faith and dwelt in the district of Riad. This illustrates the insane extremes into which all human speculations run, if a single idea—in this case that of awe, reverence, and abject submission in presence of an almighty power—is allowed to run its course without check and obtain undue preponderance.

Apart from these extreme instances we may say that the two religious theories which have survived to the present day in the struggle for existence, are monotheism and pantheism. Pantheism is, in the main, the creed of half the human race—of the teeming millions of India, China, Japan, Ceylon, Thibet, Siam, and Burmah. How deeply it is rooted in their conceptions was very forcibly impressed on me in a conversation I had on board one of the P. and O. steamers with an English missionary returning from China. He told me how he had dined one evening with an intelligent Chinese merchant, and after dinner they walked in the garden discussing religious subjects, and he tried to impress on his host the first principles of the Christian religion. It was a starlight night, and for sole reply the Chinese gentleman stretched his hand to the heavens and said, ' Do you mean to tell me all that is dead—do you take me for a fool ? ' The Chinese 'illative sense' was as absolute in its conclusions for pantheism, as that of Cardinal Newman for theism. In fact pantheism, though not the whole truth, and almost as inconsistent as polytheism with the real facts of the universe as disclosed by science, has a certain poetical truth in it, to which chords of human emotion vibrate responsively, and is perhaps not so widely in error as some of the extreme theories which treat matter as something base and brutal. Wordsworth's noble lines—

> A sense sublime
> Of something far more deeply interfused,
> Whose dwelling is the light of setting suns,

And the round ocean and the living air,
And the blue sky, and in the mind of man ;
A motion, and a spirit that impels
All thinking things, all objects of all thoughts,
And rolls through all things—

are pure pantheism, and yet we cannot but feel ourselves to a great extent in sympathy with them.

So also the well-known lines of a greater than Wordsworth, Shakespeare, are pure Buddhism:

The cloud-capp'd towers, the gorgeous palaces,
The solemn temples, the great globe itself,
Yea, all which it inherit, shall dissolve
And, like this insubstantial pageant faded,
Leave not a rack behind.   We are such stuff
As dreams are made on, and our little life
Is rounded with a sleep.

No one can read these lines without feeling that the Buddhist conception is as far as possible from being a trivial or vulgar one, and that the triviality and vulgarity are rather with those who cannot, up to a certain point, understand and sympathise with it.

The religions of the East are very philosophical, and have kept very clearly in view this fundamental distinction between the knowable and the unknowable. In the 'Century Magazine' of July 1886, there is an interesting account of a conversation between an American missionary and the Bozu or chief priest of the great temple of the Shin Sect of Buddhists at Kioto in Japan.   The priest was an intelligent and highly educated gentleman who spoke English, and was well versed in the speculations of modern philosophy.   The conversation turned on theological questions, and when pressed by the argument for a Divine Creator, from design shown in the universe implying intelligence, he replied :—

' No ; God cannot *make* matter. Only artificial things show design, only things which can be made. What do you mean by saying a thing shows design ? You only mean that by trying a man could make it.'

And he proceeded to illustrate it thus :—

' You show me a gold ring ; the ring shows design, but not the gold ; gold is an ultimate element, which can neither be made nor destroyed. When men can make a world, then they can prove that this one shows design, for the only way they know of design is by what they make.'

He went on to argue for the immortality of the soul, and as a consequence for its pre-existence and the transmigration of souls, from the conservation of energy ; and concluded his argument against the creation and government of the world by a comprehensible, anthropomorphic Creator, by adducing the existence of evil.

' There is a sickness,' he said, ' called fever and ague ; what do you call the medicine to cure that ? '

' Quinine.'

' Yes ; now we have not found that long ; a good God would not have let so many people suffer if He could have given them that. A man found it by chance. The sickness and suffering in this life are for wrong done in another life.'

We may not accept this unproved theory of the cause of sickness and suffering, but it is very interesting to find that candid and intelligent minds, brought up in a society and religious beliefs so widely different from our own, have arrived practically at the same conclusions as John Stuart Mill, Herbert Spencer, and other leaders of advanced thought in modern Europe, and drawn almost identically the same line between that

M .

which is knowable and that which is unknowable by the human mind.

But, however large-minded we may become in seeing the good in other forms of creed, we English of the nineteenth century are not going to turn either pantheists or Buddhists, and practically the contest of the present day is between the supernatural or miraculous, and the natural or scientific, hypotheses.

According to the former the operations of the universe are carried on to a considerable extent by what may be called secondary interferences of a supernatural being, who with will, intelligence, and design, like human though vastly superior, frequently interposes to alter the course of events and bring about something which natural law would not have brought about. The other hypothesis cannot be stated better than in Bishop Temple's words, that the Great First Cause created things so perfect from the first, that no such secondary interferences have ever been necessary, and everything has been and is, evolved from the primary atoms and energies in a necessary and invariable succession. The supernatural and the natural theories of the universe are thus brought into direct antagonism.

For the supernatural theory it must be conceded that it is quite conceivable, as is proved by the fact that it has been the almost universal conception of mankind for ages, and remains so still for the greater number. It is, as I have said, the inevitable first conception when men began to reflect on the phenomena of the universe, and to reason from effects to causes. I have always thought that Hume went too far in condemning miracles as absolutely incredible *a priori*. It is a question of evidence. *A priori*, I can conceive that the true explanation of the universe might have been natural law, as the general rule, supplemented by miracles ; just as readily as that it is law always, and miracle never. The verdict must be decided by the weight of evidence. The two theories must be called, face to face, before the tribunal of *fact*, and its decision must be respected. This is exactly what has been going on for the last two centuries, and specially for the last half century, and the record of decisions is now a very ample one. In every single instance law has carried the day against miracle.

Instance after instance has occurred in which phenomena which in former ages were attributed without hesitation to supernatural agencies have been conclusively proved to be due to natural laws. Take the obvious instance of thunder. When Horace wrote :—

> Jam satis terris nivis, atque diræ
> Grandinis misit Pater, et rubente
> Dextera sacras jaculatus arces
> Terruit urbem,

he wrote to a public to whom it was an undoubted article of faith that thunder and lightning, hail and snowstorms, came direct from the Father of the gods in the sky. Even to a late period this was the general faith, and the prayers in our rubric for rain or fine weather remain as a survival of the belief that these things, when unusual or in excess, are supernatural manifestations. But Benjamin Franklin said, ' No, there is nothing supernatural about lightning. I will bring it down from the clouds and manufacture it by turning a wheel.' Appeal being made to *fact*, the verdict is that Franklin was right, and that lightning-conductors protect ships and houses better than prayers or incantations.

Again, when Galileo and the Church joined issue as to whether the earth was round or flat, inspiration and authority were cited in vain for the received theory ; *fact* said it was round, and it was proved to be so by men sailing round it. The law of gravity was considered a very dangerous heresy, and for a long time pious divines held out against its conclusions, and contended that it was no better than atheism to doubt that comets were signs of God's anger sent to warn a sinful world. But Halley calculated the time of his comet's return according to the laws of gravity, and appeal being made to fact, the comet returned true to time.

This has occurred so often that few are left who doubt the universal prevalence of law in the material universe, where former generations saw miracles at every turn. Nor is the defeat of miracle less conspicuous in the spiritual world. Where former ages and rude races saw, and still see, possession by evil spirits, modern doctors see fevers, epilepsies, or insanity. Once more appeal being made to *fact*, the old medicine-men administered incantations, the new ones quinine—which cure the most patients ?

In like manner demonology and witchcraft, with all their train of cruelties and horrors, once universally believed even by men like Justice Hale, have passed into oblivion as completely as the Lamiæ, Phorkyads, and other fantastic figures of the classical Walpurgis-night. Is the world the better or the worse for this triumph of natural law over supernaturalism?

The triumph has been so complete in innumerable instances, without a single one to the contrary, that belief in the permanence and universality of natural law has become almost an instinct in all educated minds, and even those who cling to old beliefs must admit that the most cogent and irresistible evidence is requisite to establish the fact of a real supernatural interference.   It may be taken as an axiom that wherever a natural explanation is possible, a miraculous one is impossible.

Now this is just the point on which, as knowledge has increased, the evidence for miracles has become weaker, almost in the exact ratio in which the necessity for evidence has become stronger.

Take, for instance, the following case recorded by Dr. Braid of Glasgow.   Miss R. had suffered from ophthalmia and was totally blind.   She could not discern a single letter of the title-page of a book placed close to her, though some of the letters were a quarter of an inch long.   Dr. Braid placed the patient in a condition of hypnotism or artificial somnambulism, and directed the nervous force, or sustained attention of the mind, to the eyes by wafting over them.   After a first sitting of about ten minutes she was able to read a great part of the title-page, and after four more sittings she was able to read the smallest-sized print in a newspaper, and was quite cured for the rest of her life.   In another case, that of Mrs. S., blindness of the left eye had occurred owing to an attack of rheumatic fever, the structure of the eye, both external and internal, being considerably injured, and more than half the cornea covered by an opaque film.   After a few sittings the cornea became transparent, and the patient was cured.

In both these cases the blind were made to see by processes which were purely mechanical, for hypnotism was induced by the simple means of making the patient strain her attention on some fixed idea or object, commonly on a black wafer stuck on a white wall, and the stimulation of the optic nerve to greater activity did the rest. And if the blind could be made to see, *a fortiori* the deaf were made to hear, and the lame and halt to walk, by the same mechanical process. Here there is an explanation of nine-tenths of all recorded miracles by purely natural causes.

Again, take the well-known case of the Berlin book-seller, Nicolai, who, having fallen into ill-health, for a whole year saw, when awake, visions so real and palpable that he may be said to have lived in the company of dis-embodied spirits, undistinguishable from actual men and women. This is a common phenomenon in vivid dreams, but the Berlin case takes us a step farther, and shows us how subjective impressions may assume the form of objective realities, even in the case of a man wide awake, of a sceptical turn of mind, and in full possession of his reasoning faculties. Why then should we be driven to the alternative of miracle or imposture, to account for similar dreams or visions being taken for objective reali-ties by enthusiastic minds, living in an atmosphere of religious excitement, in an uncritical age, when super-natural occurrences were considered to be matters of course ? And history is full of instances which show how any supernatural germ, planted in such a medium, propagates itself and extends to millions, almost as rapidly as the bacillus germ does in an epidemic of small-pox. St. Vitus's dance, or the dancing mania, ran the round of Europe like the potato disease, and even yet survives in the hysterical affections of the sect of Shakers. The gift of tongues spread like wildfire through Irving's congregation, and only died out because it had fallen on the uncongenial soil of the nineteenth century ; even the story of the tail of the lion over the gateway of the old Northumberland House being seen by many passers-by to wag because one had asserted it, illustrates the contagiousness of nervous sympathy, and the tricks which ' strong imagination ' can play with the senses.

Another great blow has been dealt against the miraculous theory by what can only be called the singular want of intelligence displayed in the exercise of miraculous power as commonly recorded. The *raison d'être*, or effect desired to be produced by miracles, is to convert mankind from sin, or to attest a divine mission by convincing proofs. Even ordinary human intelligence—and how much more so that of a superior Being—must see that to attain this end the means must be to make the proof convincing. There is no reason in itself why it should not be so. The fact that a man who was alive and signed a will is now dead, is attested as regards the latter proposition by a proper medical certificate, and as regards the former by two credible witnesses, who are prepared to come into court, give their names and addresses, depose on oath to the signature, and stand cross-examination. If this testimony is required to establish a fact so antecedently probable as that one particular man has undergone the common fate of millions of millions of other men, that is to say, that he has died after being alive, how much more must it be requisite to establish the fact so antecedently improbable, as that one man among those many millions after having died came back to life. And yet where is the recorded miracle for which even this *minimum* amount of testimony is forthcoming ? Why are miracles so constantly performed in holes and corners, in obscure localities, among little knots of ignorant and enthusiastic adherents, attested by the vaguest hearsay evidence of unknown or incompetent witnesses, and apparently under circumstances inevitably calculated to defeat their object and engender doubts in the minds of reasonable and conscientious men. Take, for instance, the miracles now said to be wrought at Lourdes. The object must be taken to be to convert infidel France to the Catholic faith. But obviously this object would be far better attained by a single undoubted miracle wrought at Paris before a commission headed by a man like Pasteur, than by any number of miracles scarcely, if at all, distinguishable from those of Dr. Braid, alleged to occur at an obscure village in the presence of peasants and pilgrims. Or, take a higher instance, that of the demand made by the Pharisees to Jesus for a sign to attest his Messiahship. Consider the circumstances of the case, and see if it is at all possible that if he had possessed the power of working miracles he should have replied, 'Why doth this generation seek after a sign? verily I say unto you, there shall no sign be given unto this generation' (St. Mark ix. 12). In the first place the statement throws discredit upon all the miracles said to have been wrought, by the positive and explicit declaration that none should be wrought. But beyond this, the very essence of the mission of Jesus was contained in the words, 'Repent ye, for the kingdom of heaven is at hand.' He had a firm conviction that the kingdom of heaven, or a millennium of peace and goodwill, was close at hand, and its advent only retarded by the sinfulness and want of faith of his chosen people. He thought it his bounden duty to do all he could to remove the obstacle and expedite the coming of the kingdom. With this conviction, though fully seeing the risk and counting the cost, when he found that he was making no decided headway by preaching in a remote province, he determined to go to Jerusalem and make there one great effort to accomplish his object. Can it be doubted that he would use every means in his power to carry his mission to a successful conclusion? If, having the power to do so by working a miracle, he had refused, he would from his point of view have been guilty of a great sin—that of preventing the coming of the kingdom of heaven.

Again, who were the Pharisees? No doubt there were formalists and hypocrites among them, but the position of the sect in the Jewish nation was almost exactly similar to that of the English Puritans in the reign of Charles. They were the embodiment of the patriotic and religious spirit of the race, the sons of the heroic fathers who fought under Judas Maccabeus against Antiochus, the fathers of the equally heroic sons who made the last desperate stand against the legions of Titus. It was their duty, when a claim to Messiahship was advanced, before departing from the traditions of their ancestors, to require evidence. The universally expected evidence of a temporal deliverer being wanting, there remained only the evidence of miracles, which, moreover, were assigned as the test of a Messiah by all their prophets. To refuse them a sign, if a sign were possible, was to do injustice to many sincere and conscientious men. Nay, more, it was an act of cruelty if leaving them in their old faith entailed eternal punishment. The same thing applies to all records of miracles. They are never wrought under circumstances where they would be the most effective means for attaining proposed ends. They are never wrought under circumstances which leave them clear of the suspicion of being subjective illusions or misinterpretations of effects due to natural causes. They never convince any but those who are more than half convinced already.

It would be easy to multiply instances showing the inadequacy of the evidence adduced to establish such an exceptional and extraordinary fact as the occurrence of a real miracle. But it is unnecessary to do so, as all thinking minds have come, or are fast coming, to the conclusion of Dr. Temple, that ' all the countless varieties of the universe were provided for by one original impress, and not by special acts of creation modifying what had previously been made.'

It is only when we look behind the phenomena of the universe at this Great First Cause, that I see anything to object to in the definition of Dr. Temple, and of Christian philosophers generally. They assume it to be a personal Deity, who is to a great extent known or knowable, and therefore must have attributes conformable to human perceptions which are the basis of all human knowledge. In other words, however much we may purify and enlarge these attributes, He must be essentially an anthropomorphic God or magnified man. To this theory there seems to me to be this fatal objection, that it gives no account of the origin of evil, or rather that it makes the Divine Creator directly responsible for it. The existence of evil in the world is as palpable a fact as the existence of good. There are many things which to our human perceptions appear to be base, cruel, foul, and ugly, just as clearly as other things appear to be noble, merciful, pure, and beautiful. Whence come they? If the existence of good proves a good Creator, how can we escape the inference that the existence of evil proves an evil one ? This is never so forcibly impressed on me as when I read the arguments of those who insist most strongly on the conception of a one, anthropomorphic God. When Carlyle says, ' All that is good, generous, wise, right—whatever I deliberately and for ever love in others and myself—who or what could by any possibility have given it to me but One who first had it to give ? This is not logic, but axiom.' I cannot but picture to myself the sledge-hammer force with which, if he had approached the question without prepossessions, he would have come down on the cant, the insincerity, the treason to the eternal veracities, which refused to look facts in the face, and apply the same reasoning to the evil. Or if Arnold defines the Deity as the ' Something not ourselves which makes for righteousness,' how of the Something not ourselves which makes for unrighteousness ? The only escape I can find from this dilemma is to accept existing facts and not evade them. It is a fact that polarity is the law of existence. Why we know not, any more than we know the real essence and origin of the atoms and energies which are our other ultimate facts. But we accept atoms and energies, and accept the law of gravity and other laws ; why not accept also the law of polarity, and admit that it is part of the ' original impress ': one of the fundamental conditions under which the evolution of Creation from its ultimate elements is necessitated to proceed. This the human mind can understand ; beyond it is the great unknown or unknowable, in presence of which we can only feel emotions of reverence and of awe, and 'faintly trust the larger hope' that duality may somehow ultimately be merged in unity, evil in good, and 'every winter turn to spring.'

As nations advanced in civilisation there has always been a tendency among the higher and purer minds to relegate the Great First Cause further and further back into the unknown, and to divest it of anthropomorphic attributes. When Socrates said, 'that divinely revealed wisdom of which you speak, I deny not, inasmuch as I do not know it; I can only understand human reason,' he spoke the identical language of Darwin, Spencer, Huxley, and those leaders of modern thought whom theologians call agnostics. Even in religions based on the idea of a single anthropomorphic Deity the same tendency often appears among the highest thinkers. Thus Emmanuel Deutsch, in his learned work on the Talmud, tells us, 'Its first chapter treats of the Deity as conceived by Jewish philosophy. The existence of God is, of course, presupposed. But what of His attributes? Has He any? Scripture literally taken seems to affirm this. Yet taken in a higher sense, as understood by the Alexandrines, the Talmud, and the Targum, it denies it.'

The great Jewish doctors, Ibn Ezra, Jehuda Hilmi, and Maimonides, take this view of a divine origin shrouded in ineffable mystery. Maimonides says, 'If you give attributes to a thing, you define this thing, and defining a thing means to bring it under some head, to compare it with something like it. God is sole of His kind. Determine Him, circumscribe Him, and you bring Him down to the modes and categories of created things.' Even St. Paul says, 'O the depths of God. How unsearchable are His judgments, and how inscrutable His ways'; and the Creed of our own Church, in the midst of a string of definitions all implying that God is comprehensible, has the words 'the Father incomprehensible.'

It is evident that the reasons why these anticipations of the prevailing tendency of modern thought only appeared by glimpses, and among a very limited number of philosophic minds, arose from the fact that the miraculous theory of the universe everywhere prevailed. Every unusual occurrence was supposed to be owing to the direct supernatural interference of a Being acting in the main with human attributes, and therefore to be a direct refutation of the theory which denied the possibility of defining His attributes, and relegated Him to the dim distance of an incomprehensible Creator. With the utter breakdown of the miraculous theory, and the certainty that all the countless varieties of the universe arise, not from special interferences, but from one original impress, this theory of a reverent and devout agnosticism becomes impregnable and holds the field against all rivals. It, and it alone, is consistent with the facts of science, the deductions of reason, the axioms of morality, while at the same time it denies nothing, and leaves an ample background on which to paint the visions of faith, and to reflect back to us spectral images of our hopes and fears, our longings and aspirations.

Some seek for a solution of the mystery, and try to reconcile the existence of evil with that of an almighty and beneficent Creator, by assuming that in the long run everything will come right. Evolution, they say, has led constantly to higher and better things, and when carried far enough will lead to a state of society in which wars will cease, evil passions die out, and universal love and charity prevail—in other words, to a millennium.

Even if this were true, what of the untold millions of the human race who have perished in their sins while evolution was slowly working out this tardy millennium ? Are they the *chair à canons*, whom a Napoleon-like Deity sacrifices with cynical indifference, in the calculated moves of the game of Creation? Is this their idea of an all-wise and all-merciful Father who is in heaven ?

And again, is it true that evolution works constantly for good and promises to bring about such a millennium ? It is doubtless true that evolution means progress, and the ever-increasing development of the more and more complex and differentiated from the simple and uniform. But is this all for good, or all for happiness; and is not evolution, like everything else, subject to the primary and all-pervading law of polarity ? We have only to ask the question to answer it. In the case of the individual, which is the epitome of the history of the species, is development from the engaging innocence of childhood always in the direction of goodness and happiness ?

So far is this from being the case that, as individuals and societies advance, and become higher and more complex in the scale of organisation, the law of polarity asserts itself with ever-increasing force, and contrasts become sharper. The good become better, the bad worse ; and as we become less

> Like the beasts with lower pleasures,
> Like the beasts with lower pains,

if our happiness becomes more intense, so does our misery become more intolerable. I refer not merely to physical conditions, though here the contrast is most apparent. An intelligent traveller who recently circled the world, surveying mankind with a keen and impartial eye 'from China to Peru,' says, as the result of his experience, 'The traveller will not see in all his wanderings so much abject repulsive misery among human beings in the most heathen lands, as that which startles him in his civilised Christian home, for nowhere are the extremes of wealth and poverty so painfully presented.' This is perfectly true ; but it would be a rash conclusion to infer that civilised and Christian countries are worse than heathen lands, or that those who march in the van of progress and succeed in the struggle for life, have a larger dose of original sin than the laggards and those who fail.

Accumulations of population and accumulations of capital are alike causes and effects of progress in an industrial age. But you can no more have a north without a south pole, than you can have this progress without its counterpart of suffering. When an educated gentleman was, like the good vicar,

Passing rich with forty pounds a year,

how many struggles and how many heart-aches were avoided. When 'merry England' dwelt in rural hamlets and villages, the 'bitter cry' of East London could scarcely have been written. Turn it as you like, increase of population means increase of poverty. Say that only five per cent. fail in the battle of life, from their own or inherited faults ; from bad luck, ill-health, weakness of mind, adverse surroundings ; five per cent. on thirty millions is a larger figure than five per cent. on ten millions. And the lot of those who fail is aggravated by the success of those who succeed. The scale of living rises, and the cost of living increases, while competition becomes keener. Increase of population in a limited area means increased difficulty of finding employment; and the complex relations of international commerce send panics and crises vibrating throughout the world, which throw millions out of work, or reduce them to starvation wages. In simple forms of society every one accepts the condition in which he finds himself as a matter of course, while in a more complex civilisation the fiend Envy steps in, and teaches the baser natures who are failures, to regard every success as an insult and every successful man as an enemy. Hence Labour rises in mad revolt against Capital; Socialists attack society with dynamite; and Utopian theorists preach a millennium to be attained by abolishing private property and individual liberty.

If we turn to the moral aspects of the question, it is still more clear that evolution does not tend solely to the side of virtue. There is doubtless less ferocious savagery, less rude and unconscious or half-conscious crime, in civilised societies, but there is far more deliberate and diabolical wickedness. The very temptations and opportunities which, if resisted, lead to higher virtues, if succumbed to, lead to greater vice. Even the intellectual advance, if perverted, becomes the instrument of greater crimes. A chemist discovers nitroglycerine, and dynamite becomes a resource of civilisation. There is a saying that there is 'no blackguard so bad as a Scotch blackguard,' which, as a patriotic Scotchman, I take to be a tribute to the generally high intellectual and moral character of my countrymen. A powerful polarity is powerful, as the case may be, either for good or evil. Why then should we believe that evolution, which, carried thus far, has developed more strongly the contrast between good and evil, will, if carried a little farther, extinguish it by annihilating the evil ?

In fact, the good and evil resulting from the higher evolution of society are so equally balanced that it depends very much on place, time, and temperament whether we are optimists or pessimists. If my liver acts properly I am an optimist ; if it is out of order, a pessimist. Personally I incline to optimism—that is, I think that this world, if not exactly ' the best of all possible worlds,' is yet on the whole a very tolerable world, and that life to the majority, and on the average, is worth living. I think also that progress is certainly towards higher, and very probably towards happier, conditions. It seems to me that in the most advanced English-speaking communities, the condition of at least one half —viz. the female half—of the population is distinctly better, and that the working class, who form the majority of the male half, though many are worse off than formerly, are, on the whole, better fed, better clothed, better educated, and better behaved.

This, however, is perhaps very much a matter of temperament. Greater minds than mine have seen things differently and inclined to pessimism. Buddhism, and almost all Oriental religions and philosophies, are based upon it, and look to Nirvana or annihilation of personal identity as the supreme bliss. Pauline Christianity assumes that all mankind, except a few chosen vessels, are so hopelessly bad as to be predestined to eternal damnation. And even more remarkable, Shakespeare, the universal genius, who one would say had as

N

happy a temperament and led as successful a life as any
man, had his moods of despondency in which he could
say :—

> When in disgrace with fortune and men's eyes,
> I all alone bemoan my outcast state ;
> Wearying deaf heaven with my fruitless cries,
> And look upon myself, and *curse my fate.*

Or declare with Hamlet that no one would bear the ills
of life if

> He himself could his quietus make
> With a bare bodkin.

With instances like these, and the disgust of life manifested in so many modern societies by the increase of
suicides, and the spread of pessimistic theories like
those of Schopenhauer and Hartmann, who can deny
that the great magnet of modern civilisation has a
south as well as a north pole, and that progress is not
all towards perfection ?

The attempts of theologians to reconcile the existence of evil with the goodness of an almighty Creator,
by relegating the adjustment to a future life, only make
the fact of this fundamental polarity more apparent, for
their conceptions of a heaven and a hell obviously do
not reconcile, but only intensify, the opposite polarities.
The good are better, the bad worse, the happy happier,
and the wretched more miserable, in all these attempts
to define the undefinable and to reconcile divine justice
with divine mercy. All that remains really clear to
each individual is that by his efforts in this life he can
do something to keep the balance of polarities somewhat
more on the side of good, both in his own individual
existence, and in that of the aggregate of units, of which
he is one, which is called society or humanity.

The great advantage of this form of religious hypothesis, which for want of a better name I call Zoroastrianism, is that, in the first place, it gets rid of the
antagonism between religion and science, for there is no
possible discovery of science which is irreconcilable with
the fact that there is a necessary and inevitable polarity
of good and evil, and in the background a great unknown, which may be regarded with those feelings and
aspirations which are inseparable from human nature.
And secondly, there is the still greater advantage that
we can devote ourselves with a whole heart and sincere
mind to the worship of the good principle, without
paltering with our moral nature by professing to love
and adore a Being who is the author of all the evil and
misery in the world as well as of the good. If it were
really true that there were such a Being as theologians describe, who created the immense majority of the
human race vessels of wrath doomed to eternal punishment, either from pure caprice or to avenge the slight
offered to Him by the disobedience of a remote ancestor,
what would be the attitude of every healthy human
soul towards such a Being? Rather that of Prometheus
or Satan, than of Gabriel or Michael ; of heroic defiance
than of abject submission. We may gloss this over in
words, but the fact remains, and it is difficult to over-
estimate the amount of evil which has resulted in the
world from this confusion of moral sentiments which
has made good men do devil's work in the belief that
it had divine sanction.

The horrors of demonology and witchcraft had their
origin in texts of the Old Testament ; religious wars
and persecutions arose out of the fundamental error that
intellectual acceptance of doubtful dogmas was the one

thing necessary for salvation ; and ruthless cruelty was justified by an appeal to God's anger with Saul for refusing to hew in pieces the captive Amalekites. A follower of Zoroaster would see at once that these were works of Ahriman and not of Ormuzd, and that in taking part in them he was deserting the standard under which he had enlisted, and doing deeds of darkness while pretending to serve the Prince of Light. This idea of being a soldier enlisted in the army of light seems to me to afford one of the strongest practical inducements to hate what is evil and cleave to what is good. A bad deed or foul thought is felt to be not only wrong but dishonourable : a disloyal going over to the enemy and abandonment of the chief under whom we had enlisted, and of the comrades with whom we had served. This is a very strong motive, and even in the humble ranks of the Salvation Army we can see how powerfully it operates to make men true to their banner.

Indeed a great deal of what is best in genuine Christianity seems to me to resolve itself very much into the worship of Jesus as the Ormuzd or personification of the good principle, and determination to try to follow his example and do his work. It happens to me to receive a good many circulars from the devoted men and women who are doing so much charitable work to assist the poor and fallen, and I observe that the appeals are almost constantly made in the name of Jesus. When the Salvation Army made an appeal the other day to its members for funds to prosecute their campaign, it was touching to read the replies and see men parting with an overcoat or giving up their beer, and women going without a new bonnet or cup of tea, to contribute their mite. But always for the 'love of Jesus,' for the 'Saviour's sake,' as an offering to the 'dear Redeemer.' Theological Christianity says that the one thing needful is to believe in the Catholic Faith as defined by the Athanasian Creed, without which we shall 'without doubt perish everlastingly.' Practical Christianity has completely dropped the Holy Ghost as a sort of fifth wheel to the coach, and relegated the Father into ever vaguer and greater distance; while it has fastened more and more on the figure of Jesus of Nazareth as the practical living embodiment of the good principle of the universe. In a word, Christianity, as it has become more reasonable, more charitable, more pure, and more elevated, has approximated more and more to Zoroastrianism, and for practical purposes modern Christians are, to a great extent, without knowing it, worshippers of Ormuzd, with Christ for their Ormuzd.

To this I see no sort of objection. The tendency to personify abstract principles in something which is warmer, dearer, nearer to ourselves, is ineradicable in human nature; and especially among the great masses of mankind who cannot rise to the height of philosophical speculations. It is impossible in the present age to invent new personifications, or to revive old ones. Jesus has the immense advantage of being in possession of the field, with all the accumulated love and reverence of nineteen centuries of followers. It would be difficult to invent a better ideal or a more perfect example. No doubt the ideal, like all human conceptions, is not absolutely perfect; it is subject to the law of polarity, and its excellences, if pushed to the 'falsehood of extremes,' in many cases become faults. It would not do in practice if smitten on one cheek to turn the other, or to take no thought for the morrow and live like the sparrows. The opposition between the flesh and the spirit is also stated so absolutely, that it is apt to lead to a barren and ignoble asceticism. But those are elements which, practically, are not likely to be pushed to excess, and which serve rather to mitigate the tendencies of modern civilisation to an undue preponderance of the opposite polarities of selfishness, worldliness, and sensuality. Courage, hardihood, self-reliance, foresight, a love of progress, and a desire to attain independence, will always remain prominent virtues, especially of the stronger races, and the gentler teachings of Christianity will long be wanted as an influence to soften, to elevate, and to purify. By all means, therefore, let Christians remain Christians, and see in Christ their Ormuzd, or personification of the good principle. Only let them remember that there are two sides to every question, and cease to entertain hard and bitter thoughts towards those who follow the truth after a different fashion. Let them delight rather to discover unity in the spirit than differences in the letter, and instead of anathematising with Athanasius those who dissent by one hair's breadth from the Catholic faith, strive with St. Paul after that charity which 'suffereth long and is kind : beareth all things, believeth all things, hopeth all things, endureth all things.'

This will be easier if they recollect that love and reverence for Jesus, as the personification of the good principle, is in no way connected with the supernatural dogmas and legends which have come down from superstitious ages, and which are seen every day, more and more clearly, to stand in direct contradiction to the real facts and real laws of the universe. He is the bright example of the highest ideal of human virtue, not on account of miracles, but in spite of them; not because he was a transcendental abstraction with attri-butes altogether outside of human experience or conception; but because he was a man whom other men can love and other men can strive to imitate. The dogmas and miracles may quietly fade out of sight, as so many articles of the Athanasian Creed have already done, like mists before the rising rays of larger knowledge and purer morality, and yet the essence of Christianity will remain, as a worship of the good and beautiful, personified in the brightest example which has been afforded—that of Jesus, the son of the carpenter of Nazareth.

CHAPTER XII.

CHRISTIANITY AND MORALS.

Christianity based on morals—Origin of morality—Traced in Judaism—
Originates in evolution—Instance of murder—Freedom of will—Will
suspended in certain states of brain—Hypnotism—Mechanical theory
—Pre-established harmony—Human and animal conscience—Analysis
of will—Explained by polarity—Practical conclusion.

THE great advantage which Christianity possesses over
most other religions is that it is based to a much greater
extent on the solid foundation of an elevated morality. The creeds of ancient Egypt, of Buddhism, and of
Confucianism contain many excellent moral precepts ;
and the injunctions to 'do unto others as you would be
done by,' and to 'love your neighbour as yourself,' are
to be found long before the Sermon on the Mount.
But these religions in the main followed other lines of
development, and branched off either into metaphysical
conceptions or into formal rites and ceremonies. With
the exception of Judaism, of which Christianity is the
lineal descendant, no religion has ever to the same extent become to the great mass of its adherents a rule
of conduct and an incentive, strengthened by divine
sanction, to lead pure and upright lives. This is the
sense in which Christianity has always been understood
by the vast majority of Christians, and its corruptions
have come much more from above than from below ;

from theologians, priests, and politicians, than from the instincts of the millions ; and this it is which enables it to retain such a wonderful vitality even in modern times, when faith in dogmas and miracles has been so greatly weakened. In order to appreciate the solidity of this basis it is necessary to understand the origin of morals, and to see that the fundamental precepts of moral law are not mere chance inventions of a few exceptional minds, or the teachings of doubtful revelations, but are the necessary growth and products of human nature, in the course of the evolution of society from rude beginnings to a high civilisation. This gives them a certainty and sanction which could be derived from no other source, and makes them what in fact they have become—almost primary instincts of the natural and normal mind in civilised communities. I proceed, therefore, to endeavour to trace shortly the process by which moral laws have originated and grown up to their present certainty and cogency in the course of evolution.

As I have already said, the element of morality is one of the latest to be developed in religious conceptions. The first impressions of savage races reflect the feelings of vague superstitious terror with which they regard unknown phenomena and powers. They are afraid of ghosts and afraid of thunder, long before they rise to a belief in a future state of rewards and punishments, or to the notion of an almighty Being acting by natural laws. In a higher state of development they personify natural powers in gods, who have no more idea of morality than if they were so many parallels of latitude or degrees of longitude ; and they invent tribal gods, who are simply great chiefs, bound by no laws, but granting favours when appeased and inflicting injuries when angry. By slow degrees, as civilisation advances, moral ideas are evolved, and the more enlightened minds begin to attribute moral attributes to their deities. Earnest men, prophets, and reformers take up these ideas and preach them to the world, and, if circumstances are favourable and the soil prepared, they take root and become popular convictions, surviving in the struggle for life, and becoming stronger from generation to generation.

This evolution of moral ideas is most clearly traced in the religious history of the Jews. In their earlier conceptions Jehovah is represented with all the traits of a jealous and capricious Oriental sultan. The one virtue in his eyes is implicit obedience; the one unpardonable crime, anything that looks like disrespect. David is the man after God's own heart, though he commits crimes of the foulest description, and treats as nullities the moral commandments against adultery and murder. But when he takes a census of his people Jehovah is offended, and, with a total disregard of justice, visits his anger, not on the offender, but on the innocent people whom he decimates by a pestilence. In like manner, Abraham is favoured because he is ready to obey the inhuman command to sacrifice his son; while Saul loses Jehovah's favour because he hesitates to massacre his captives in cold blood. The first ideas of a higher moral sense appear with the prophets in the troubled times of the later kings—when poor little Palestine was being ground between the upper millstone of Assyria and the nether one of Egypt. Sufferings and persecutions, anxieties and tribulations, wrought a ferment in the Jewish mind from which new ideas were generated. Sacrifices had been duly offered, and yet the enemies of Jehovah waxed and his chosen people waned. It must be that He was offended with them because He required something better than the blood of bulls—justice and mercy. So taught the popular preachers of the day—men like Isaiah and Amos—and by degrees their words found acceptance. It was not, however, until the Captivity that these ideas of morality were wrought into the Jewish nation so as to become, so to speak, flesh of their flesh and blood of their blood, as they have remained ever since. Whether it was contact with the more advanced moral ideas of religions like those of Buddha and Zoroaster, or, more probably, their sufferings from the cruelty and injustice of their conquerors, the Captivity certainly made them a new nation, attached ardently to morality and mono- theism—thus effecting in a few years, and by purely human agencies, what, according to received beliefs, centuries of miraculous dispensation had failed to ac- complish. How speedily and how effectually the work was done appears from that most interesting narrative of the domestic life of a middle-class Jew of Nineveh, the Book of Tobit. The simple piety and homely household virtues are almost identically the same as those of many a Jewish family living to-day in Lon- don or Frankfort. From that time forward Jewish morality maintains a high level, and in the age im- mediately preceding Christianity it had attained great purity and spirituality in the school of the early doc- tors of the Talmud, and of the Jewish colony of Alex- andria. The Sermon on the Mount, beautiful as it is, is but an admirable *résumé* of maxims which are to be found in the works of Philo and other Jewish teachers, and which were current in the synagogues of the day. Hillel, who was president of the Sanhedrin when Christ was born, when asked what was the law, replied, ' Do not unto another what thou wouldst not have another do unto thee. This is the whole Law, the rest is mere commentary.' And again, 'Do not judge thy neighbour until thou hast stood in his place.'

The Talmud anticipates in a wonderful degree not only the moral precepts of the Gospel, but to a great extent its phraseology and technical terms. ' Redemption,' ' grace,' ' faith,' ' salvation,' ' Son of man,' ' Son of God,' ' kingdom of heaven,' were all, as Deutsch shows, not invented by Christianity, but were household words of contemporary Judaism. In one respect only Christianity shows a higher evolution of morality than Judaism —viz. its universality. Pure Judaism hardly rises above the idea of ' neighbour,' or those who were of the same race or common faith ; while Christianity, as enlarged by St. Paul, embraces all mankind, and may truly say : ' Humani nihil a me alienum puto.'

The idea that morality and religion are products of a slowly developing evolution is denounced by many as degrading and materialistic. In many the instinct of the 'good' is so strong that it seems to them sacrilege to attempt to explain it. They insist that it is either a universal instinct implanted from the first in all mankind, or else that it has been so implanted by a divine revelation. They forget that, to use the vigorous phraseology of Carlyle, 'It matters not whether you call a thing pan-theism or pot-theism ; what really concerns us is to know whether it is *true*.' Now it admits of no question that, whether we like it or not, the evolutionist theory of morality is the true one. Take an extreme instance, that of murder. We feel an instinctive horror at the idea, and even a brutal ruffian like Bill Sikes becomes an accursed thing to himself and his companions when he has transgressed the commandment 'Thou shalt do no murder.' But is it so everywhere, and was it so always? By no means ; the Fiji islander kills and eats a stranger or enemy without scruple ; the Red Indian and the Dyak are not accounted men until they have murdered some one and brought home his scalp or his head as a trophy. Even at a late period among ourselves murder was considered to be rather as a civil injury, to be met by compensation, than as a crime ; and a regular tariff was established of the amount to be paid according as the victim was a slave or a freeman.

The origin and progress of the idea that murder is a crime can almost be traced step by step. The wife of a rude savage does something which offends him ; a violent perception of anger flashes from the visual organ to the perceptive area of the brain, and a reflex action flashes from it along the motor nerve to the muscles of the arm. He strikes and kills her, almost as unconsciously and instinctively as he walks or breathes. But other perceptions follow on the act. He finds next day that he has no one to cook his food; the image of her dying face photographed on his brain is an unpleasant one ; and thus by degrees a series of secondary perceptions get attached to the primary one of striking when he feels angry. If he gets another wife who again provokes him, the primary perception calls up the secondary ones, and the nerve-centres of his brain, instead of being solicited only in one direction, are acted on in opposite ways by conflicting impressions. He hesitates, and, as the primary impulse of passion is probably the more evanescent, the restraining impulses prevail, and every time they prevail they acquire more strength. Gradually they extend to a conviction that it is both inconvenient and disagreeable to kill any one with whom he is closely related either by family or tribal ties, and that, in a word, murder does not pay, and is wrong, unless practised on an enemy. This idea accumulates by heredity, and evidently those tribes or races in whom it is strongest will have an advantage in the struggle for life and be most likely to survive.

From this point the idea may be traced historically, deepening and widening from generation to generation as civilisation advances, until in the higher races it assumes the form of an instinctive abhorrence of murder in the abstract, as we find it at the present day.

It is a mistake to suppose that the foundations of morality are in any way weakened by thus tracing them up to their first origins. On the contrary, if we consider the matter rightly, they are placed on a much more solid and unassailable basis. If we say that moral laws depend on a universal instinct implanted in all mankind, faith in them is shaken whenever we read in history, or hear from the report of travellers, of whole nations, constituting from first to last the immense majority of the human race, who had none of those ideas which we now consider fundamental. If, again, we base them on divine precepts miraculously conveyed, every discovery of science and development of thought which weakens faith in miracles impairs the basis of morals. And on this theory, hopeless contradictions arise within the sphere of those very moral laws which we seek to establish ; as in reconciling the justice and mercy of the Creator in revealing this inspired code only to limited portions of the human race, and under conditions which leave large scope for legitimate doubt, and which, in point of fact, failed to ensure recognition for its moral precepts among His own chosen people for a long period after its promulgation.

But on the scientific theory of the evolution of morality by natural laws it stands on an impregnable footing. No one can deny that, as a matter of fact, such instincts do prevail, and have become part of the nature of all the best men and best races, and that each successive generation tends to fix them more firmly Mathematical laws are not the less certain because they can be traced back to counting on the fingers, and moral laws will continue to have a certainty and cogency, scarcely inferior to the axioms of mathematics, although we can trace them back to origins as rude as the attempts of the Australian savage to extend his perceptions of number beyond 'one, two, and a great many.'

The real difficulty is not in tracing the origin of these instincts of morality, but in that fundamental difficulty which underlies all theories of reconciling the consciousness of free-will with the material attributes with which it is indissolubly associated. Without freedom of will there can be no conscience, no right or wrong in acting in accordance or otherwise with the instincts of moral law, however those instincts may have been derived. Now it is certain that the will, like life, memory, consciousness, and other mental functions, is, so far as human knowledge extends, indissolubly connected with matter and natural laws, in the form of certain motions of the cells which form the grey substance of the nerves and of the nervous ganglia of which the cortex of the brain is the most considerable. This is conclusively proved by experiment. We know that, by removing certain portions of the brain of a dog or of a pigeon, we can destroy the power of motion while preserving the will, and by removing certain other portions we can destroy the will while preserving the powers of motion. Take away a certain portion of the brain of a pigeon, and although it retains the power of taking food, it has so totally lost the will to exercise this power that it will starve in the midst of abundance, though it can be kept alive by placing the food in its mouth. In like manner, in the human brain there are certain portions which, if destroyed by injury or disease, will paralyse the power of giving effect to the will by muscular movements, while the destruction of other portions will paralyse the will which originates such movements. Numerous cases are recorded in medical treatises in which the will is completely paralysed for the performance of certain functions, and in such cases the anatomist can lay his finger on the spot where the brain is affected, and when the brain is dissected after the death of the patient, it will be found that his prediction is verified, and that this region of the brain really was diseased. In sleep also, and in abnormal states of the brain such as somnambulism, and mesmerism or hypnotism, the action of the will is suspended. Hypnotism affords the most remarkable instances, for here the will seems to be transferred from the Ego or individuality of the patient to that of the operator, and the currents of nervous energy which induce motion in A are set going by impulses in the mind of A, not caused by his own will, but by that of B, conveyed by words, gestures, or other subtle indications. A ludicrous instance of this is recorded by Dr. Braid, in which an old lady, who had a true puritanical abhorrence of dancing as sinful, being hypnotised, began capering about the room when a waltz tune was struck up, on being told to do so by the operators.

There are some other curious effects produced by hypnotism, in the way of inducing a sort of double consciousness and memory, which makes people in this condition totally forget things which they remember when awake, and remember things which were totally forgotten in the waking state.

These and a variety of other instances point to the conclusion that man is only a conscious machine. In other words, that the original impress, to use Dr. Temple's words, was so perfect that it provided a pre-established harmony not only for the innumerable phenomena of the material universe as unfolded by evolution, but for the still more innumerable phenomena of life in all its manifestations and all its complex relations to outward environment. I say of *life*, for we clearly cannot confine the theory to human life. A dog, who with the two courses before him of doing wrong and chasing a rabbit, or doing right and remaining at his master's heel, chooses one of them, is in exactly the same position as Hercules between the rival attractions of virtue and pleasure. If Hercules acted as a machine, yielding to the pre-established preponderance of the stronger attraction, so did the dog; but if Hercules exerted free-will and felt the approval or blame of conscience, so did the retriever. There is no fundamental distinction, but merely a question of degree, between human conscience and the shame which a dog feels when it knows that it has done wrong, and the

O

pleasure which it manifests when conscious that it has behaved properly.

Shall we thus conclude, as Leibnitz and other great philosophers have done, in favour of the mechanical theory ? But if we do, how are we to account for the instinctive ineradicable feeling, which comes home to every one with a conviction even stronger than the evidence of the senses, that we really have a choice between opposite courses, and can decide on our own actions—a conviction which is obviously the foundation of all conscience and of all morality ?

Let us try to analyse more closely what Will really means, and under what conditions it is manifested. The circuit which connects any one single perception with action, through sensory nerve, sensory centre, motor centre, motor nerve and muscle, is as purely mechanical as that of an electric circuit. Reflex motions such as breathing, and even more complex motions which by repetition have become reflex or instinctive, are also mechanical and involve no exercise of will. But when perceptions become complex, and one primary evokes a number of secondary perceptions—in other words, when the cells of the corresponding portions of grey matter in the cortex of the brain are set vibrating by a variety of complex and conflicting molecular motions, the feeling of free-will inevitably arises. We feel the conviction that there is a something which we call soul, mind, or in the last analysis, ' I myself I,' which sits, as Von Moltke might do, in a cabinet receiving con-flicting telegraphic messages from different generals, and deciding then and there what order to flash out in reply.

What can we say to this ? That it is like space and

time, one of the categories of thought, or primary
moulds in which thought is cast. We do not know
what space and time really are in their essence, or why
they are the necessary conditions of thought, any more
than we do in the case of will. They may be illusions,
but we accept them, and of necessity accept them, as
facts. For all practical purposes it is the same to us,
as if we understood their essence and knew them to be
realities. A man can no more doubt that he is an
individual being, with a will which, in a great many
cases, enables him to decide which of a variety of
impulses shall prevail, than he can hesitate, if he is
furnishing a room, to regulate his purchase of carpeting
and paper by space of three dimensions, without regard
to possible speculations as to quaternions.

Perhaps the principle of polarity may assist us in
understanding that both theories may be true; or rather
that matter and spirit, necessity and free-will, may be
opposite poles of one fundamental truth which is beyond
our comprehension. We cannot shake off this principle
of polarity, and arrive at any knowledge, or even conception, of the absolute truth in regard to the atoms,
energies, and natural laws, which make up the universe
of matter and of all the ordinary and material functions
of life; why should we expect to do so in the higher
manifestations of the same life, which have been arrived
at in the later stages of one unbroken course of evolution from monad to man?

This, at any rate, is the theory which best satisfies
my own mind and enables me to reduce my own individual chaos into some sort of a cosmos. I draw from
it the following conclusions :—

For all practical purposes assume that 'right is

right,' and that the moral instincts, however they have been formed, are imperative laws.   Assume also that

Man is man and master of his fate,

and that we have, to a great extent, the power of deciding what to do and what not to do.   But in doing so, keep the mind open to all conclusions of science, and admit freely that these assumptions are indissolubly connected with natural laws and with material organs, and that man is to a very great extent dependent on his environment and his place in evolution, both for his moral code and for the force of will and conscience which enable him to conform to it.   Learn therefore the lesson of a large toleration and of charity in thought and deed, towards those who, from inherited constitution or unfortunate conditions of education and outward circumstances, fall under the sway of the principle of evil, and lead bad, useless, and unlovely lives.   Had you and I, reader, been in their place, should we have done better?

CHAPTER XIII.

ZOROASTRIANISM.

Zoroaster an historical person—The Parsees—Iranian branch of Aryan family—Zoroaster a religious reformer—Scene at Balkh—Conversion of Gushtasp—Doctrines of the 'excellent religion'—Monotheism—Polarity—Dr. Haug's description—Ormuzd and Ahriman—Anquetil du Perron—Approximation to modern thought—Absence of miracles—Code of morals—Its comprehensiveness—And liberality—Special rites—Fire-worship—Disposal of dead—Practical results—The Parsees of Bombay—Their probity, enterprise, respect for women—Zeal for education—Philanthropy and public spirit—Statistics—Death and birth rates.

ZOROASTRIANISM is commonly supposed to derive its name from its founder Zoroaster, a Bactrian sage or prophet, who lived in the reign of King Gushtasp the First. Zoroaster's name has come down to us from antiquity in much the same relation to this form of religion as that of Moses to Judaism, or of Sakya-Mouni to Buddhism. As in those cases, certain learned commentators have endeavoured to show that the alleged founder was purely mythical and had no real historical existence, basing their argument mainly on the fact that a number of supernatural attributes, and embodiments of metaphysical and theological ideas, became attached to the name, just as a whole cycle of solar myths became associated with the name of Hercules. But this seems to be carrying scepticism too far. Experience shows that religions have generally originated in the crystallisation of ideas floating in solution at certain periods of the evolution of societies, about the nucleus of some powerful personality. Nearly all the great religions of the world, such as Buddhism, Confucianism, Christianity, and Mahometanism, clearly had historical founders, and it would be hypercritical to deny that such a man as Jesus of Nazareth really lived because many of his sayings and doings may be traced to applications, more or less erroneous, of ancient prophecies, or because his human nature became transfigured into the Logos and other metaphysical conceptions of the Alexandrian philosophy.

In the case of Zoroaster, the argument for his historical existence seems even stronger, for his name is connected with historical reigns and places, and his genuine early history contains nothing supernatural or improbable. He is represented as simply a deep thinker and powerful preacher, like Luther, who gave new form and expression to the vague religious and philosophical ideas of his age and nation, reformed its superstitions and abuses, and converted the leading minds of his day, including the monarch, by the earnestness and eloquence of his discourses. At any rate, for my purpose I shall assume his personality, for my object is not to write a critical essay on the origin and development of the Zoroastrian religion, but to show that in its fundamental ideas and essential spirit it approximates wonderfully to those of the most advanced modern thought, and gives the outline of a creed which goes further than any other to meet the practical wants of the present day, and to reconcile the conflict between faith and science. This will be most clearly and vividly shown by assuming the commonly accepted historical existence of Zoroaster to be true, and by confining myself to the broad, leading principles of his religion, without dwelling on its varying phases, or on the mythical legends and ritualistic observances which, as in the case of all other old religions, have crystallised about the primitive idea and the primitive founder.

Zara-thustra, or, as he is commonly called, Zoroaster, and the religion which goes by his name, are known to us mainly from the sacred books which have been preserved by the modern Parsees. The Parsees, a small remnant of the Persians who under Cyrus founded one of the mightiest empires of the ancient world, flying from their native country to escape from persecution after the Mahometan conquest, formed a colony in India, and are now settled at Bombay. They form a small but highly intelligent community, who have preserved their ancient religion, and, fortunately, some considerable fragments of their sacred scriptures. The oldest of these are written in the Gata dialect of the Avesta or Zend language, which is contemporary with Sanskrit, and bears much the same relation to it as Latin does to Greek. The primitive Aryan family at some very remote period became divided into two branches, and radiated from their Central Asian home in two directions. The Hindoo branch migrated to the south into the Punjaub and Hindostan ; the Iranian westwards, into Bactria and Persia ; while other successive waves of Aryan migration in prehistoric times rolled still further westwards over Europe, obliterating all but a few traces of the aboriginal population.

The period of this separation of the Iranian and Hindoo races must be very remote, for the Rig-Veda is probably at least 4,000 years old, and the divergence between its form of Sanskrit and the Gata dialect of the Zend is already as great as that between two kindred European languages such as Greek and Latin. The divergence of religious ideas is also evidently of very early date. In the Hindoo, and all other races of the primitive Aryan stock, the word used for gods and good spirits is taken from the root 'div,' to shine. Thus, Daeva in Sanskrit, Zeus and Theos in Greek, Deus in Latin, Tius in German, Diews in Lutheranism, Dia in Irish, Dew in Kymric, all mean the bright or shining one represented by the vault of heaven. But in Iranian the word has an opposite sense, and the ' deevs ' correspond to our 'devils.'

The primitive Aryan religions were evidently all derived from a contemplation of the powers and phenomena of nature. The sky, with its flood of light and vault of ethereal blue, was considered to be the highest manifestation of a Supreme Power ; while the sun and moon, the stars and planets, the winds and clouds, the earth and waters, were personified, either as symbols of the Deity or as subordinate gods. The original simple faith was thus apt to degenerate into a system of polytheism, and, as the gods came to be represented by visible forms, into idolatry.

Zoroaster appears to us, like Mahomet at a later age and among a ruder people, as a prophet or reformer who abolished these abuses and restored the ancient faith in a loftier and more intellectual form, adapted to the use of an advanced and civilised society. The records of his life and teaching have fortunately been preserved in so authentic a form, that distant as he is from us we can form a singularly accurate idea of who he was and what he taught.

Some 3,200 years ago a sight might have been seen in the ancient city of Balkh—the famous capital of Bactria, the ' Mother of Cities '—very like that witnessed some fourteen centuries later at our own Canterbury. The king and his chief nobles and courtiers were assembled to hear the discourse of a preacher who proposed to teach them a better religion. Gushtasp listened to Zoroaster, as Ethelbert listened to Augustine, and in each case reason and eloquence carried conviction, and the nation became converts to the new doctrine.

This conversion was effected without miracles, for it is expressly stated in the celebrated speech of the prophet, preserved in the 30th chapter of the Yasna, that he relied solely on persuasion and argument. Ferdousi, the Persian Homer, thus describes the first interview between Zoroaster and Gushtasp : ' Learn,' he said, ' the rites and doctrines of the religion of excellence. For without religion there cannot be any worth in a king. When the mighty monarch heard him speak of the excellent religion, he accepted from him the excellent rites and doctrines.'

The doctrines of this ' excellent religion ' are extremely simple. The leading idea is that of monotheism, but the one God has far fewer anthropomorphic attributes, and is relegated much farther back into the vague and infinite, than the god of any other monotheistic religion. Ahura-Mazda, of which the more familiar appellation Ormuzd is an abbreviation, means the ' All-knowing Lord ; ' he is said sometimes to dwell in the infinite luminous space, and sometimes to be identical with it. He is, in fact, not unlike the inscrutable First Cause, whom we may regard with awe and reverence, with love and hope, but whom we cannot pretend to define or to understand. But the radical difference between Zoroastrianism and other religions is that it does not conceive of this one God as an omnipotent Creator, who might make the universe as he chose, and therefore was directly responsible for all the evil in it; but as a Being acting by certain fixed laws, one of which was, for reasons totally inscrutable to us, that existence implied polarity, and therefore that there could be no good without corresponding evil.

Dr. Haug, who is the greatest authority on all questions connected with the Zend scriptures, says: 'Having arrived at the grand idea of the unity and indivisibility of the Supreme Being, Zoroaster undertook to solve the great problem which has engaged the attention of so many wise men of antiquity and even in modern times, viz. how are the imperfections discernible in the world, the various kind of evils, wickedness, and baseness, compatible with the goodness, holiness, and justness of God? This great thinker of remote antiquity solved this difficult question philosophically, by the supposition of two primæval causes, which, though different, were united, and produced the world of material things as well as that of spirit. These two primæval principles are the two moving causes in the universe, united from the beginning, and therefore called twins. They are present everywhere—in the Ahura Mazda, or Supreme Deity, as well as in man.'

They are called in the Vendidad Spento Mainyush, or the 'beneficent spirit,' and Angro Mainyush, or the 'hurtful spirit.' The latter is generally known as Ahriman, the Prince of Darkness; and the former as Ormuzd, is identified with Ahura Mazda, the good God, though, strictly speaking, Ahura Mazda is the great unknown First Cause, who comprehends within himself both principles as a necessary law of existence, and in whom believers may hope that evil and good will ultimately be reconciled.

Anquetil du Perron, the first translator of the Zendavesta, in his ' Critical View of the Theological and Ceremonial System of Zar-thurst,' thus sums up the Parsee creed : ' The first point in the theological system of Zoroaster is to recognise and adore the Master of all that is good, the Principle of all righteousness, Ormuzd, according to the form of worship prescribed by him, and with purity of thought, of word, and of action, a purity which is marked and preserved by purity of body. Next, to have a respect, accompanied by gratitude, for the intelligence to which Ormuzd has committed the care of nature (i.e. to the laws of nature), to take in our actions their attributes for models, to copy in our conduct the harmony which reigns in the different parts of the universe, and generally to honour Ormuzd in all that he has produced. The second part of their religion consists in detesting the author of all evil, moral and physical, Ahriman—his productions, and his works ; and to contribute, as far as in us lies, to exalt the glory of Ormuzd by enfeebling the tyranny which the Evil Principle exercises over the world.'

It is evident that this simple and sublime religion is one to which, by whatever name we may call it, the best modern thought is fast approximating. Men of science like Huxley, philosophers like Herbert Spencer, poets like Tennyson, might all subscribe to it; and even enlightened Christian divines, like Dr. Temple, are not very far from it when they admit the idea of a Creator behind the atoms and energies, whose original impress, given in the form of laws of nature, was so perfect as to require no secondary interference. Admit that Christ is the best personification of the Spenta Mainyush, or good principle in the inscrutable Divine polarity of existence, and a man may be at the same time a Christian and a Zoroastrian.

The religion of Zoroaster has, however, this great advantage in the existing conditions of modern thought, that it is not dragged down by such a dead weight of traditional dogmas and miracles as still hangs upon the skirts of Christianity. Its dogmas are comprised in the statement that there is one supreme, unknown, First Cause, who manifests himself in the universe under fixed laws which involve the principle of polarity. This is hardly so much a dogma as a statement of fact, or of the ultimate and absolute truth at which it is possible for human faculty to arrive. No progress of science or philosophy conflicts with it, but rather they confirm it, by showing more and more clearly with every discovery that this is in very fact and deed the literal truth. Religion, or the feeling of reverence and love for the Great Unknown which lies beyond the sphere of human sense and reason, shines more brightly through this pure medium than through the fogs of misty metaphysics; and we can worship God in spirit and in truth without puzzling our brains as to the precise nature of the Logos, or exercising them on the insoluble problem how one can be equal to three, and at the same time three equal to one.

As regards miracles, which are another millstone about the neck of Catholic Christianity, the religion of Zoroaster is entirely free from them. There are, it is true, a few miraculous myths about him in some of the

later writings in the Pehlvi language, as of his conception by his mother drinking a cup of the sacred Homa,
but these are of no authority and form no part of the religion. On the contrary, the original scriptures which
profess to record his exact words and precepts disclaim
all pretension to divine nature or miraculous power, and
base the claims of the 'excellent religion' purely on
reason. This is an immense advantage in the 'struggle
for life,' when every day is making it more impossible
for educated men to believe that real miracles ever
actually occurred, and when the evidence on which
they were accepted is crumbling to pieces under the
light of critical enquiry. The Parsee has no reason
to tremble for his faith if a Galileo invents the telescope or a Newton discovers the law of gravity. He
has no occasion to argue for Noah's deluge, or for the
order of Creation described in Genesis. Nay even, he
may remain undisturbed by that latest and most fatal
discovery that man has existed on the earth for untold
ages, and, instead of falling from a high estate, has
risen continuously by slow and painful progress from
the rudest origins. How many orthodox Christians
can say the same, or deny that their faith in their
sacred books and venerable traditions has been rudely
shaken ?

The code of morality enjoined by the Zoroastrian
religion is as pure as its theory is perfect. Dr. Haug
enumerates the following sins denounced by its code,
and considered as such by the present Parsees : Murder,
infanticide, poisoning, adultery on the part of men as
well as women, sorcery, sodomy, cheating in weight
and measure, breach of promise whether made to a
Zoroastrian or non-Zoroastrian, telling lies and deceiv-

ing, false covenants, slander and calumny, perjury, dis
honest appropriation of wealth, taking bribes, keeping
back the wages of labourers, misappropriation of religious property, removal of a boundary stone, turning
people out of their property, maladministration and
defrauding, apostasy, heresy, rebellion. These are positive injunctions. The following are condemnable from a
religious point of view : Abandoning the husband; not
acknowledging one's children on the part of the father;
cruelty towards subjects on the part of a ruler ; avarice,
laziness, illiberality and egotism, envy. In addition
there are a number of special precepts adapted to the
peculiar rites of the Zoroastrian religion which aim
principally at the enforcement of sanitary rules, kindness to animals, hospitality to strangers and travellers,
respect to superiors, and help to the poor and needy.

It is evident that this is the most complete and comprehensive code of morals to be found in any system
of religion. It comprises all that is best in the codes
of Buddhism, Judaism, and Christianity, with a much
more ample definition of many vices and virtues which,
even in the Christian religion, are left to be drawn as
inferences rather than inculcated as precepts. Thus,
laziness, cheating, selfishness, and envy are distinctly
defined as crimes, and their opposites as virtues, and
not merely left to be inferred from the general maxims
of 'loving your neighbour as yourself,' and 'doing unto
others as you would be done by.' The comprehensiveness and liberal spirit of the code is also remarkable,
for we are repeatedly told that these rules of morality
apply to non-Zoroastrians as well as to Zoroastrians.
The application of religious precepts to practical life
is another distinguishing feature. Thus kindness to

animals is specially enjoined, and it is considered a sin to ill-treat animals of the good creation, such as cattle, sheep, horses, or dogs, by starving, beating, or unnecessarily killing them. With true practical wisdom, however, the 'falsehood of extremes' is avoided, and this precept is not, as in the case of Brahminism and Buddhism, carried so far as to prohibit altogether the taking of animal life, which is expressly sanctioned when necessary. This sober practical wisdom, or what Matthew Arnold calls 'sweet reasonableness,' is a very characteristic feature of Zoroaster's religion, and very remarkable as having been taught at so early a period in the history of civilisation.

Another precept, which might well have been made by an English board of health in the nineteenth century, is not to pollute water by throwing impure matter into it.

The only special Parsee rites which would be unsuited for modern European society, are the worship of the sacred fire and the disposal of the dead. It is true that the former is distinctly understood to be merely a symbol of the Deity, and used exactly as water is in baptism, or as the ascending flame of candles and smoke from swinging incense are in the Catholic ritual, to bring more vividly before the minds of the worshippers the idea of the spirit soaring upwards towards heaven. Still, in modern society fire is too well understood as merely a particular form of chemical combination, and is too familiar as the strong slave and household drudge of man, to acquire a leading place in a religious ritual where it has not been hallowed by the usage of a long line of ancestors and the traditions of a venerable antiquity. All that can be said is, that if religious rites and ceremonies are to be maintained in an age when science has become the prevailing mode of thought, appropriate symbolism, especially that of music, must more and more take the place of appeals to the intellect on metaphysical questions, and of repetitions of traditional formulæ which have lost all living significance.

Another Parsee rite, which is even less adapted for general usage, is that of disposing of the dead on towers of silence, where the body moulders away or is devoured by birds of prey. It originates in a poetical motive of not defiling the pure elements, fire, earth, or water, by corruption; but it is obviously unsuited for the conditions of civilisation and climate which prevail in crowded cities under a humid sky.

There is little prospect therefore of any general conversion to the sect of Zoroastrians; but what seems probable is the gradual transformation of existing modes both of religious and secular thought into something which is, in principle, very closely akin to the 'excellent religion' taught by the Bactrian prophet.

The miraculous theory of the universe being virtually dead, the only theory that can reconcile facts with feelings, and the ineradicable emotions and aspirations of the human mind with the incontrovertible conclusions of science, is that of a remote and more or less unknown and incomprehensible First Cause, which has given the original atoms and energies so perfect an impress from the first, that all phenomena are evolved from them by fixed laws, one of the principal of such laws being that of polarity, which develops the ever-increasing complexities and contrasts of the inorganic and organic worlds, of moralities, philosophies, religions, and human societies.

True religion consists in a recognition of this truth, a feeling of reverence in presence of the unknown, and, above all, a feeling of love and admiration for the good principle in whatever form it is manifested, in the beauties of nature and of art, in moral and physical purity and perfection, and all else that falls within the domain of the Prince of Light, in whose service, whether we conceive of him as an abstract principle, or accept some personification of him as a living figure, we enlist as loyal soldiers, doing our best to fight in his ranks against the powers of evil.

The application of the all-pervading principle of polarity is exemplified in the realm of art. The glorious Greek drama turned mainly on the conflict between resistless fate and heroic free-will, and is typified in its highest form by Æschylus, when he depicts Prometheus chained to the rock hurling defiance at the tyrant of heaven. Our own Milton, in like manner, gives us the spectacle of the fallen archangel opposing his indomitable will and fertile resources to the extremity of adverse circumstance and to Almighty power.

The greatest of modern dramas, Goethe's ' Faust,' turns so entirely on the opposition between the human soul striving after the infinite, and the spirit *der verneint*, who combats ideal aspirations with a cynical sneer, that it might well be called a Zoroastrian drama. It is a picture of the conflict between the two opposite principles of good and evil, of affirmation and negation, of the beautiful and the ugly, personified in Faust and Mephistopheles, and it is painted on a background of the great mysterious unknown. ' Wer darf ihn nennen ? '

Who dares to name Him,
Who to say of Him, ' I believe ' ?

P

> Who is there ever with a heart to dare
> To utter, 'I believe Him not'?

So in poetry, Tennyson, the poet of modern thought, touches the deepest chords when he asks—

> Are God and Nature, then, at strife?

and paints in the sharpest contrast on the background of the unknown, the conflict between the faith that

> God is love indeed,
> And love creation's final law,

and the harsh realities of nature, which

> Red in tooth and claw
> With ravine shrieks against the creed;

or again in his later work, 'The Ancient Sage,' he says—

> Thou canst not prove the Nameless, O my son!
> For nothing worthy proving can be proven,
> Nor yet disproven.

In like manner in the works of art which embrace a wider range, and hold up the mirror to human nature, as in Shakespeare's plays, and the novels of Walter Scott and other great authors, the interest arises mainly from the polarity of the various characters. We care little for the goody-good heroes or vulgar villains, but we recognise a touch of that nature which makes all the world akin in a Macbeth drawn by metaphysical suggestion to wade through a sea of blood; in Othello's noble nature caught like a lion in the toils by the net of circumstances woven by a wily hunter; in Falstaff, a rogue, a liar, and a glutton, yet made almost likeable by his ready wit, imperturbable good-humour, and fertile resources. Shakespeare is, in fact, the greatest of artists, because he is the most multipolar. He has poles of sympathy in him which, as the poles of carbon attract so many elements and form so many combinations, enable him to take into his own nature, assimilate, and reproduce every varied shade of character from a Miranda to a Caliban, from an Imogen to a Lady Macbeth, from a Falstaff to an Othello. Sir Walter Scott and all our great novelists have the same faculty, though in a less degree, and are great in exact proportion as they have many poles in their nature, and as those are poles of powerful polarity. The characters and incidents which affect us strongly and dwell in the memory are those in which the clash and conflict of opposites are most vividly represented. We feel infinite pity for a Maggie Tulliver dashing her young life, like a prisoned wild bird, against the bars of trivial and prosaic environment which hem her in ; or for a Colonel Newcome opposing the patience of a gentle nature to the buffets of such a fate as meets us in the everyday world of modern life, the failure of his bank and the naggings of the Old Campaigner. On a higher level of art we sympathise with a Lancelot and a Guinevere because they are types of what we may meet in many a London drawing-room, noble natures drawn by some fatal fairy fascination into ignoble acts, but still retaining something of their original nobility, and while

Their honour rooted in dishonour stands,

appearing to ordinary mortals little less than ' archangels ruined.' Or even if we descend to the lowest level of the penny dreadful or suburban drama, we find that the polarity between vice and virtue, however coarsely delineated, is that which mostly fascinates the uncultured mind.

The affinity between Zoroastrianism and art is easily explained when we consider that in one respect it has a manifest advantage over most Christian forms of religion. Christianity in its early origins received a taint of Oriental asceticism which it never shook off, and which in the declining centuries of the Roman empire, and in the barbarism and superstition of the Middle Ages, developed into what may be almost called a devil-worship of the ugly and repulsive. The antithesis between the flesh and the spirit was carried to such an extreme and false extent, that everything that was pleasant and beautiful came to be regarded as sinful, and the odour of sanctity was an odour which the passer-by would do well to keep on the windward side of. This leaven of asceticism is the rock upon which Puritanism, monasticism, and many of the highest forms of Christian life have invariably split. It is contrary to human nature, and directly opposed to the spirit of the life and doctrines of the Founder of the religion. Jesus, who was 'a Jew living among Jews and speaking to Jews,' adopted the true Jewish point of view of making religion amiable and attractive, and denouncing, as all the best Jewish doctors of the Talmud did, the pharisaical strictness which insisted on ritualistic observances and arbitrary restrictions. In no passages of his life does the 'sweet reasonableness' of his character appear more conspicuous than where we find him strolling through the fields with his disciples and plucking ears of corn on the Sabbath, and replying to the formalists who were scandalised, 'The Sabbath was made for man, not man for the Sabbath.' The ascetic bias subsequently introduced may have been a necessary element in counteracting the corruption of Rome ; but the pendulum in its reaction swung much too far, and when organised in the celibacy of the clergy and monastic institutions asceticism became the source of great evils. Even at a late period we can see in the reaction of the reign of Charles II. how antagonistic the puritanical creed, even of men like Cromwell and Milton, proved to the healthy natural instinct of the great mass of the English nation. And at the present day it remains one of the main causes of the indifference or hostility to religion which is so widely spreading among the mass of the population. Children are brought up to consider Sunday as a day of penance, and church-going as a disagreeable necessity ; while grown-up men, especially those of the working classes, resent being told that a walk in the country, a cricket-match, or a visit to a library or museum on their only holiday, is sinful.

In view of the approximation between the Zoroastrian religion and the forms of modern thought it is interesting to note how the former works among its adherents in actual practice. For, after all, the practical side of a religion is more important than its speculative or philosophical theories. Thus, for instance, the Quakers have a faith which is about the most reasonable of any of the numerous sects of Christianity and nearest to the spirit of its Founder, and yet Quakerism remains a narrow sect which is far from being victorious in the 'struggle for life.' Mahometanism, again, while dying out among civilised nations, shows itself superior to Christianity in the work of raising the barbarous, fetish-worshipping negroes of Africa to a higher level. And Mormonism, based on the most obvious imposture and absurdity, is the only new religion which, in recent times, has taken root and to a certain extent flourished.

Tried by this test, Zoroastrianism has made good its claim to be called the ' excellent religion.' Its followers, the limited community of Parsees in India, are honourably distinguished for probity, intelligence, enterprise, public spirit, benevolence, tolerance, and other good qualities. By virtue of these qualities they have raised themselves to a prominent position in our Indian empire, and take a leading part in its commerce and industrial enterprise. The chief shipbuilder at Bombay, the first great native railway contractor, the founder of cotton factories, are all Parsees, and they are found as merchants, traders, and shopkeepers in all the chief towns of British India, and distant places such as Aden and Zanzibar. Their commercial probity is proverbial, and, as in England, they have few written agreements, the word of a Parsee, like that of an Englishman, being considered as good as his bond. Their high character and practical aptitude for business are attested by the fact that the first mayor, or chairman of the Corporation of Bombay, was a Parsee who was elected by the unanimous vote both of Europeans and natives.

The position of women affords perhaps the best test of the real civilisation and intrinsic worth of any community. Where men consider women as inferior creatures it is a sure proof that they themselves are so. They are totally wanting in that delicacy and refinement of nature which distinguishes the true gentleman from the snob or the savage, and are coarse, vulgar brutes, however disguised under a veneer of outward polish. On the other hand, respect for women implies self-respect, nobility of nature, capability of rising to high ideals above the sordid level of animal appetite and the selfish supremacy of brute force.

The Parsees in this respect stand high, far higher than any other Oriental people, and on a level with the best European civilisation. The equality of the sexes is distinctly laid down in the Zoroastrian scriptures. Women are always mentioned as a necessary part of the religious community. They have the same religious rites as the men. The spirits of deceased women are invoked as well as those of men. Long contact with the other races of India, and the necessity for some outward conformity to the practices of Hindoo and Mahometan rulers, did something to impair the position of females as regards public appearances, though the Parsee wife and mother always remained a principal figure in the Parsee household ; and latterly, under the security of English rule, Parsee ladies may be seen everywhere in public, enjoying just as much liberty as the ladies of Europe or America. Nor are they at all behind their Western sisters in education, accomplishments, and, it may be added, in daintiness of fashionable attire. In fact, an eager desire for education has become a prominent feature among all classes of the Parsee community, and they are quite on a par with the Scotch, German, and other European races in their efforts to establish schools, and in the numbers who attend, and especially of those who obtain distinguished places in the higher schools and colleges, such as the Elphinstone Institute and the Bombay University. Female education is also actively promoted, and no prejudices stand in the way of attendance at the numerous girls' schools which have been established, or even of studying in medical colleges, where Parsee women attend lectures on all branches of

medical science along with male students.   Those who
know the position of inferiority and seclusion in which
women are kept among all other Oriental nations can
best appreciate the largeness and liberality of spirit of a
religion which, in spite of all surrounding influences,
has rendered such a thing possible in such a country as
India.

Another prominent trait of the Parsee character is
that of philanthropy and public spirit.   In proportion
to their numbers and means they raise more money for
charitable objects than any other religious sect.   And
they raise it in a way which does the greatest credit to
their tolerance and liberality.   For instance, the Parsees
were the principal subscribers to a fund raised in Bom
bay in aid of the 'Scottish Corporation,' and quite
recently a Parsee gentleman gave 16,000l. towards the
establishment of a female hospital under the care of
lady doctors, although the benefit of such an institution
would be confined principally to Mahometan and Hindoo
women, Parsee women having no prejudice against em-
ploying male doctors.

The public spirit shown by acts like this is the trait by
which the Parsee community is most honourably distinguished, and in respect of which it must be candidly
confessed it far surpasses not only other Oriental races,
but most European nations, including our own.   Whatever the reason may be, the fact is certain that in
England, while a great deal of money is spent in charity,
lamentably little is spent from the enormous surplus
wealth of the country on what may be called public
objects.   There is neither religious influence nor social
opinion brought to bear on the numerous class who
have incomes far beyond any possible want, to teach

them that it should be both a pleasure and a pride to associate their names with some act of noble liberality. A better spirit we may hope is springing up, and there have been occasional instances of large sums applied to public purposes, such as parks and colleges, by private individuals, principally of the trading and manufacturing classes, such as the Salts, Crossleys, Baxters, and Holloways; but on the whole the amount contributed is miserably small. It is probably part of the price we pay for aristocratic institutions that those who inherit or accumulate great fortunes consider it their primary object to perpetuate or to found great families. Be this as it may, a totally different spirit prevails among the Parsees of Bombay, where it has been truly stated that hardly a year passes without some wealthy Parsee coming forward to perform a work of public generosity. The instance of Sir Jamsedjee Jijibhoy, who attained a European reputation for his noble benevolence, is only one conspicuous instance out of a thousand of this 'public spirit' which has become almost an instinctive element in Parsee society.

How far the large and liberal religion may be the cause of the large and liberal practice, it is impossible to say. Other influences have doubtless been at work. The Parsees are a commercial people, and commerce is always more liberal with its money than land. They are the descendants of a persecuted race, and as a rule it is better to be persecuted than to persecute. Still, after making all allowances, it remains that the tree cannot be had which bears such fruits; the religion must be a good one which produces good men and women and good deeds.

Statistical facts testify quite as strongly to the high

standard of the Parsee race, and the practical results which follow from the observance of the Zoroastrian ritual. A small death-rate and a large proportion of children prove the vigorous vitality of a race. The Parsees have the lowest death-rate of any of the many races who inhabit Bombay. The average for the two years 1881 and 1882 per thousand was for Hindoos 26·11; for Mussulmans 30·46; for Europeans 20·18; for Parsees 19·26. The percentage of children under two years old to women between fifteen and forty-five was 30·27 for Parsees, as against Hindoos 22·24, and Mussulmans 24·9, showing incontestably greater vitality and greater care for human life.

Of 6,618 male and 2,966 female mendicants in the city of Bombay, only five male and one female were Parsees.

These figures speak for themselves. It is evident that a religion in which such results are possible cannot be unfavourable to the development of the ' mens sana in corpore sano ; ' and that, although we may not turn Zoroastrians, we may envy some of the results of a creed which inculcates worship of the good, the pure, and the beautiful in the concerns of daily life, as well as in the abstract regions of theological and philosophical speculation.

CHAPTER XIV.

FORMS OF WORSHIP.

> Not vainly did the early Persian make
> His altar the high places and the peak
> Of earth-o'ergazing mountains, and thus take
> A fit and unwall'd temple, where to seek
> The spirit, in whose honour shrines are weak,
> Uprear'd of human hands. Come, and compare
> Columns and idol-dwellings, Goth or Greek,
> With nature's realms of worship, earth and air,
> Nor fix on fond abodes to circumscribe thy prayer !
>
> *Childe Harold*, iii. 91.

A SHREWD Scotch-American ironmaster—Andrew Carnegie—in an interesting and instructive record of ex-
periences during a voyage round the world, gives the
following description of the worship of the modern
Parsees, as actually witnessed by him at Bombay :—

'This evening we were surprised to see, as we
strolled along the beach, more Parsees than ever before,
and more Parsee ladies richly dressed, all wending their
way towards the sea. It was the first of the new moon,
a period sacred to these worshippers of the elements ;
and here on the shore of the ocean, as the sun was sinking in the sea, and the slender silver thread of the

crescent moon was faintly shining on the horizon, they congregated to perform their religious rites.

'Fire was there in its grandest form, the setting sun, and water in the vast expanse of the Indian Ocean outstretched before them. The earth was under their feet, and wafted across the sea the air came laden with the perfumes of " Araby the blest." Surely no time or place could be more fitly chosen than this for lifting up the soul to the realms beyond sense. I could not but participate with these worshippers in what was so grandly beautiful. There was no music save the solemn moan of the waves as they broke into foam on the beach. But where shall we find so mighty an organ, or so grand an anthem?

'How inexpressibly sublime the scene appeared to me, and how insignificant and unworthy of the unknown seemed even our cathedrals "made with human hands," when compared with this looking up through nature unto nature's God! I stood and drank in the serene happiness which seemed to fill the air. I have seen many modes and forms of worship—some disgusting, others saddening, a few elevating when the organ pealed forth its tones, but all poor in comparison with this. Nor do I ever expect in all my life to witness a religious ceremony which will so powerfully affect me as that of the Parsees on the beach at Bombay.'

I say Amen with all my heart to Mr. Carnegie. Here is an ideal religious ceremony combining all that is most true, most touching, and most sublime, in the attitude of man towards the Great Unknown. Compare it with the routine of an ordinary English Sunday, and how poor and prosaic does the latter appear! There is nothing which seems to me to have fallen more completely out of harmony with its existing environment than our traditional form of church service. The sermon has been killed by the press and has become an anachronism. There was a time when sermons like those of Latimer and John Knox were living realities ; they dealt with all the burning political and personal questions of the day, and to a great extent did the work now done by platform speeches and leading articles. If there are national dangers to be denounced, national shortcomings to be pointed out, iniquity in high places to be rebuked, we look to our daily newspaper, and not to our weekly sermon. The sermon has in a great majority of cases become a sort of schoolboy theme, in which traditional assumptions and conventional phrases are ground out, with as little soul or idea behind them as in the Thibetan praying-mill. In the course of a long life I have gained innumerable ideas and experienced innumerable influences, from contact with the world, with fellow-men, and with books ; but although I have heard a good many sermons, I cannot honestly say that I ever got an idea or an influence from one of them which made me wiser or better, or different in any respect from what I should have been if I had slept through them. And this from no fault of the preachers. I have heard many who gave me the impression that they were good men, and a few who impressed me as being able and liberal-minded men—nor do I know that, under the conditions in which they are placed, I could have done any better myself. But they were dancing in fetters, and so tied down by conventionalities that it was simply impossible for them to depart from the paths of a decorous routine.

The fact is that the whole point of view of our

religious services, especially in Protestant countries, has become a mistaken one. It is far too much an appeal to the intellect and to abstract dogmas, and too little, one to the realities of actual life and to the vague emotions and aspirations which constitute the proper field of religion. In the great reaction of the Reformation it was perhaps inevitable that an appeal should be made to reason against the abuses of an infallible Church; and as long as the literal inspiration of the Bible and other theological premises were held to be undoubted axioms by the whole Christian world, there might be a certain interest in hearing them repeated over and over again in becoming language, and in listening to sermons which explained shortly conclusions which might be drawn from these admitted axioms. But this is no longer the case. It is impossible to touch the merest fringe of the questions now raised by the intellectual side of religion in discourses of half an hour's length; even if the preacher were perfectly free, and not hampered by the fear of scandalising simple, pious souls by plain language. Spoken words have to a great extent ceased to be the appropriate vehicle for appealing either to religious reason or to religious emotion—books for the former, music for the latter, are infinitely more effective. Music especially seems made to be the language of religion. Not only its beauty and harmony, but its vagueness, and its power of exciting the imagination and stirring the feelings, without anything definite which has to be proved and can be contradicted, fit it to be the interpreter of those emotions and aspirations which fill the human soul in presence of the universe and of the Great Unknown. Demonstrate, with St. Thomas Aquinas or

Duns Scotus, how many angels can stand on the point of a needle, and I remain unaffected ; but let me hear Rossini's 'Cujus Animam,' or Mozart's 'Agnus Dei,' and I say, ' Thus the angels sing.'

In this respect the Roman Catholic Church has retained a great advantage over reformed churches. Whatever we may think of its tenets and principles, its forms of worship are more impressive and more attractive. The Mass, apart from all dogma and miracle, is a mysterious and beautiful religious drama, in which appropriate symbolism, vocal and instrumental music, all the highest efforts of human art, are united to produce feelings of joy and of devoutness. The vestment of the priest, his gestures and genuflexions, the Latin words chanted in stately recitative, the flame of the candles pointing heavenwards, the burning incense slowly soaring upwards, the music of great masters, not like our dreary and monotonous psalmody, but in fullest harmony and richest melody—all combine to attune the mind to that state of feeling which is the soul of religion.

In this respect, however, what I have called the Zoroastrian theory of religion affords great advantages. It connects religion directly with all that is good and beautiful, not only in the higher realms of speculation and of emotion, but in the ordinary affairs of daily life. To feel the truth of what is true, the beauty of what is beautiful, is of itself a silent prayer or act of worship to the Spirit of Light; to make an honest, earnest, effort to attain this feeling, is an offering or act of homage. Cleanliness of mind and body, order and propriety in conduct, civility in intercourse, and all the homely virtues of everyday life, thus acquire a higher significance, and any wilful and persistent disregard of them becomes an act of mutiny against the Power whom we have elected to serve. Such moral perversion becomes impossible as that which in the Middle Ages associated filth with holiness, and adduced as a title to canonisation that the saint had worn the same woollen shirt until it fell to pieces under the attacks of vermin. We laugh at this in more enlightened days, but we often imitate it by setting up false religious standards, and thinking we can make men better by penning them up on Sundays in the foul air and corrupting influences of densely peopled cities.

The identification of moral and physical evil, which is one of the most essential and peculiar tenets of the Zoroastrian creed, is fast becoming a leading idea in modern civilisation. Our most earnest philanthropists and zealous workers in the fields of sin and misery in crowded cities are coming, more and more every day, to the conviction that an improvement in the physical conditions of life is the first indispensable condition of moral and religious progress. More air, more light, better lodging, better food, more innocent and healthy recreation, are what are wanted to make any real impression on the masses who have either been born and bred in an evil environment, or have fallen out of the ranks and are the waifs and stragglers left behind in the rapid progress and intense competition of modern society. Hence we see that the devoted individuals and charitable institutions who take the lead in works of practical benevolence direct their attention more and more to the rescue of children from bad surroundings ; to sending them to new and happier homes in the colonies, to country retreats for the sickly, and excursions for the healthy; and to providing clubs and reading-rooms as substitutes for the gin-palace and public-house. The latest development of this idea, that of the 'People's Palace' in the East End of London, is a noble offering to the 'Spirit of Light,' by whatever name we choose to call him, in opposition to the 'Spirit of Darkness.'

To the Zoroastrian, prayer assumes the form of a recognition of all that is pure, sublime, and beautiful in the surrounding universe. He can never want opportunities of paying homage to the Good Spirit and of looking into the abysses of the unknown with reverence and wonder. The light of setting suns, the dome of loving blue, the clouds in the might of the tempest or resting still as brooding doves, the mountains, the

> Waste
> And solitary places where we taste
> The pleasure of believing what we see,
> Is boundless, as we wish our souls to be;

the ocean lashed by storm, or where it

> All down the sand
> Lies breathing in its sleep,
> Heard by the land—

these are a Zoroastrian's prayers.

And even if, 'in populous cities pent,' he is cut off from close communion with nature, opportunities are not wanting to him of letting his soul soar aloft with purifying aspirations. A glimpse of the starry sky, even if seen from a London street, may bear in on him the awful yet lovely mystery of the Infinite. Good books, good music, true works of art, may all strengthen his love of the good and beautiful. A dense fog, or

Q

drizzling rain may obscure the outward view, but with the inner eye he may stand listening to the lark cr under the vernal sky, and while his

> Heart looks down and up,
>   Serene, secure;
> Warm as the crocus-cup,
>   As snowdrops pure,

thank the Good Spirit that it has been given to man to write, and to him to read, verses of such exquisite perfection as Shelley's ' Ode to a Skylark ' and Tennyson's ' Early Spring.' Above all, where men congregate in masses, in the great centres of politics, of commerce, of literature, science, and art, he can hear best

> The still sad music of humanity,
> Not harsh nor grating, but of ample power
> To chasten and subdue,

and associate himself with movements in which his little individual effort is exerted towards making the world a little better rather than a little worse than he found it.

This, rather than wrangling with his fellow-mortals about creeds and attempts to name the unnameable, believe the unbelievable, and define the undefineable, seems to me to be the religion of the future. Call it by what name you like, I quarrel with no one as long as he can find

> Sermons in stones and good in everything.

CHAPTER XV.

PRACTICAL POLARITIES.

Fable of the shield—Progress and conservatism—English and French colonisation—Law-abidingness—Irish land question—True conservative legislation—Ultra-conservatism—Law and education—Patriotism —Jingoism and parochialism—True statesmanship—Free trade and protection—Capital and labour—Egoism and altruism—Socialism and *laissez faire*—Contracts—Rights and duties of landlords—George's theory—State interference — Railways—Post Office — Telegraphs— National defence—Concluding remarks.

A WELL-KNOWN fable tells how in the olden time two knights were riding in opposite directions along a green road overarched by the trees of an ancient forest. It was a bright morning in early summer, with the green leaves freshly bursting in contrasted foliage ; the sun had just risen over the tops of the trees in clouds of golden and crimson glory ; dewdrops were glittering like diamonds on every twig and blade of grass ; and the joyous birds carolling their loudest song to greet the opening day.

Everything was fresh and cheerful as of a newborn earth, and so were the spirits of the two youthful knights, who were pricking forth in search of adventures. He whose face was turned towards the West, where the rising sun had last set, wore a primrose scarf over his cuirass, and had on his shield a quaint device, which,

on closer inspection, might be seen to be a tombstone
with the inscription,

'I was well, would be better, and here I am.'

He rode along musing on the heroic legends of the past,
and wishing that he had been a knight of Arthur's round
table to ride out with the blameless king against invad-
ing heathen.

The second knight, whose face was turned towards the
rising sun, bore an azure shield with a different device.
On it was depicted the good Sir James Douglass
charging the serried Paynim army, and, as he charged,
flinging before him into the hostile ranks the casket
containing the heart of Robert Bruce, and shouting for
battle-cry—

Go thou aye forward, as was thy wont.

As he rode his fancy wrought the fairy web of a
day-dream, in which he saw himself delivering the fair
princess Liberty from the fiery dragon Prejudice and
the stolid giant Obstruction.

The knights met just where an ancient oak of mighty
bulk stretched overhead a huge branch across the path,
as some aged athlete might stretch out an arm rigid
with gnarled and knotted muscles, to show younger
generations how Olympian laurels were won when
Pollux or Hercules plied the cestus. From this branch
a shield hung suspended.

'Good morrow, fair knight,' said he of the primrose
scarf; 'prithee tell me if thou knowest what means this
golden shield suspended here.'

'I marvel at it myself, good Sir Knight,' responded
the other; 'but you mistake in calling the shield golden;
it is of silver.'

'Your eyes must be of the dullest,' said the first knight, 'if you mistake gold for silver.'

'Not so dull as yours,' retorted the other, 'if you mistake silver for gold.'

The argument waxed hot, and, as usual in such cases, as tempers grew weak adjectives grew strong. Soon, like the old Homeric heroes when Greek met Trojan

Far on the ringing plains of windy Troy,

winged words of fire and fury darted from each mouth, and epithets were exchanged, of which 'stupid old Tory' and 'low, vulgar Radical' were among the least unparliamentary. At length the fatal words 'You lie' escaped simultaneously from both, and on the instant spears were couched, steeds spurred, and, red with rage, they encountered each other in full career. Such was the momentum that both men and horses rolled over, even as the Templar went down before the spear of Ivanhoe within the lists of Ashby-de-la-Zouch. But, like the redoubted knight Brian de Bois-Guilbert, each sprang to his feet and drew his sword, eager to redeem the fortune of war in deadly combat. Like two surly boars with bristling backs and foaming tusks quarrelling for the right of way in Indian jungle, or tawny lions in Numidian desert tearing one another to pieces for the smiles of a leonine Helen, the heroes clashed together, cutting, slashing, parrying, foyning, and traversing, until at length, bleeding and breathless, they paused for a moment, leaning on their swords to recover second wind.

Just then an aged hermit appeared on the scene, drawn thither by the sound of the combat.

'Pause, my sons,' he said, 'and tell me what is the cause of this furious encounter'

'Yonder false villain protests,' said the one, 'that the shield which hangs there is of gold.'

'And that lying varlet persists that it is of silver,' said the other.

The hermit smiled, and said, 'Hold your hands, good sirs, for a single moment, and use your remaining strength to exchange places and look at the opposite side of the shield.'

They obeyed his words, and found to their confusion that they had been fighting in a quarrel in which each was right and each wrong.

'Father,' they said, 'we are fools. Grant us thy pardon for our folly and absolution for our sin.'

'Absolution,' said the hermit, 'is soon granted for faults which arise from the innate tendency of poor human nature. Wiser and older men than you are prone to see only their own side of a question. Come, then, with me to my humble hermitage; there will I dress your wounds and offer you my frugal fare; happy if from this lesson you may learn for the rest of your lives, before indulging in vehement assertions and proceeding to violent extremities, to "look at the other side of the shield."'

The application of this fable to the polarity of politics will be obvious to every intelligent reader. As the earth is kept in its orbit by the due balance of centripetal and centrifugal forces, so is every civilised society held together by the opposite influences of conservative and progressive tendencies. The conservative tendency may be likened to the centripetal force which binds the mass together, while the progressive one resembles that centrifugal force which prevents it from being concentrated in a rigid and inert central body without life or

motion. As Herbert Spencer truly says, ' from antagonistic social tendencies there always results not a
medium state, but a rhythm between opposite states.
Now the one greatly preponderates, and presently, by
reaction, there comes a preponderance of the other.'
So it is with the antagonism of conservative and liberal
tendencies. In the societies of the ancient world, and
to the present day in the East, the conservative tendency
unduly preponderates, and they crystallise into inert
masses in the form of despotisms, and of sacerdotal or
administrative hierarchies. At times the pent-up forces
which make for change accumulate, and, as in the
French Revolution, explode with destructive violence,
shattering the old and bringing in new eras. But unless the balance between liberty and order is tolerably
preserved in the individual citizens whose aggregate
forms the society, after a period more or less prolonged
of violent oscillations they crystallise anew into fresh
forms, in which another military dynasty, or it may be
administrative centralisation under the name of a re-
public, again asserts the preponderance of the centripetal
force.

The happiest nations are those in which the individual character of individual citizens supplies the
requisite balance. An ideal society is one in which
every citizen is at the same time liberal and conservative ;
law-abiding, and yet with a strong instinct for liberty
of thought and action, for progress and for individual
independence. It is among the Teutonic races, especially
when they are placed in favourable conditions as in new
countries, or in old countries where for ages

> Freedom has widened slowly down,
> From precedent to precedent,

that this happy ideal is most nearly realised. Hence it is that these races are more and more coming to the front and surviving in the struggle for existence.

The contrast of English and French colonisation affords a striking instance of this difference of races. A century and a half ago France stood as well as England in the race for colonial supremacy. She had the start of us in Canada, and her pioneers had explored the Great Lakes, the Mississippi, and a large part of the continent of North America west of the Rocky Mountains. To-day there are sixty millions of an English-speaking population in that continent, while French is scarcely spoken beyond the single province of Quebec. Political events had doubtless something to do with this result ; but it has been mainly owing to the innate qualities of the two races, for even the genius of Chatham might have failed to establish our supremacy if it had not been backed by the superior intelligence, energy, and staying power of the English colonists. The ultimate cause of the triumph of the English over the French element in America and India is doubtless to be found in the stronger individualism of the former. The character of the French is eminently social, they like to live in societies, and shrink from encountering the hardships and still more the isolation of the life of early settlers. They like to be administered, and shrink from the responsibility of hewing out, each for themselves, their own path in the relations of civil life or in the depths of primæval forests.

It is so to the present day, and they fail conspicuously in creating a large French population even at their own doors in Algeria ; while in their more distant colonies they conquer and annex, but to see their com-

merce fall into the hands of English, Germans, and
Chinese, as in Cochin China, or to stagnate as in New
Caledonia. As a witty French writer puts it, the trade
of a remote French colony may be summed up as—
imports, absinthe and cigars ; exports, stamped paper
and red-tape. Individualism in this case has been fairly
pitted against Socialism, and has beaten it out of the
field by the verdict of Fact, which is more conclusive
than any amount of abstract argument.

To return, however, to the field of politics. Where
the essential quality of being law-abiding is wanting
in individuals, it is hopeless to look for real liberty.
The centripetal force in societies, as in planets, must be
supplied somehow, or they would fly into dissolution ;
and if not by the integration of the tendencies of the
individual units, then by external restrictions. Socialists may be allowed to make inflammatory harangues
in a non-explosive atmosphere, but hardly to let off
their fireworks in a powder-magazine. In order, however, that a nation shall be law-abiding, it is essential
that the great majority should feel that, on the whole, the
law is their friend. It is not in human nature to love
that which injures, or to respect that which is felt to be
unjust. The volcanic explosion of the French Revolution was due to the feeling of the French nation, with
the exception of a few courtiers, nobles, and priests,
that the existing order of things was their enemy, and
law a tool in the hands of their oppressors. Even
among English-speaking races we find, in the unfortunate instance of Ireland, that under specially unfavourable circumstances the same effects may be
produced by the same causes. What has English law
practically meant for centuries to an average peasant of

Kerry or Connemara ?   It has meant an irresistible malevolent power, which comes down on him with writs of eviction to compel him to pay a high rent on his own improvements.   More than half the population of Ireland consists of tenants and their families occupying small holdings, paying less than 10*l.* a year of rent. Of an immense majority of these small holdings two things may be safely asserted : first, that the total gross value of the produce is insufficient, after paying the rent, to leave a decent subsistence for the cultivator. Secondly, that this rent is levied to a great extent on the improvements of the tenant or his predecessors. Throughout the poorer parts of Ireland the greater part of the soil, in its natural state of bog or mountain, is not worth a rent of a shilling an acre ; but some poor peasant, urged by the earth-hunger which results from the absence of other sources of employment, squats upon it, builds a wretched cottage, delves, drains, fences, and reclaims a few acres of land so as to bear a scanty crop of oats and potatoes.   When he has done so the landlord or landlord's agent comes to him and says, ' This land is worth ten or fifteen shillings an acre, according to the standard of rents in the district, and you must pay it or turn out ; ' and the law backs him in saying so by writs of eviction and police.   Put yourself in poor Pat's place, and say if you would love the law and be law-abiding.

It would take me too far from the scope of this volume into the field of contemporary politics if I attempted to point out who is to blame for this state of things, or what are the remedies.   It is enough to say that this is the real Irish problem, and to point to it as an instance of the calamitous effects which inevitably follow when the instincts of a whole population are brought by an unfavourable combination of circumstances into necessary and natural antagonism with the laws which they are bound to obey.

Conservative legislation, by whatever party it is introduced, really means making the law correspond with the common sense and common morality of all except the criminal and crotchety classes, so that the majority may feel it to be their friend. For instance, the most truly conservative measure of recent times was probably that which legalised trades' unions and gave working-men full liberty to combine for an increase of wages. The old legal maxim, that such combinations were illegal as being in restraint of trade, was so obviously an invention of the members of the upper caste who wore horsehair wigs, to give their fellows of the same caste who employed labour an unfair advantage, that it could not fail to cause feelings of discontent and exasperation among the masses of working-men. By its repeal the sting has been taken out of Socialism, and the British working-man has come to be, in the main, a reasonable citizen, on whom incitements to violence in order to inaugurate Utopias, fall as lightly as the howlings of the barren east wind on the chimney-tops. It has led also to reasonable and peaceful adjustment of disputes between employers and labourers by arbitration and sliding-scales instead of by strikes and lock-outs. In the United States of America the law-abiding instinct is even stronger. We find that strikes attended with violence are almost always confined mainly to the foreign element of recently imported immigrants, and that the native-born American citizen considers the laws as his own laws, and is determined to have them respected.

The balance between the conservative and progressive tendencies is, however, at the best, always imperfect, and inclines too much sometimes in one and sometimes in the other direction. In England the conservative tendency has had on the whole too much preponderance. I do not speak of political institutions, for in these of late years the balance has been pretty equally preserved ; but in practical matters there is still a good deal of old-fashioned stolid obstruction. This is most apparent in law and in education. The common or judge-made law, though on the whole well-intentioned and upright, is fettered by so many technicalities and musty precedents, that it fails in a great many instances to be, what civil law ought to be, a cheap, speedy, and intelligible instrument for enforcing honest dealings between man and man. One of our greatest railway contractors once said to me, ' If I want to make an agreement which shall be absolutely binding, I make it myself on a sheet of note-paper ; if I want to have a loophole, I send it to my lawyer to have it drawn up in legal language and engrossed on sheets of parchment.' Another man of large experience in commercial and financial matters laid down this axiom : ' If you want to know what is the law in a doubtful case, reason out what is the common-sense view of it, and assume that the direct opposite is probably the law.' These may be extreme instances, as all such epigrammatic sentences generally are, but it is undeniable that they have a considerable basis of substantial truth ; and that law, with its dilatory processes, its enormous expense, and its uncertain conclusions, may be, and often is, not an instrument of justice, but a weapon in the hands of an unscrupulous adventurer or of a dishonest rich man, to extort blackmail or to defeat just claims.

Again, what nation but England would tolerate so long a system of land law, so bristling with antiquated technicalities, so tedious, and so expensive, as almost to amount to a prohibition of the transfer of land in small quantities ; or could let the private interests of a mere handful of professional lawyers stand in the way of a codification of laws and a registration of titles?

Education is another subject which shows how difficult it is to move the sluggish ultra-conservative instincts of the English mind in the direction of progress, when not stimulated by political conflict. What is education ? The word tells its own story; it is to *draw out*, not to *cram in* ; to unfold the capacities of the growing mind, strengthen the reasoning faculty, create an interest in the surrounding universe ; in a word, to excite a love of knowledge and impart the means of acquiring it. For the mass of the population, education is necessarily confined in a great measure to the latter object. The three R's—reading, writing, and arithmetic —are indispensable requisites, and the acquirement of these, with perhaps a few elements of history and geography, absorbs nearly all the time and opportunity that can be afforded for attendance at school. For any culture beyond this the great majority must depend on themselves in after life. But there are a large number of parents of the upper and middle classes who can and do keep their children at school for eight or ten years, and spend a large sum of money in giving them what is called a higher education. What is there to show for this time and money, even in the case of the highest schools, which ought to give the highest education? On the credit side, a little Latin and less Greek, plenty of cricket and athletics, good physical training, and, best of all, on the whole a manly, honourable, and gentlemanlike spirit. But on the debit side, absolute ignorance, except in the case of a few unusually clever and ambitious boys, of all that a cultivated man of the nineteenth century ought to know. No French, no German, and, what is worse, no English. The average boy can neither write his own language legibly nor grammatically, and, if he goes straight from a public school into a competitive examination, stands an excellent chance of being plucked for spelling. And, what is worst of all, he not only knows nothing, but cares to know nothing; his reasoning faculty has never been cultivated, and his interest in interesting things has never been awakened. What is the first lesson he has had to learn ? 'Propria quæ maribus dicantur mascula dicas,' that is, words appropriated to males are called masculine—a lesson which elicits as much reasoning faculty, and creates as much interest, as if he had been made to commit to memory that things made of gold are called golden. Suppose instead of this that the lesson had been that two volumes of hydrogen combine with one volume of oxygen to form water. The exercise to the memory is the same, but how different is the amount of thought and interest evoked, especially if the experiment is made before the class and each boy has to repeat it for himself! How many new subjects of interest would this open up in the mind of any lad of average intelligence! How strange that there should be airs other than the air we breathe, which can be

weighed and measured, and that two of them by combining shall produce their exact weight of a substance so
unlike them as water! Or if the exercise of a class
were to look through a microscope at the leaf of a plant
or wing of an insect, and try who could best draw what
they had seen and write a description of it in a legible
hand and in good English, how many faculties would
this call into play compared with the dull routine of
parsing a Latin sentence or writing a halting copy of
Greek iambics! Even grammar, the one thing which is
supposed to be taught thoroughly, is taught so unin-
telligently that it awakens no interest beyond that of a
parrot learning by rote. From 'propria quæ maribus'
the scholar passes to 'as in præsenti perfectum format
in avi,' without an attempt to explain what language
really means, how it originates from root-words, and
how these inflections of 'as' and 'avi' are part of the
devices which certain families of mankind, including
our own, have invented as a mechanism for attaching
shades of meaning, such as present and past, to the
primitive root. Even the alphabet intelligently taught
opens up wide fields of interesting matter as to the
history of ancient nations, and their successive attempts
to analyse the component sounds of their spoken words,
and to pass from primitive picture-writing to phonetic
symbols. But the instructors of the budding manhood
of the *élite* of the nation, like Gallio, 'care for none
of these things,' and the organisation of our higher
schools seems to be stereotyped on the principle that they
are made for teachers rather than for scholars, and that
their chief *raison d'être* is to enable a limited number of
highly respectable gentlemen from the Universities to
realise comfortable incomes with a maximum of holi-

days and a minimum of trouble. And the parents support the system because so many of them really reverence rank more than knowledge, and are willing to compound for their sons growing up ignorant, idle, and extravagant, if by any chance they can count a lord or two among their acquaintance.

Mr. Francis Galton, in the course of his interesting inquiries as to the effect of heredity and education on character and attainments, took the very practical course of addressing a set of questions to some hundred and eighty of our most distinguished men as to the hereditary qualities of their ancestors, and the various influences which they considered had done most to promote or to retard their success in life. Of course he received a variety of answers, 'quot homines tot sententiæ,' but upon one point there was a striking unanimity. 'They almost all expressed a hatred of grammar and the classics, and an utter distaste for the old-fashioned system of education. There were none who had passed through this old high and dry education who were satisfied with it. Those who came from the greater schools usually did nothing there, and have abused the system heartily.'

And yet the system goes on, and the Eton Latin grammar will probably be taught, and hexameters written, for another generation. Surely the needle swings here too strongly towards the negative or ob-structive pole.

The instances are so numerous in social and practical life in which it is necessary to look at both sides of the shield that the difficulty is in selection. Take the case of patriotism. Patriotism is beyond all doubt a great virtue—in fact, the fertile mother of many of the

higher and heroic virtues. Who does not sympathise
with the legends of Wallace and William Tell, and scorn
with Walter Scott

> the man with soul so dead
> Who never to himself has said,
> This is my own, my native land!

And yet how thin a line of partition separates it from
narrow-minded arrogance and insolent ignorance! Reflected in the latter form from Paris, in hysterical shouts
now of 'À Berlin, à Berlin!' and now 'À bas perfide
Albion!' we call it 'Chauvinism,' and recognise it as an
unlovely exhibition. But call it 'Jingoism,' and let it
take the form of the bellowings of some stupid bull, as
the red flag, now of a French and now of a Russian
scare, crosses his line of vision, and we are blind to its
deformity. Still there is another side to the shield, for
even 'Jingoism,' which is only another word for patriotism run mad, is more respectable than the opposite
extreme of a sordid and narrow minded parochialism,
which shrinks behind the 'silver streak,' measures everything by the standard of pounds, shillings, and pence,
and, with what Tennyson calls

> The craven fear of being great,

groans over the responsibilities of extended empire.
The growth of such a spirit among prominent politicians of the advanced Liberal school seems to me one
of the most alarming symptoms of the day; but I take
comfort when I reflect that the most democratic community in the world, that of the United States, is precisely
the one which has shown most determination to maintain its national greatness, if necessary by the sword,
and has made the greatest sacrifices for that object. If

R

the 'copperheads' were a miserable minority in America, why should we be afraid of our 'English copperheads' ever becoming a majority in Old England?

In this, as in all similar cases, it is evident that true statesmanship consists in hitting the happy mean, and doing the right thing at the right time ; and that true strength stands firm in the middle between the two opposite poles, while weakness is drawn by one or other of the conflicting attractions into

The falsehood of extremes.

When Sir Robert Peel some forty years ago announced his conversion by the unadorned eloquence of Richard Cobden, and free trade was inaugurated, with results which were attended with the most brilliant success, every one expected that the conversion of the rest of the civilised world was only a question of time, and that a short time. Few would have been found bold enough to predict that forty years later England would stand almost alone in the world in adherence to free-trade principles, and that the protectionist heresy would not only be strengthened and confirmed among Continental nations such as France and Germany, but actually adopted by large and increasing majorities in the United States, Canada, Australia, and other English-speaking communities. Yet such is the actual fact at the present day. In spite of the Cobden Club and of arguments which to the average English mind appear irresistible, free trade has been steadily losing ground for the last twenty years, and nation after nation, colony after colony, sees its protectionist majority increasing and its free-trade minority dwindling.

It is evident there must be some real cause for such a universal phenomenon.   In countries like France and Russia we may attribute it to economical ignorance and the influence of cliques of manufacturers and selfish interests ; but the people of Germany, and still more of the United States, Canada, and Australia, are as intelligent as ourselves, and quite as shrewd in seeing where those interests really lie.   They are fettered by no traditional prejudices, and their political instincts rather lie towards freedom and against the creation of anything like an aristocracy of wealthy manufacturers.   And yet, after years of free discussion, they have become more and more hardened in their protectionist heresies.

What does this prove ?   That there are two sides to the shield, and not, as we fancied in our English insularity, only one.

Free trade is undoubtedly the best, or rather the only possible, policy for a country like England, with thirty millions of inhabitants, producing food for less than half the number, and depending on foreign trade for the supplies necessary to keep the other half alive. It is the best policy also for a country which, owing to its mineral resources, its accessibility by sea to markets, its accumulated capital, and the inherited qualities, physical and moral, of its working population, has unrivalled advantages for cheap production.   Nor can any dispassionate observer dispute that in England, which is such a country, free trade has worked well. It has not worked miracles, it has not introduced an industrial millennium, the poor are still with us, and it has not saved us from our share of commercial depressions.   But, on the whole, national wealth has greatly increased, and, what is more important, national well-being has increased with it, the mass of the population, and especially the working classes, get better wages, work shorter hours, and are better fed, better clothed, and better educated than they were forty years ago.

This is one side of the shield, and it is really a golden and not an illusory one. But look at the other side. Take the case of a country where totally opposite conditions prevail: where there is no surplus population, unlimited land, limited capital, labour scarce and dear, and no possibility of competing in the foreign or even in the home market with the manufactures which, with free trade, would be poured in by countries like England, in prior possession of all the elements of cheap production. It is by no means so clear that protection, to enable native industries to take root and grow, may not in such cases be the wisest policy.

Take as a simple illustration the case of an Australian colony imposing an import duty on foreign boots and shoes. There is not a doubt that this is practically taxing the immense majority of colonists who wear and do not make these articles. But, on the other hand, it makes the colony a possible field for emigration for all the shoemakers of Europe, and shoemaking a trade to which any Australian with a large family can bring up one of his sons. Looking at it from the strict point of view of the most rigid political economist, the maximum production of wealth, which is the better policy ? The production of wealth, we must recollect, depends on labour, and productive labour depends on the labourer finding his tools—that is, employment at which he can work. A labourer who cannot find work at living wages is worse than a zero : he is a negative quantity as far as the accumulation of wealth is concerned. On the other hand, every workman who finds work, even if it may not be of the ideally best description, is a wealth-producing machine. What he spends on himself and his family gives employment to other workmen, and the work must be poor indeed if the produce of a year's labour is not more than the cost of a year's subsistence. The surplus adds to the national capital, and thus capital and population go on increasing in geometrical progression. The first problem, therefore, for a new or a backward country is to find 'a fair day's wages for a fair day's work,' for as many hands as possible. The problem of making that employment the most produc-tive-possible is a secondary one, which will solve itself in each case rather by actual practice than by abstract theory.

This much, however, is pretty clear, that in order to secure the maximum of employment it must be varied. All are not fit for agricultural work, and, even if they were, if the conditions of soil and climate favour large estates and sheep or cattle runs rather than small farms, a large amount of capital may provide work for only a small number of labourers. On social and moral grounds, also, apart from dry considerations of political economy, progress intelligence and a higher standard of life are more likely to be found with large cities, manufactures, and a variety of industrial occupations than with a dead level of a few millionaires and a few shepherds, or of a few landlords and a dense population of poor peasants. If protection is the price which must be paid to render such a larger life possible, it may be sound policy to pay it, and the result seems to show that neither it nor free trade is inconsistent with rapid progress, while, on the other hand, neither of them affords an absolute immunity from the evils that dog the footsteps of progress, and from the periods of reaction and depression which accompany vicissitudes of trade.

Here, as in other cases, there are two sides of the shield, and true statesmanship consists in seeing both, and doing the right thing, at the right place, and at the right time. If free trade is, as we believe, ultimately to prevail, it will be an affair of time. The real trial of protection comes when it has stimulated production to a point which gluts the home market and leaves a surplus which must be exported. Exports of articles the cost of which has been artificially raised by protection, cannot compete in the world's market with the cheaper products of free-trade countries. Vicissitudes therefore of prosperity and depression must tend to become more frequent and more severe, and, if production goes on, a point must be reached where, at whatever cost, it must either be arrested or made capable of competing in the wider market. The United States are probably not far from such a point, and it would have been already reached but for the immense and unexhausted resources of that vast continent. In France the point has apparently been reached, and we find that, with a lower scale of wages than in England, it is becoming more and more difficult every day to maintain that lower scale, and the export trade of its manufactured goods to foreign markets.

Protection, leading to higher wages and profits than can be permanently maintained, and artificially enhancing the cost of living to the working classes, threatens, more and more every day, to introduce strained relations between capital and labour in most countries of Europe.

The relation between capital and labour affords a good

instance of the inevitable error of applying hard and fast logical conclusions to the complex and ever-varying problems of actual life. Ricardo and other distinguished writers on political economy have assumed that the two constitute a fundamental antagonistic polarity. Wealth, they say, is the joint product of capital and labour, and, as in the case of a cake which has to be divided between C and L, the more C gets the less is left for L, and *vice versâ*. The theory sounds plausible : but what says fact? In the most unmistakable manner it pronounces, as the outcome of practical experience, that the profits of capital and the wages of labour rise and fall together. High profits mean high wages, rising profits rising wages, falling profits falling wages. It has been proved so in a thousand instances, and not one can be quoted where the one factor has varied in an inverse, and not in a direct, ratio with the other. It is obvious that there must be some fallacy in Ricardo's argument. The fallacy is this : he assumes the cake to be of fixed dimensions, whereas in point of fact it varies, sometimes diminishing to zero, or even to a negative quantity, at others expanding to many times its original size. A new gold-field is discovered in a remote country, and forthwith profits rise to cent. per cent., and wages to a pound a day ; a bad season and depression of trade overtake an old country, and the gross value of the produce of many a farm is insufficient to cover expenses and depreciation, even if the labourers worked for nothing. The polarity is therefore confined to the limited and temporary case of the division of the profit, where there is a profit, in particular trades and in individual instances. And this is regulated mainly by the accustomed scale of wages and standard of living of the work-

men, and their opportunities of finding employment
elsewhere if dissatisfied with the terms offered to them.
On the whole, it may be said that capital has the best of
it on a rising, and wages on a falling, market. A manu-
facturer or mine-owner's profit may rise from five to
twenty per cent. without quadrupling the rate of
wages; but, on the other hand, it may fall from twenty
per cent. to five, or even for a time below zero, without
a proportionate diminution in the price paid for labour.
Capital is, in fact, the great insurer of labour, the fly-
wheel which regulates the motion of the industrial
machine. This will be best illustrated by a practical
instance. The Brighton Railway Company for several
consecutive years paid no dividend, or only a trifling
amount, on the shareholders' capital, but during the
whole of this time it gave steady employment at good
wages to upwards of ten thousand workmen. The
Blaenavon Coal and Iron Company in South Wales was
for many years a losing concern, and successive capitalists lost the best part of a million pounds in it, until at
length it was reorganised with a small capital and became a fairly prosperous concern. During the whole
of this time it gave employment at fair wages to several
thousand workmen. Which had the best of it in these
two cases, capital or labour, and where would the workmen have been on any communistic or co-operative system? In fact it will be apparent to any one who will
study dispassionately the statistics of any line of in-
quiry, such as the scale of wages, the price of provisions,
the accumulations of savings banks and provident
societies, &c., for the last twenty years, that the working
classes have had the lion's share of the vast increase
which has taken place in the wealth and income of

the nation. I am glad that it is so, for it is better, both morally and politically, that the condition of the masses should be improved, and their standard of living raised, than that capital should accumulate too exclusively in large masses.

Still there is a good deal to be said for such large accumulations. Let us go to the United States of America for an illustration, where everything is on a large scale, and colossal fortunes have been made in a few years. The *modus operandi* by which most of these fortunes have been made may be described according to the way we look at it, either as railway jobbing or as pioneering the way in useful enterprise. The construction of the first railway across the continent to California is a typical instance. A clique or syndicate of wealthy speculators make surveys and estimates of a line across deserts and over mountain ranges, and ascertain pretty accurately what it will cost. They form a company with a capital of double that cost, and by subventions from the Government, grants of land, and sale of mortgage bonds, raise the half really required, and hold the other half in shares as profit in paper. The line is made, and if the traffic turns out well, and there is a period of speculation in the money market, the paper is turned into dollars, and, if the line really costs, say, 10,000,000*l.* or 20,000,000*l.*, the promoters realise an equal amount as profit.

This has two sides to it : it is doubtless bad for the public to have to pay rates which give a return on twice the actual cost, and the possession of a close monopoly in the hands of a few millionaires may be abused to the detriment of individual traders. But, on the other hand, the railway could not have been made in any other way. If it had been necessary to wait until the slow growth of population insured such a traffic as would induce the ordinary public to subscribe for shares at par, you might have waited for twenty years before a single mile of railway was made west of the Mississippi. Nor is this all: the enormous profit realised in the first of these enterprises led to a rush of rich speculators into the lottery of pushing railways ahead of traffic, in which there were such magnificent prizes. The continent was covered by new railways built to create new traffic rather than to provide for that which already existed. And the traffic was created, though, as the lottery contained blanks as well as prizes, many of the original promoters were ruined. The second great line spanning the continent—the Northern Pacific—ruined two successive sets of promoters, and is only now beginning to be moderately successful.

But the final result has been that while British India, which went on what may be called the respectable system of getting a pound's worth of work for every pound raised, has only 12,000 miles of railway, the United States, under the speculative system, has got 120,000 miles. I cannot doubt that the national wealth of America is greater at the present day than if there had been no Jay Goulds or Vanderbilts, and the construction of her railways had been delayed on the average for twenty years.

The contrast between labour and capital or free trade and protection is only a particular case of the larger polarity between what is called in scientific language egoism and altruism, or, in more popular phraseology, individualism and socialism. According to one theory, the best result is obtained by leaving individuals as free as possible to act on their own suggestions of their duties and interests, and confining the intervention of the State to enforcing laws for the protection of life and property, and such measures as are obviously necessary for the safety of society. According to the other theory, the State ought to interfere wherever the results of individual liberty lead to abuses, and should endeavour to create a society as near to ideal perfection as possible, by administering and regulating the public and private affairs of its citizens. It is obvious that the question has two sides, that extreme conclusions in either direction are, as is always the case, invariably false. Individualism carried too far would disintegrate society. It would be impossible to leave it to the short-sighted selfishness of every citizen to say whether an army and navy should be maintained for national defence, and taxes should be levied for their support.

Individualism also easily passes over into a hard and cruel selfishness, which recognises no obligation beyond the letter of the law, and acts practically on the principle of 'Every one for himself, and the devil take the hindmost.' It is this phase of individualism which makes enthusiasts and men of strong moral and religious sympathies declaim so vehemently against *laissez faire*, and cry aloud, like Carlyle, for a hero or benevolent despot who is to scourge humanity into the practice of all the virtues.

On the other hand, Socialism, if not confined within rigid limits of experience and common sense, is even more destructive in its consequences. Civilised society is based on the security of private property and the observance of contracts. If these are liable, not merely to be regulated in extreme and exceptional cases, but to be absolutely condemned in principle, as by Socialists of the Proudhon school, who declare, ' La propriété c'est le vol ; ' or overruled and set aside whenever they are thought to conflict with humanitarian scruples or sentimental aspirations, society would be dissolved into its elements, to crystallise anew about some military dictator or other strong form of repressive government, who could restore it to a state of stable equilibrium in accordance with these fundamental laws.

No society based on the community of goods has ever existed, except on a very limited scale and for a very short time, under some strong temporary influence such as religious excitement. In the early Christian Church it only existed as long as its members were a handful of humble individuals who were impressed with the idea that the end of the world was close at hand, and that sacrifices made on earth would be repaid at an early day with compound interest in heaven. They acted on what was almost as much a principle of enlightened selfishness as if they had placed their money on the best possible security at the highest possible interest.

The only existing society, as far as I am aware, which has everything in common, is a small sect of Shakers in the United States, which owes its limited success to two conditions—first, that there is no marrying or giving in marriage; secondly, that a member invented a patent rat-trap—conditions which are hardly likely to survive in the struggle for life and become a type for general adoption.

The nearest approach to Communism in practical operation on a large scale is that of the village communities of Russia and parts of India, which certainly show no signs of being progressive types destined to gain ground. On the contrary, they fail to fulfil what is the first condition of an agricultural community, that of obtaining a fair average produce from the soil, and the more enterprising and intelligent moujiks or ryots invariably seek to obtain something which they can call their own and are not obliged to share with the idle and improvident. A conclusive objection to all schemes of Socialism or Communism is, that they not only crush out all individual initiative and enterprise in material life, but that they also destroy all incentives to individual charity and benevolence. Why make sacrifices to help others, if they are already helped at your expense by the State? This is no theoretical objection, but has been proved practically by the history of the poor laws. What scope for individual charity was there in a parish like that in Buckinghamshire, where under the old poor law the rate had risen to twenty shillings in the pound, and the cultivation of the soil was abandoned? Or even in less extreme cases, any one who is acquainted with remote rural parishes inhabited by cotters and small farmers must be aware that the poor law operates strongly to destroy the feeling of manly independence and family affection which induced the poor to support their own aged and infirm relatives.

In many parts of Scotland with which I am personally acquainted men who a generation ago would have thought it a disgrace to ask for help to support an aged father or mother, now think it only fair play, after having contributed for years to the poor rate, to try and get something out of it in return.

Altruism, as Herbert Spencer well puts it, if carried to excess, defeats itself, for in annihilating egoistic vices it annihilates egoistic virtues, and the result is zero—a result which, as 'nature abhors a vacuum,' can happily never be attained, and the precepts of the Sermon on the Mount must always remain maxims of private morality, rather than of State regulation.

It is of little use, however, to deal with such generalities; as long as we confine ourselves to extreme instances on either side, it is as easy as it is idle to refute them. Profitable discussion only begins when we enter on the wide intermediate space which lies between the extreme frontier provinces, and, instead of arguing for absolute conclusions, endeavour to discover the happy mean in doubtful cases, where there really are limitations of time and circumstance, and a good deal which may be reasonably said on each side of the question.

Take for instance the case of contract, which has been so much discussed with reference to the Irish question. Nothing can be clearer than that the enforcement of contracts is one of the principal duties of a government. The principle of *caveat emptor* may occasionally lead to results not altogether consistent with strict morality; but there will always be fools in the world, and it is better they should pay for their folly than that the State should be perpetually interfering in the vain attempt to protect them. The bargain may be a bad one, but it is far better that men should be held to their bargains than that every loser should have a loophole provided to escape by appealing to some legal quibble or State-provided tribunal of arbitration.

But there are limits to this salutary principle. The .

contract must be a free one, freely entered into by parties who meet on equal terms. If it is a compulsory one, which the weaker party has practically no option of refusing, the case is altered. Thus, in the case of children, it is absurd to say that they are free agents in contracting for the disposal of their labour, and the State properly interferes by Factory Acts to limit the number of hours for which they are to work. So in the relations between landlord and tenant, whenever they meet on equal terms, and the tenant has an option of either taking or refusing to take a farm at the rent asked, both sides must be held to their bargain, however disadvantageous it may turn out for either of them. But if the landlord is practically omnipotent, and the tenant has no alternative but to promise to pay an impossible rent or to be turned out on the roadside and die of starvation, it is by no means so clear that the State should enforce the bargain unless the landlord submits to equitable terms. Or again, if the rent is not due to the intrinsic value of the land, but is a confiscation of the tenant's improvements, it is far from being self-evident that the law should look only at landlords' rights and forget all about landlords' duties.

It is a question rather of fact than of argument or assertion, whether such a state of things does or does not prevail at any particular time in any particular country. If the contracts were fair bargains entered into by free agents, they ought to be enforced whether prices have risen or fallen, leaving it to the humanity and self-interest of landlords to make reasonable reductions. But if they were no more equal bargains than those of slaves or factory-children, the State might fairly interfere to attach equitable conditions to the enforcement of inequitable contracts.

The antithesis between the rights and duties of property, especially in the case of land, is one which raises many nice and difficult questions. Some theorists, like Henry George, are for solving it by ignoring the rights altogether. According to them, private property in land is the source of all the evils that afflict modern society ; poverty, depressions of trade, low profits, and low wages are caused by the constant drift towards high rents, due to the possession by a small section of the community of a monopoly in that which is as much a necessity of existence as air or water. Abolish private property in land, and straightway you will have the millennium.

In this extreme form the fallacy of the argument is obvious. You cannot stop at land, but must have the courage of your opinion, and go the full length, with Proudhon, of denouncing all property as robbery. For if the right of individual property is the first condition of civilised society, you can hardly exclude that form of it which, in all ages and all countries, has been practically the most powerful incentive to progress and civilisation.

Compare the United States of America under their homestead laws, with Russia under a system of village communes ; or the California of to-day with that of fifty years ago under the Jesuit padres; and you will see that the desire to acquire property in land has been what may be called the high-pressure steam supplying the motive power to reclaim continents and multiply population.

Nor in principle is there any argument for the confiscation of land which would not equally apply to the

confiscation of any other sort of property, when theorists, philanthropic at other people's expense, thought
that the owner had more than was good for him, or had
acquired it as an unearned increment, without working
for it. Suppose two men, A and B, employed as engine-
drivers on an American railway, have each saved a
hundred dollars. The railway has been a failure : intended to reach a distant terminus, it has stopped half-
way in a desert, for want of funds, and for years has
paid no dividend. The hundred-dollar shares are only
worth ten, and the land at the distant terminus is only
worth ten dollars an acre. But A and B are sharp
fellows, and see that if speculation ever revives the line
will probably be completed, and both shares and land
will become valuable. A buys ten shares with his
hundred dollars, and B ten acres of land. The boom
comes, the capital is found, the line completed, and the
shares rise to par, and the land to a hundred dollars
an acre. A and B have each realised nine hundred
dollars by what may be described, as you like to put
it, either as an unearned increment or as providence
and foresight. On what principle can you confiscate
B's nine hundred dollars because it is in land, and leave
A's untouched because it is in shares?

On the other hand, there is no doubt that when we
come to more complex cases, in which land is held in
large masses, fenced in, not by the natural right of a
man to the produce of his own exertions, but by artificial legal systems of inheritance and settlement, we are
on neutral ground, where fair discussion is possible as
to the limitations and conditions under which the State
may afford its protection. Landed property is more
the creature of law, and runs greater risks in case of

s

revolution or communistic legislation, than personal
property, which is more easily concealed or transferred.
It is not unreasonable, therefore, that it should pay a
higher insurance in the form of taxation, and especially
when it passes by inheritance or settlement, when the
new owner's title is to a great extent artificial and the
creation of the law.   No one can dispute the abstract
justice of a succession duty on all property, landed or
personal, in proportion to its amount, passing by operation of law : the only question can be as to the amount,
and the expediency of confining it within limits that
shall not trench on confiscation or impair the desire to
accumulate capital.   And in the case of land, there is
no doubt that there are a good many instances in which
the question of the ' unearned increment ' is raised more
forcibly than in the case of ordinary property.   Take a
practical instance within my own knowledge, for an
illustration is often better than an argument.   There
was a mountain property in Wales which, as a sheep or
cattle farm, might be worth at the outside 800l. a year.
Coal and iron were discovered under it, capitalists sank
pits and erected works, two or three sets lost their
money ; but the works were carried on, a large amount
of labour was employed, and in course of time a town
of some eight or nine thousand inhabitants sprang
up.   The proprietor's 800l. a year grew into 8,000l.
from fixed rents and royalties, which he has enjoyed
for the last thirty years, through good times and bad,
without being called on to contribute a penny towards
schools, churches, roads, sewers, water, or any of the
local objects necessary for the civilised existence of the
population of eight thousand whose labour has added
to his wealth.   I do not blame him: the law told him

to do what he liked with his own, and it probably never occurred to him that he was under any moral obligation to go beyond the law.   But I do think that the law would have been more just, and better for the interests of the community, if it had made some portion of this unearned increment of 7,000*l.* a year liable for a contribution towards the sanitary and other objects essential for the decent existence of the town which had grown up on this property and given it this increased value.   I cannot help thinking that centuries of landlord legislation, and of a public opinion based mainly on that of the wealthy and specially of the landed classes, have made our laws in many respects too favourable to the predominant interests, and that the swing of the pendulum now is, and properly is, in the direction of recognising the duties as well as the rights of property.

We must take care, however, not to let it swing too far in this direction, for of the two evils it is better to put up with occasional cases of hardship and oppression on the part of bad landlords than to endanger the security of property by reforms pushed to extremes at the dictation of impulsive masses, designing demagogues, or sentimental philanthropists.

Herbert Spencer, in his works on Sociology, often dwells with great force on the evils which arise from State interference.   There can be no doubt that it is very undesirable that the State should become a sort of Jack-of-all-trades, and undertake branches of business which can be conducted by private enterprise.   It is undesirable for two reasons : first, because the work is certain to cost more and be worse done ; secondly, for the still more important reason that it tends to extinguish individual enterprise, strangle progress with red-tape, and teach a nation to look, like children to outside guidance, rather than, like men to their own. Still the question has two sides. Whatever individual enterprise can do should be left to it; but there are, in the complex conditions of modern society, a number of things which cannot be done by individuals, and which must either be left undone or done by the State, or by some local authority, joint-stock company, or other quasi-monopoly sanctioned by the State. Thus, if it were a question of bringing coals from Newcastle by sea, no one would suggest that the State should interfere with the private enterprise of individual shipowners. But to bring them by land requires railways, and railways can only be built by capitals beyond the reach of private individuals. If the State had not delegated a portion of its powers to joint-stock companies, not a ton of coal would ever have been brought by land to London.

And if the State may thus occasionally delegate its powers with advantage to the community, there are cases in which it may, with equal advantage, undertake itself branches of the nation's business. For instance, the Postal Service. The advantages of a cheap and uniform system for the collection and delivery of letters throughout the whole kingdom are so great that they far outweigh any theoretical objections to State interference. Possibly some of the larger towns might have been as well or better served by private enterprise, but no non-paying district would have had a post-office, and the enormous commercial and educational benefits of the penny post would have been in a great measure lost to the community.

The case of telegraphs is not so clear. Probably, on the whole, the advantages of a uniform State management preponderate, but there are drawbacks which make it doubtful. Even at a sixpenny rate a great deal of the telegraphic communication of the large towns and active centres of business is taxed to make up for the deficiency of the rest of the kingdom. And invention and improvement in telegraphy are no doubt checked to a considerable extent by creating a State monopoly whose first duty it is to try to satisfy its masters at the Treasury by making the system pay.

When we come to railways we are on debateable ground, and it is fairly arguable that they should be worked by the State for the public good. But the objections here outweigh the advantages. Every one who has any practical experience of the working of railways must be aware that the simplicity and uniformity of the penny postal system are totally inapplicable, and that the traffic of the country requires, above all things, great freedom and elasticity in meeting, day by day, the varying contingencies which arise. Here is an illustration : In a certain town in France, on a railway worked by the State, it was determined to have a *fête* in order to raise funds for a hospital, and, as an attraction, to bring down from Paris a small troop of actors and have a play in the evening. The question turned on the railway consenting to give them a reduced fare for the return journey. The manager of the railway was quite willing, but said that he had no power to alter the tariff without permission from the Minister of Public Works. The permission was applied for, and the result was that it arrived exactly on the day twelve months after the *fête* had been held.

Contrast this with the case of the general manager of the London and North Western Railway sitting in his office at Euston and receiving half a dozen telegrams asking him to quote special rates, one perhaps for beef from Chicago to London, another for emigrants from Hamburg to New York *via* Liverpool, and all requiring telegraphic answers then and there, if the business is to be done at all.

Again, if railways had been in the hands of the State, I do not suppose that we should have had half our present mileage; for the Treasury would never have sanctioned the outlay of public money on lines which could not show the prospect of a fair return on the capital, and it would have vetoed any multiplication of trains or reduction of rates which threatened loss to the exchequer. I can speak with some authority on this point, for I have been both Chairman of a railway company and Secretary of the Treasury, and I am certain that, in the former capacity, I have introduced important innovations, such as excursion trains and cheap periodical tickets, by which the public have greatly benefited, which I should have vetoed in the latter capacity.

Still there may be exceptional cases, as that of Ireland, where an unreasonable number of poor companies, in a poor country, wrangling among themselves, and giving a bad service at an excessive cost, intensify social and political evils, where the arguments in favour of a State purchase may outweigh the objections; and the extent and nature of State control over British railways is always a question fairly open to discussion.

In other departments, the supply of articles such as water and gas, and the enforcement of sanitary conditions, are probably best left to local authorities: in the latter case, under some central supervision to see that the duty is not evaded. Wherever neglect involves danger to others, as in the case of small-pox and other contagious epidemics, it is clear that the decision cannot be left to individuals, and the State is bound to interfere to enforce rational precautions.

So also the State is bound to undertake trades which are essential for the protection of the nation against foreign enemies. Our dockyards and arsenals may, and doubtless do, often make mistakes and turn out expensive work ; but we could not safely leave the building of ironclads and supply of cannon solely to private enterprise, for there is no such large and steady demand for such articles as would induce a number of private firms to erect works and keep up establishments adequate to supply the wants which might arise in an emergency. In all such matters, therefore, of national defence we must put up with a certain amount of drawbacks incidental to State management, and confine ourselves to endeavouring to reduce them to a minimum. And this is to a great extent within the power of the nation and its Parliament, by applying common-sense principles of business to national expenditure, and seeing that while on the one hand we get as nearly as possible a pound's worth of work for every pound spent, on the other hand we do not spend nineteen shillings uselessly, because some Chancellor of the Exchequer wants to gain momentary popularity by the ' penny wise and pound foolish ' economy of docking the extra shilling off the necessary estimates. In private life a man gets on by knowing when to spend as well as when not to spend, and true economy has no greater foe than spasmodic parsimony alternating almost certainly with spasmodic extravagance. It would be

easy to multiply instances, for there are few phases
of political and practical life to which the principle of
polarity does not apply, where extremes are not false,
and where there is not a good deal to be said on both
sides of the question. But the very obviousness of the
principle makes it difficult to deal with it generally
without degenerating into commonplace, while to trace
its application exhaustively in any one instance would
require a volume. Those who wish to pursue the
subject further will do well to study the works of
Herbert Spencer, where they will find the application
of general principles to all the problems of sociology
treated with a depth of philosophic insight and an
abundance and aptness of illustration which I cannot
pretend to equal. My ambition is of a humbler nature.
I do not expect to set the Thames on fire, or to produce
a revolution in modern thought; but I do hope that the
views which I have endeavoured to express may do
somewhat to make some readers more tolerant and
charitable in their judgments, less bitter and one-sided
in controversy; and that whatever truth there may be
in my ideas will contribute to form a small part, neither
more nor less than it deserves, of the great body of truth
which is handed down from the present to succeeding
generations, and which becomes, long after I am there
to witness it, the inheritance of the human race in the
course of its evolution.

And now, before I take my final leave of the reader,
let me for a few moments throw the reins on the neck
of fancy, and suppose myself standing with that group
of Parsees by the shore of the Indian Ocean, listening to
its murmured rhythm, inhaling the balmy air, watch-
ing the silver crescent of the new moon, and musing

on the wise sayings of the ancient sage; the sum of
the reflections which I have tried to embody in the
preceding pages would take form and crystallise in the
following sonnet :—

Hail ! gracious Ormuzd, author of all good,
Spirit of beauty, purity, and light ;
Teach me like thee to hate dark deeds of night,
And battle ever with the hellish brood
Of Ahriman, dread prince of evil mood—
Father of lies, uncleanness, envious spite,
Thefts, murders, sensual sins that shun the light,
Unreason, ugliness, and fancies lewd—
Grant me, bright Ormuzd, in thy ranks to stand,
A valiant soldier faithful to the end ;
So when I leave this life's familiar strand,
Bound for the great Unknown, shall I commend
My soul, if soul survive, into thy hand—
Fearless of fate if thou thine aid will lend.

INDEX.

T

THE END.

PROBLEMS OF THE FUTURE.

By SAMUEL LAING.

Demy 8vo, 3s. 6d.   Sixteenth Thousand.

SOME OPINIONS OF THE PRESS.

From THE DAILY NEWS.

"The versatile and accomplished author of these thoughtful and often suggestive coutributions in aid of younger seekers after knowledge, is himself a good example of that indefatigable and insatiable intellectual curiosity, which is the motive and secret of all true science.

"All, or nearly all, the questions which are at present occupying the foremost men of science are here discussed in the clear, simple, and untechnical language of one who has mastered the subjects sufficiently to make his deepest thoughts run clear in words."

From THE MANCHESTER GUARDIAN.

"Those who read with pleasure and sympathy Mr. Laing's former volumes on 'Modern Science and Modern Thought,' and 'A Modern Zoroastrian,' will give a no less cordial welcome to this new work from the same fluent pen. He addresses himself to that increasingly large number of both men and women who have acquired some elementary ideas about Science and its drift, and who want to know more. Such persons can have no more engaging guide than Mr. Laing. His knowledge is wide, and he has what specialists seldom have, a sense of proportion. In the volume before us he deals with a very varied range of subjects, but always in a pleasant, cheery way."

From THE SCOTSMAN.

"Mr. Laing addresses himself to the semi-scientific reader, and seeks to bring him abreast of the most advanced thought and research of the day upon such questions as the origin and phenomena of solar heat, the physical composition of the universe, the date and duration of the glacial period, and the origin and antiquity of man."

From THE GLASGOW HERALD.

"Mr. Laing has produced one of the most remarkable and interesting volumes which it has been our good fortune to read for some time. . . . The most adverse critics would scarcely deny that he has written a most interesting and suggestive book."

From THE LONDON DAILY TELEGRAPH.

"Mr. Laing makes out a formidable list of problems which, though we have been probing and discussing them for centuries, still await the solution of yet unborn philosophers. He wishes to know what manner of religion will eventually tumble from the great crucible of scepticism and investigation to which he thinks all old beliefs must submit. He wishes to learn where astronomy is to limit its aspirations, and whether chemists are to reduce the elements to one, or to find something more remote than the primæval atoms. How soon will Europe consent to turn her multitudinous sabres into ploughshares, and when shall we settle on a satisfactory basis the laws of taxation and finance, population and food?"

From THE ILLUSTRATED LONDON NEWS.

"A veteran public man, who has during forty years past, after gaining high mathematical honours at Cambridge, been constantly employed in Board of Trade official administration, or in the duties of a member of Parliament, or as Finance Minister of India, or as Chairman of the Brighton Railway Co., is not likely to be a dreamy idealist, or a scholastic bigot. He has a vast acquired fund of practical common-sense, a trained faculty of induction and experimental reasoning, the habit of looking all round the different sides of a question, and then hitting the central point, and that of reducing to just proportion and co-ordination.

"Accordingly, Mr. Laing's summaries of the general propositions concerning the physical constitution of the visible universe, the origin and development of the forms of organic life, and the laws determining the progress of mankind to secular welfare, added to our stock of knowledge within the last thirty-four years, are very useful reading. . . . This instructive volume also contains several essays of a political character, on the huge military armaments of Europe, on taxation and finance, on the increase of population and the prospects of an adequate food-supply, concerning which the opinions of Mr. Laing should have considerable weight."

From VANITY FAIR.

"Mr. Laing resembles Mr. Gladstone in one thing—that in spite of having been immersed all his life in business, politics, and economics, he seems always to have time to write essays *de omnibus rebus et quotuodem aliis*; but there is this difference, that while Mr. Gladstone claims to be original and critical and fails to establish such a position —Mr. Laing merely claims to expound in forcible and lucid terms to semi-scientific readers, the results of modern science and thinking, and in such his purpose succeeds admirably. . . . 'Armed Europe,' 'Taxation and Finance,' and 'Population and Food,' are written by one who has thought before he writes, and writes well what he thinks, and this remark applies broadly to the whole work."

A MODERN ZOROASTRIAN.

By SAMUEL LAING

Demg 8vo, 3s. 6d. Eleventh Thousand.

SOME OPINIONS OF THE PRESS.

From THE ST. STEPHEN'S REVIEW.

" We undertake to predict that this work will be acknowledged as the most remarkable scientific and philosophical work of 1887. It is abstruse in abstract thought, but it is simple enough in intelligent language to be understood by the people. Those who have read Mr. Laing need scarcely be told how deftly he weaves the crushing proof round and round his arguments, or how skilfully he advances new dogma, which on the face of it is unanswerable. There are points in the book which are of supreme interest to the non-scientific reader, and, indeed, it teems with topical matter."

From THE LITERARY WORLD.

"The reception given to Mr. Laing's former work, 'Modern Science and Modern Thought,' has induced him to publish this most interesting and fascinating book, which will be read and re-read by all students of philosophy and science with avidity and delight."

From THE SECULAR REVIEW.

"If our readers' would like to form an acquaintance with a book replete with the grandest generalisations and most daring speculations that do not spring from imaginative ideation, but rest on the foundation of physical phenomena, we recommend them to a thoughtful perusal of Mr. Laing's 'Modern Zoroastrian.' They will find the pith and epitome of much that is most salient in the writings of Darwin, Huxley, and Haeckel put with a terseness and perspicuity for which Mr. Laing stands unrivalled."

From THE AYRSHIRE POST.

" We wonder if any of our readers have ever read that most interesting and fascinating book entitled, 'A Modern Zoroastrian.' If not, we would recommend them to make an early acquaintance with it."

From THE LITERARY GUIDE.

"The work is executed with a strong, supple, and well-trained hand. Mr. Laing's philosophy is peculiarly practical. While metaphysicians and theologians are straying into bogs here and pathless wilds there, he keeps resolutely to the beaten path of common sense."

From THE POPULAR SCIENCE MONTHLY (*New York*).

" This book, like many others of late date, is evidence of two facts : first, that the traditional religion has lost its hold on most scientifically educated minds, and secondly, that such minds are not content without some religion. The author's views are well expressed, and readers having a taste for this class of subjects will find the book an interesting one."

MODERN SCIENCE AND MODERN THOUGHT.

By SAMUEL LAING.

Demy 8vo, 3s. 6d.   Twenty-third Thousand.

SOME OPINIONS OF THE PRESS.

From THE TIMES.

"Mr. Laing is a man of active mind, and he has had a busy and rather multifarious life. He is on good terms with his work, his fellow-workers, and his fellow-thinkers. He treads a beaten path. If he does not pretend to originality it is because science is not original except to those who devote themselves to some one field of investigation. He reports what is known, or believed, or not believed, by the majority of scientific men. The character of the work is foreshadowed in its divisions and titles. Two hundred pages are given to 'Science,' followed by about one hundred professedly given to 'Thought.' The thought, however, is scientific, and it is science that dominates from the first page to the last. In the first part Mr. Laing exhibits with much power and effect the immense discoveries of science, and its numerous victories over old opinions whenever they have had the rashness to challenge conclusions with it. These discoveries are not so familiar to the world at large but that any ordinary reader may learn much from a writer combining matter and style, and conveying solid information in simple yet striking language. In a comparatively small compass are here displayed the results of recent inquiries into the composition and constitution of the earth and of the universe, into the nature and laws of matter, into the development of organised and animated existence, into the history of man, into the myths of all races and the faiths of all people ; into force, motion, electricity, light, and heat. As one turns over the glowing pages one is tempted to lament that a man so qualified to instruct and to illustrate should have been almost exclusively occupied in absorbing official and practical duties."

From THE PALL MALL GAZETTE.

" Apart from the uselessness and undue multiplication of all such books, Mr. Laing's brief statement of an agnostic creed is good enough and sensible enough in its own way. It is the expression of a sensible, well-read, compromise-loving Briton's final conclusions upon religious matters. The first part is a rapid and clearly written *résumé* of all that modern science and modern criticism have done to sap the foundation of current theologies and the current dogmas. This *résumé* is admirably done. Mr. Laing manages to condense into a few short chapters an amount of salient information on matters astronomical, geological, archæological, and historical; and withal he condenses it cleverly. . . . The evidence of geology against the Mosaic cosmogony; the evidence of biology, and especially of evolutionism, against the story of creation; the evidence of the palæolithic flints and the reindeer age cave-men against the naïve history of Adam and Eve; the evidence of human development against the entire Biblical conception of man's importance in the scheme of nature—all marshalled with considerable skill, and enforced by excellent and typical examples. The anxious but unlearned inquirer who really wishes to know how much recent researches have effected towards undermining the groundwork of the existing creeds, cannot do better than turn to Mr. Laing's pleasantly written pages."

From THE WESTMINSTER REVIEW.

"From the first page to the last the book is charmingly written, with temperance and wisdom that will win a hearing for the author from many who may not share his views."

From THE SCOTSMAN.

"His task Mr. Laing has discharged in a business-like manner. In his first part he has presented the chief results of modern scientific investigations with singular terseness and lucidity, and what is more, he has contrived to indicate by simple and impressive illustrations the methods by which those results have been attained. And this he has done in a style so simple and elementary, yet so sufficient for his purpose, that any fairly intelligent reader who has never been able to give attention to scientific subjects may fully grasp the sum of the knowledge he seeks to impart. . . . These chapters are of genuine interest, as showing the conclusions of a practical man who belongs neither to the philosophers nor the theologians, but has intelligently studied the researches and reasonings of both, and has formed his judgment between them on the principles of common sense, and by means of the ordinary rules by which men weigh evidence in ordinary life."

From THE MORNING POST.

"Mr. Laing's book is of a useful and reliable character. . . . There is much in the book which will be useful to those for whom it is intended."

HUMAN ORIGINS.

By SAMUEL LAING.

With Illustrations. Demy 8vo, 3s. 6d. Sixteenth Thousand.

SOME OPINIONS OF THE PRESS.

The Times says :—" Mr. Laing's present purpose is to use recent researches into the history of the ancient nations of the world as a rough 'measuring-rod' for gauging the duration of the prehistoric periods of human existence. . . . This is Mr. Laing's plan, and its execution is divided into two parts ; in the first Mr. Laing recapitulates the results, carried up to the latest date, of the labours of Egyptologists and Assyriologists, with a glance at civilisation which, like the Chinese, cannot be traced back to such a remote era. In the second he reviews once more the evidence for the Neolithic and Palæolithic ages, and the Quaternary and Tertiary periods. . . . Mr. Laing performs an operation of great utility to the general reader."

The Globe says :—" Mr. Laing's theme is the antiquity of man, and his treatment of it is pleasant and profitable. . . . The various views concerning the origin of man receive unbiassed attention in the readable volume."

The Daily Graphic says :—" Mr. Samuel Laing's books have a peculiar interest for all those who have neither time nor opportunity to be in the vanguard of scientific progress, but yet like to follow within measurable distance prompted by some reliable coach. But Mr. Laing is more than a coach, he is never anything but interesting. He never seeks to obscure his own point of view ; but few people have the requisite moderation for writing on controversial matters in his uncontroversial way."

The Review of Reviews says :—" In the present volume Mr. Laing describes, with great lucidity of expression and clearness of exposition, the theories which now obtain as to the origin and evolution of the human race. . . . Stimulating and informative to the last degree, and sufficiently popular to be understood by the veriest tyro in science. He presents the latest results arrived at by modern science in as clear and lucid a manner as possible, and every one who has mastered his volumes will be as much abreast of scientific thought as the general reader can ever hope to be."

Black and White says :—" Mr. Laing has been inspired to put his great knowledge to a laudable use, and compose for us clearly, in one volume, the teaching of modern science upon the origin and antiquity of man. . . The book is wonderfully interesting and surprisingly cheap."

The National Observer says :—" It is clearly written, the facts it records are of stupendous interest."

Science (New York) says :—"This is an exceedingly well-written and interesting summary of all the theories, facts, and mysterious questions connected with the origin of mankind on earth, by a somewhat remarkable man whose previous works met with a wide circulation in England. . . . His various publications present the results of wide and discriminating reading and research, in a logical, concise, yet comprehensive style, for the benefit of those who have not the time to look into such matters for themselves."

The Glasgow Herald says :—" The author of this book is a well-known writer upon various philosophical, scientific, and historical subjects. Not only is he possessed of a large fund of information, but his style is generally clear and intelligent, while the arrangement of his matter is almost invariably satisfactory. The present work is devoted mainly to support and illustration of the theory of evolution. Although here and there he seems to take too much for granted, the volume is fresh, attractive, and pleasing. Especially should it be found valuable by the young and those who, from the pressure of the ordinary avocations of life, have neither the time nor the education to fit them for becoming specialists. The advances made in modern days in the investigation of the various problems of science and history have been so great that Mr. Laing is entitled to all praise for publishing so many of their results in a semi-popular form which is intelligible without being slipshod or slovenly. It should be mentioned that 'Human Origins' is profusely and successfully illustrated. It is a book to awaken thought and to stimulate criticism."

The Daily Chronicle says :—" In the present work Mr. Laing attacks some theories of the highest importance, and on the whole with a fulness of knowledge and an ability which leaves little to be desired. . . . The reader will find many questions canvassed in Mr. Laing's pages with a clearness, a literary power, and an amount of scientific knowledge which is seldom insufficient and never wearisome."

The Birmingham Gazette says :—" Mr. S. Laing, who is well known to a large circle of readers as an original thinker on problems relating to the history, unwritten and recorded, of this globe, has just published a volume on 'Human Origins,' which is likely to be the cause of considerable controversy. His subject is a vast one, and only his wide reading and erudition justify him in choosing it. Mr. Laing is a wonderfully lucid writer, and he marshals his immense array of facts with the utmost precision. No one can rise from the reading of one of his chapters without feeling that a great amount of useful and valuable information has been gained, and that light has been plentifully cast upon obscure subjects."

Truth says :—" More admirable than its admirable predecessors."

The Guardian says :—" The immediate object of this book is to demonstrate the immense antiquity of man. This is done by following up in detail the two distinct lines of evidence from history and science. . . . All this is set forth in broad outline with lucidity ; and these chapters will be found very useful to any one who desires to know in a general way what are the conclusions which modern investigation has reached on these topics, and on what sort of arguments these conclusions rest."

The Melbourne Argus says :—" Mr. Laing writes with much force and clearness, so plainly as to be easily understanded of the people."

The Newcastle Chronicle says :—" Mr. Laing condenses a great mass of various information ; his matter is admirably arranged ; and his style is as admirably adapted to its purpose by its clearness and simplicity. 'Human Origins' is an absorbing and stimulating book, and it will well repay the perusal even of those who may dissent upon this point or that from the author's conclusions and suggestions."

F. M. EVANS AND CO., LTD., PRINTERS, CRYSTAL PALACE, S.E.